Fate is beautiful in its imperfections

Elisabeth Baldwin is a mother of heroes with mental stability, as well as manipulators and abusers (nowhere without them). Her female characters don't play superheroes trying to save their lovers from inner demons. They learn to respect and love themselves and grow with every challenge in life. Elisabeth is goddess of weird humor, aesthetic collages, catchy playlists, and writing chapters at night.

Let's keep in touch

Website: elisabethbaldwin.com

Instagram: @elisbaldwin

Forbidden series:

Forbidden Secret
Forbidden Freedom
Forbidden Love

Forbidden secret

Elisabeth Baldwin

First Published in 2022 by Elisabeth Baldwin
This paperback edition published in 2024

Copyright © 2022 by Elisabeth Baldwin
Cover and internal design © 2023 by Anastasia Grishchenko

All rights reserved. No part of this publication may be reproduced, distributed, or transmitted in any form or by any means, including photocopying, recording, or other electronic or mechanical methods, without the prior written permission of the publisher, except in the case of brief quotations embodied in critical reviews and certain other noncommercial uses permitted by copyright law.

The story, all names, characters, and events portrayed in this book are fictitious. Any similarity to real persons, living or dead, is purely coincidental and not intended by the author.

All brand names and product names used in this book are trademarks, registered trademarks, or trade names of their respective holders. Author is not associated with any product or vendor in this book.

ISBN: 979-8-322-62760-9

To those who still believe in real love.
Do not allow your heart to grow hardened by the past.

PS. With this book, I seemingly predicted a man just like Alexander for myself. Be careful, for after reading, you might encounter your true love.

Playlist

"Secrets" by OneRepublic
"As you Are" by The Weeknd
"Don't Speak" by No Doubt
"Young and Beautiful" by Lana Del Rey
"Trop Beau" by Lomepal
"Wicked Game" by Chris Isaak
"Wildest Dreams" by Taylor Swift
"Arcade" by Duncan Laurence
"Enjoy The Silence" by Depeche Mode
"Madness" by Muse
"Love Me Like You Do" by Ellie Goulding
"With or Without You" by U2
"Stay with Me" by Sam Smith
"Torn" by Natalie Imbruglia
"Secret Love Song" by Little Mix ft. Jason Derulo
"Bleeding Love" by Leona Lewis

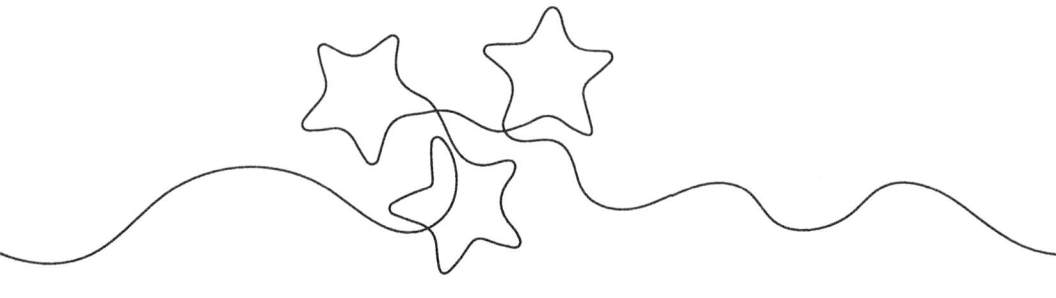

Prologue

The city night spreads before my feet. Its lights are so bright that it seems the stars have scattered over the earth. The sky is clear, and the moon smiles down on me with its crescent. Everything predicts an unforgettable night.

I can hear him even before he opens the door to the hotel room and takes the step across the threshold. In the reflection of the panoramic windows of the skyscraper, I see how the stranger freezes in the doorway and stares at me. Apparently, he is deciding whether he should go further or take a step back before it's too late. But I have already made up my mind.

"Beautiful night, isn't it?" I remark, turning to face him, my chin resting on my shoulder.

He hangs a "Do Not Disturb" sign on the handle and locks the door.

"Like any clear summer night," he says in a hoarse voice. Its timbre shooting waves of electricity through my skin. So soulful, enveloping...

Casually discarding his black suit jacket onto a nearby chair, he moves closer, his presence enveloping me from behind. In the dim twilight of the room, his masculine features are accentuated by the play of shadows. I know nothing about this man — his name, his occupation, his daily routines or habits — and yet, the uncertainty only heightens my senses, quickening my pulse and causing my breath to hitch.

I'm not sure how I found myself on this exhilarating escapade.

"Look," the stranger puts one hand on my bare shoulder, hooking the thin strap of the dress with his long fingers, and the other points to the sky. "That is the constellation, Ursa Major."

He connects the stars with invisible lines, forming the familiar shape of the Great Bear. But I can't focus on anything except for the heat of his breath against my neck.

"Beautiful," I whisper softly. He pulls the hairpin from my hair, and it tumbles down in chestnut curls over my shoulders.

"Just like you are," he tickles my ear with his lips, sliding his hand up my neck and brushing the strands over my back.

I see him glancing at our reflection in the glass. His hand grabs my chin and runs his thumb over my lips, outlining their contour. The fingers of his free hand gently pull the zipper of my dress, freeing the fabric from my body. It falls to the floor, leaving me in nothing but panties and heeled sandals.

He also looks at our reflection in the glass. It is so vulgar and dirty it takes my breath away. At this moment, his palms inquisitively explore my body, navigating every curve. A long groan escapes my throat. A smirk plays at the corners of his mouth, and I find myself wanting to wipe away that self-satisfied grin. I run my parched tongue across my lips, looking defiantly into the stranger's eyes.

In one moment, something changes in him. The expression on his face becomes gloomy, the lights of the city night shining in the pools of his black pupils.

Without hesitation, he jerks my panties down and they fall to my ankles. Sharp, burning pain explodes where the lacing of my panties has been. I scream and push my palms against the cool surface of the window.

"Stand still," he breathing heavily.

The sound of a belt buckle being undone echoes louder in my ears than my own heartbeat. Excitement mingles with a sensation I never associated with intimacy before: fear. Panic tightens around my chest as adrenaline floods my veins, the realization of my vulnerability sinking in.

Me and the stranger alone. A room in a hotel where no one will hear me and come running to help if something goes wrong...

As I struggle to gather my thoughts, I fail to notice him undressing completely, his gaze fixated on the shifting emotions on my face. I bite my lip. Broad shoulders, strong torso with sculpted muscles, powerful buttocks, and shins. Light tan on the skin. A snake tattoo coils around his waist.

I meet brown eyes in the reflection and swallow nervously. I have my back to him, still leaning against the glass, which makes my palms go cold. His eyes wander over me, scanning every millimeter, and leaving marks on my body.

The stranger's gaze penetrates my very being, flooding every cell with his presence until multicolored spots dance before my eyes.

My throat is torn from screaming, and I can no longer control myself. Lust overwhelms fear, and I lean back into his embrace, only to be held in place, denied the contact I crave. My cheek smudges the window, smearing the remains of my makeup.

Conflicting sensations wash over me — pain and pleasure, mingling in a dizzying whirl. His hands ruthlessly burn my skin, bringing bruises to the surface, as his lips cover my shoulder with gentle kisses, outlining every mole.

I'm entirely at his mercy, consumed by his presence until I forget who I am and where I am, lost in a haze of heightened sensations that bring both ecstasy and confusion. The presence of the stranger is so much around and inside of me.

"I'll call you a cab," the stranger says, wiping his damp hair with a towel after a shower.

He stands naked in the middle of the room without any embarrassment, and watches as I pull my hair back into a tight bun with shaking hands. When I finally succeed, I tug at the hem of my dress and turn around to face the man. The cool air from the air conditioner irritates my heated skin, bringing to life my emotionally inflamed brain.

"Thanks, but there's no need," I manage a strained smile.

I'm at a loss for how to act around him. After all, we seem to be no one to each other, despite the fact that just fifteen minutes ago, we were drowned in a whirlpool of orgasm, divided in two.

All I want is to flee this hotel room and retreat to the comfort of home. A shower, some soft pajamas, and a snug blanket sound like the perfect antidote to this surreal encounter.

" Are you sure you wouldn't like to freshen up before you go?" The stranger asks, throwing a towel on the bed — the same bed where my high heels were entangled in the sheets while he explored every inch of my body, igniting waves of sweet agony.

I shake my head to get the dirty pictures out of my mind. My lower abdomen unbearably burning.

"I'm sure," I croak, then clear my throat. "I'll call a taxi myself, thanks."

I quickly make my way to the door, grabbing my bag from the bedside table. The strap of the dress, as luck would have it, flies off my shoulder, revealing my breast just as I run past him. With trembling fingers, I hastily readjust the fabric.

"What is your name?" The question flies at my back, but I pretend not to hear it and slam the door behind me so hard that the vibrations reverberated throughout the corridor.

I don't need to know his name any more than he needs to know mine. We're just two strangers who shared a night together and will never cross paths again.

Chapter 1

Sophie

"What a day," my colleague sighs, her exhaustion palpable. "I'm drained. I can't muster any more energy for work. We really should check our horoscopes. Some days, astrologers advise against even signing contracts. And it feels like Mercury is in retrograde today."

I grin at her words and toss my coffee cup into the trash. It's amusing how seriously some people take these things. Personally, I only believe in magnetic storms that leave me with a pounding headache.

"Maybe you should spend less time on women's sites, Stella, and more on architectural ones," I tease, winking at her. She just rolls her eyes in response and opens the door.

We exit the office of the architectural firm where I work as an intern, silently praying for a miracle that will secure me a permanent position as an architect. It's an uphill battle, given that the company only accepts candidates with a master's degree. Here, qualifications reign supreme. But with no funds for a two-year master's program, I've resorted to shamelessly telling my boss that I'll complete my studies after my one-year internship and continue working simultaneously.

The meager hourly wage of an intern barely covers the essentials: food, rent, with a scant amount left over for leisure. But the permanent employees of our prestigious firm enjoy the highest salaries in the city. Stella, having worked here as an architect for three years, has already secured a loan for an apartment in a posh residential area and bought herself a brand-new car.

I want the same. It's not for nothing that I endured years of sleepless nights in a decrepit dormitory with cracked walls, preceded by a year of daily commutes from a neighboring city to attend preparatory courses.

"Today's Friday," Stella remarks matter-of-factly, fishing out the keys to her sleek red Audi. "Any plans?"

"I'm meeting Christine for dinner at the restaurant, maybe hitting a club afterwards," I reply with a shrug, though I know the evening will likely end after dinner — I'm not in the mood for a wild night out.

"With your wealthy friend, the retired model's daughter?" Stella quips with a chuckle.

"That's your perspective," I retort, rolling my eyes. Stella's occasional fits of baseless jealousy can be tiresome. "I know who she really is…"

I barely have time to defend my best friend before a car horn blares behind us.

"Speak of the Devil," Stella exclaims, flipping her red hair. "Alright, go have some fun. See you on Monday!"

I nod to her and make my way towards the bright turquoise Mini Cooper, driven by Christine, who's already waving frantically, urging me to hurry.

"Hey there!" Christine greets me with a kiss on the cheek as I slip into the passenger seat. "Hurry, we have a restaurant reservation in fifteen minutes, and we still have to get through the traffic jams."

"Don't grumble," I say with a grin, fastening my seatbelt.

Christine is always the life of our small group of friends. Her boundless positivity and optimism could make even the happiest person envious. In a way, we balance each other out: I'm the brooding introvert, while she's the vibrant, cheerful extrovert.

I met Christine during my preparatory courses at university. Despite my usual reluctance to make new friends, we hit it off quickly.

"I can tell someone needs a pick-me-up," Christine says, playfully pinching my cheek. "You need to forget about that asshole!"

My smile falters at the mention of Liam. It's been two months since our breakup, but not a day goes by without thoughts of him and tears shed into my pillow. Though this week, I managed to break my own record — I didn't think about him for three whole days, because my mind was preoccupied with someone else…

"Why the long face?" Christine asks, sounding irritated. "Come on, cheer up. We're going to have fun, not attend a funeral. Though, with your outfit, it does look like we're burying someone."

"What's wrong with my pantsuit?"

"It screams gray desk jockeys," Christine retorts. "Did you even check the weather this morning? It's scorching outside. Didn't you roast alive in that thing?"

"It's just a normal suit," I mutter, shedding my jacket to reveal a white sheer blouse with a puffy bow at the neck. "Better?"

"Much," Christine beams, turning onto the street we need. "You're completely out of shape, Sophie" she scolds me gently but firmly. "You can't let a man dictate your happiness."

"What would you do if your three-year relationship ended?" I ask her. "And he didn't just leave. He left for another woman."

"Me?" She grins broadly. "I'd hit every party in town and relish my newfound freedom."

"I'm not wired like that," I reply, turning to watch the passing cars outside the window.

"Oh, Soph, you just need to find a guy for one night and that's it! You'll forget about Liam right away," Christine declares, her tone brimming with certainty.

I bite my lip, contemplating whether I should divulge the events of Tuesday night, if only to deter Christine from offering such advice in the future. Gathering my courage, I decide to speak up.

"I already tried that; it didn't work for me," I reply, attempting to keep my voice neutral.

"What?!" Christine erupts, her voice echoing through the car as she slams on the brakes, causing me to lurch forward. Fortunately, the seat belt keeps me in place, sparing me from any serious jolt.

"Are you insane?!" I rub my shoulder where the belt left a mark on my skin.

"What did you do?!" Christine demands, her eyes wide with curiosity. "You didn't even tell me! Spill it! I need to know all the details!"

I manage to buy myself some time as Christine expertly maneuvers the car into a parking spot, showcasing her impressive parallel parking skills.

Chapter 2

Sophie

"**S**top stalling and spill the beans!" Christine practically claps her hands together as the waiter takes our order and leaves us alone at a table by the window.

I take a sip of water, using the moment to gather my thoughts. Flashes of that night dance through my mind: intertwined hands, heated skin, the city lights painting the backdrop, his warm breath mingling with mine... I shake my head, attempting to dispel the memories and the resulting blush creeping onto my cheeks.

"What's the big deal?" I shrug. "I followed your suggestion, went to that hotel restaurant, sat at the bar, and ordered a cocktail."

"So, what happened next?" Christine's impatience is palpable as she rubs her hands together, eager for the juicy details.

"A man sat down beside me..."

"How old was he?" She interrupts, her curiosity piqued.

"I'm not entirely sure," I purse my lips. "But I'd say early thirties."

"I've never done anything like that. So, what happened next?" She prods, her excitement barely contained.

"We talked, had some drinks," I gloss over the moment when his hand lingered on my knee, sending shivers down my spine. "Then he settled the bill and asked if I wanted to go up to his room. I said yes."

Christine squeals with excitement, causing people around us to cast curious glances our way. Embarrassed, I hide my face in my hands, the cool touch of my fingers offering a brief respite from my flushed cheeks. But Christine seems unfazed by the attention, as if she's ready to broadcast my escapades to the world.

"And how was it?" She leans closer, locking eyes with me. "Did he dominate you? Was he a total freak? Did you enjoy it? Was he better than Liam?"

"Nothing like that. We had sex, and then I went straight home," I mumble, avoiding the explicit details, feeling increasingly uncomfortable in my seat.

"He turned out to be boring, didn't he?" Christine assumes, wearing a sympathetic expression.

"No, it's just one-night stands aren't my thing," I explain, knowing I'm not being entirely honest. I lie to my best friend without a hint of guilt. If it had been anyone else, I probably wouldn't have enjoyed it, but there was something captivating about the stranger. His charisma, his charm — they swept me off my feet. And his voice, deep and alluring, wrapped around me, making me succumb to his every word.

"Come on, it must have helped a little, right?" Christine asks skeptically.

"No, it didn't," I lie again, knowing that what truly helped wasn't the night with a stranger but the stranger himself, who managed to push thoughts of Liam out of my mind and replace them with himself.

"There is something seriously wrong with you," Christine snorts. "You're defective."

Ignoring her remark, I smile as the waiter approaches with our dishes. I accept the food under Christine's probing gaze, knowing she's itching to ask more questions.

"Why are we always talking about me?" I beat her to it. "How are you doing? Have you patched things up with your mom?"

The change of topic sobers Christine, and she looks down at her salad. Family matters have always been difficult for her, even though she tries to hide it. I remember this and shamelessly use it to divert the conversation.

"Mom completely lost it. Remember when I told you she burned all our family albums? Well, she went on to torch all the pictures and portraits of herself hanging on the walls. Remember how many there were?"

I remember vividly. I've spent countless nights at Christine's house and know her mother, Laura, quite well. She's an imposing woman — tall, slender, and once a model in her youth. But unable to accept leaving the industry and facing the fact that she was no longer being booked by agencies after giving birth, she turned to alcohol to numb her pain. It had a devastating impact on Christine's life, as Laura spiraled into madness.

"Is she still drinking?" I ask as Christine's phone rings for the fifth time that evening. "Who's blowing up your phone?"

"It's my dad," Christine sighs. "Living with Mom has become unbearable, so I've been staying at Dad's place for the past week. I'll wait until things calm down before going back."

Her revelation surprises me as much as if she had claimed to have seen a live mammoth wandering around the city center. According to Christine's anecdotes, she seldom communicated with her father. He and her mother had split up before Christine was born, and she only saw him once every five years, with the rest of the time consisting of alimony payments and purchases from Christine and Laura's "Wish Lists."

"I thought you had cut ties with him," I remark, genuinely taken aback.

"We hadn't spoken, but I had to reach out. Otherwise, I would've gone insane. Though I might just go crazy with him around too. Suddenly, twenty-two years later, he realizes he has a daughter and starts trying to lecture me like I'm still a little girl. Plus, he's got a new woman who walks around half-naked in the apartment," Christine rolls her eyes. "She acts like I don't even exist."

"You should have told me," I say, setting my fork down. "I would have offered you a bed at my place."

Christine waves off the suggestion, twirling her smooth black hair with her fingers. "Don't be silly. I wouldn't want to put you in an awkward spot. You have your studio, and my dad has a spacious apartment. Besides, he still has to play the part of a father every now and then," she adds with a wry smile, attempting to mask her sadness.

I feel terrible. What kind of friend am I? I hadn't even noticed the significant changes in Christine's life and failed to offer her support.

"By the way," Christine interjects suddenly, pulling out a golden envelope from her bag. "There's a silver lining to my moving out. My dad decided to throw me a birthday party," she announces, handing me an invitation adorned with elegant white lettering. "Here's yours. Cocktail dress code."

Another reminder of my negligence as a friend. I had completely forgotten Christine's upcoming birthday. I grimace as I glance at the invitation and note the venue: one of the most lavish restaurants in the city.

"Yeah, Dad's splashing the cash," she remarks, correctly interpreting my reaction. "I guess he's trying to make up for all the missed birthdays at once."

Ever since hearing Christine's tales about her father, I've harbored a deep-seated aversion towards him. Growing up in a stable family, it's hard for me to comprehend how someone could abandon their own child and simply compensate with money: Christine sports designer clothes, drives an expensive car, and Laura hasn't worked since her daughter was born. Regardless of how affluent and successful he may be, it's clear that he's morally bankrupt.

As expected, our evening concludes with a light salad, a single glass of wine, and a shared dessert. After dinner, Christine drops me off at home before heading to her father's place. He'd been bombarding her phone with messages all evening, demanding to know her whereabouts and when she plans to come back home.

Tonight, I find myself not dwelling on my past relationship. Instead, my mind drifts back to the enigmatic stranger's burning touch. Christine was right about one thing: another man managed to divert my attention from heartache. Yet, a new dilemma now plagues my thoughts: I'm consumed with regret, to the point of trembling, for not disclosing my name to him. Perhaps, had I done so, our conversation might have continued, leading to who knows what possibilities...

Chapter 3

Sophie

I scrutinize my reflection in the elevator mirror as it ascends to the panoramic restaurant atop the hotel, where we're celebrating Christine's birthday. I hope my bodycon black satin dress with straps and heeled sandals fits the cocktail dress code. My gaze fixates on the strap, a smile involuntarily playing on my lips as I recall the stranger's fingers brushing against it. Running my hands through my straightened hair, I use my little finger to smooth the contour of my red lipstick.

The elevator door opens, and I step into the restaurant, nervously clutching a gift box. The room is crowded with unfamiliar faces, and I'm not even sure that Christine knows all of them. The gathered men and women resemble shareholders at a corporate meeting rather than attendees at a young woman's twenty-third birthday celebration.

"Soph!" Christine breaks free from the crowd and rushes towards me, her golden short dress shimmering under the lights, matching her pumps perfectly. "I'm so glad to see you. You won't believe it. Of everyone here, I only know you and a few of our classmates. I have no clue who these people are. They don't even know me but they congratulate me and give me expensive gifts," she gestures towards her brand-new Cartier watch adorning her wrist.

Nervously, I fidget with the package in my hands. Inside is an ordinary set of cosmetics; although it is her favorite brand. It lacks luster compared to others gifts.

"Happy birthday," I say, handing Christine the gift. "I wish you many, many happy moments."

She beams with delight as she begins to unwrap it. I wave my hands to stop her from opening it now, because I am extremely ashamed and afraid to see the disappointment on her face.

"This is my favorite mascara and lipstick!" she exclaims upon discovering the gift. "You're a lifesaver! I ran out and couldn't find them anywhere. They were sold out everywhere!"

Christine hugs me tightly and kisses me on both cheeks. Her reaction makes my lips stretch into a smile that is instantly replaced by bewilderment. I feel a familiar nervous vibration spreading across the entire surface of my skin, even before I see the reason.

"Oh, there he is," Christine whispers, and I turn around in the direction she's looking.

Lightning shoots through me as I meet the dark gaze of the man who has exited the elevator. I recognize him immediately, and the memory of the snake tattoo encircling his waist under that black suit jacket makes my body tingle.

Without taking his eyes off me, he heads straight in our direction. On his arm is a tall, curvaceous and long haired blond. I want to run away, but my legs seem to be rooted to the floor. I fiddle with the hem of Christine's dress like a little girl and ask her to show me where the restroom is, but she can't hear me. Like me, Christine is captivated by the presence of the stranger.

As he draws nearer, the spacious hall suddenly feels suffocating. My breath catches, my palms grow clammy, and my heart pounds in my chest. What is he doing here? Who is this woman next to him?

"Thank you for a wonderful evening," Christine opens her arms and hugs the approaching man, who continues to look at me from behind her shoulder. "The party is absolutely fabulous, dad."

Dad. This word reverberates in my ears, sending a jolt through me. I swallow nervously, feeling the vein on my temple pulse. I sense the man wishing Christine a happy birthday and saying something about a brighter future, but I can't hear anything, as if I'm trapped in a vacuum. It never occurred to me that the Stranger from the hotel could be someone's father, let alone the father of my best friend.

"Soph," Christine shakes my shoulder, attempting to snap me out of my daze. I blink, trying to force a smile onto my face. It must come out crooked, for the blonde beside him furrows her brow at the sight of me.

"Soph, this is my dad, Alexander Bailey," Christine introduces me to the dark-haired man. "Dad, this is my best friend."

"Does your friend have a full name, or is her name Soph?" Alexander's voice carries a hint of amusement, sending goosebumps skittering across my skin as if I'm wrapped in something velvety.

"Sophie Williams," Christine answers on my behalf, her arm enveloping my shoulders like a mother who is infinitely proud of her daughter. I feel uncomfortable.

"Nice to meet you, Sophie," Alexander's lips curl up slightly as he extends his hand towards me. I stare at it as if it's an unfamiliar object, invisible burns tracing along my skin where his fingers once caressed me.

"It's mutual," I manage to squeak, my voice rising an octave as I offer my trembling hand. Lightning seems to strike as he wraps his fingers around mine, leaning down to kiss the back of my hand, his intense gaze never faltering from mine.

How did I not notice the striking resemblance between Christine and the stranger before? The hue of his brown eyes, the sheen of his black hair, the profile of his straight nose and well-defined cheekbones. While Christine has a defined dimple in her chin, the Stranger's dimple is less noticeable due to his short beard.

"Alex," the blonde interjects, her voice drawn in as she clings tighter to Alexander's elbow. "Let's go say hello to Duncan. He's been trying to get your attention."

Alexander releases my hand and turns towards the man mentioned by her.

"Excuse us, girls," he says before leaving. The blonde trots after him.

"Oh," Christine rolls her eyes. "Dad is so mannered, and Lola is just Velcro. Always stuck to him."

I ignore her comment, my gaze fixed on Alexander's broad back as he engages with a group of people. My cheeks turn red as I realize the absurdity of the situation: a week ago, during dinner, I reveled in dirty memories about my best friend's father, looking straight into her eyes. I urgently need a glass of cool water.

Chapter 4

Sophie

All evening I avoid his familiar heavy gaze, and at the sight of his dark-haired head I try to lose myself in the crowd. I pretend to look with intense interest at the restaurant's exquisite decor, which deserves attention. The transparent dome spanning overhead offers an unobstructed view of the night sky: the first stars are already sparkling, and the moon comes into its own, seeing off its bright day partner.

With the first rays of the setting sun, the restaurant workers had turned on subdued lights and placed candles on the tables. All this painfully reminds me of that night, but every time the memories pop up, I struggle to pack them back into the "black box" in my head.

Christine is constantly occupied by people I don't know. They wish her happy birthday, wondering why they haven't heard about Alexander Bailey's daughter before, and continue to overwhelm her with expensive gifts. I keep myself busy by wandering around the hall, stopping, from time to time, to talk with former classmates.

My patience lasts until the moment when one of the guys once again asks how my relationship with Liam is going and why he is not here. I'm trying to avoid direct answers because I do not intend to discuss my private life.

From this day forward, my number one rule is: never date classmates, guys from the same company or strangers who may be the father of your best friend.

I make another attempt to hide when I realize that I will not be able to get Christine's attention for some time. She is being pulled along by a group of people, seemingly saying something funny, because she starts laughing.

I'm not sure how I will be able to talk to her again without noticing the resemblance to her father. I hope these feelings will fade with time.

After asking one of the waiters where the restroom is, I give him my glass of champagne and go in the direction indicated. Trying to find the right door in a dimly lit hallway, and cursing under my breath when I can't find a single sign.

"Are you lost?" The familiar voice makes my legs give way.

His hands deftly grab me by the waist and do not allow me to shamefully fall to the floor. I expect Alexander to pull away from me, but this doesn't happen. His fingers only tighten their grip the fabric of my dress. I try to take a step back, but I can only hear the seams splitting.

"I need to go to the restroom," I mumble unclearly, my teeth starting to chatter from nerves, and my body trembling.

Alexander lets go with one hand. But before I can exhale in relief, his fingers find my chin and force me to raise my head until his dark eyes meet mine.

"Someone can see us," I say in a barely audible voice. If someone notices us, then trouble is inevitable. Especially if Christine is the one who sees us.

My former Stranger is silent. He presses with his gaze, suppresses my will. Alexander's fingers smear on my lips, just like in the hotel room. I swallow convulsively, but the trembling only intensifies, and it seems to me that I am about to faint.

"Did you befriend Christine on purpose to get close to me?" He finally breaks his silence.

My eyes widen involuntarily at his unexpected suggestion. I bat my eyelashes in confusion, trying to figure out exactly what he means.

"Me? No. Christine and I have been friends for six years," I murmur as if under hypnosis, looking at the reflections of the moon in his pupils. "I didn't know you and her... You are her... I didn't know."

His hand squeezes my jaw firmly, making my mouth open involuntarily, and my cheeks begin to ache. Squinting his eyes, he studies every millimeter of my face for another moment, and then harshly releases it.

I stagger back, clinging to the ledge of the parquet with my heels, and grab the first door handle I can find. But luck is clearly not on my side today, and Alexander does not intend to let me go so easily. He grabs my hand and pulls again.

"You won't tell her anything, understand?" He mutters through clenched teeth, squeezing my wrist so hard that my fingertips start to numb.

"I have no intention to tell her," I look at him defiantly because I can't stand being taken for a fool. "This would ruin my friendship with Christine. I'm not stupid."

"I really hope so," he says hoarsely and with a sharp movement presses me with all the weight of his body to the wall. Even in the semi-darkness of the corridor, I can see how his brown eyes grow even darker. "Otherwise, you will regret it very much."

His lips cover mine in a greedy kiss. My breath catches, and my legs go limp. The intensity of this man is impossible to resist, and I surrender, allowing him to dominate my body. While just a few meters away, his daughter — my best friend laughs out loud. She must never know about us.

Chapter 5

Sophie

Alexander releases me only when many voices in the restaurant begin to chant "Happy Birthday to you", interspersed with the rustling of sparklers, which are usually set on a cake.

Without saying a word, he pulls a handkerchief from the pocket of his perfect jacket and wipes my lipstick from his lips. Not for one second does he take his piercing gaze from my eyes. After making sure that there are no more stains appear on the white fabric, Alexander turns around and walks briskly away.

I take a deep breath in through my nose, realizing that I haven't been breathing all this time. The sound of my heart beats loudly in my ears. What just happened?

It turned out that the restroom was right in front of me. Entering it, I lock the door, rechecking the lock several times. I rest my trembling hands on the cool ceramic rim of the sink and lift my head to look at my reflection in the mirror. Lipstick is smeared over half of my face, my chest heaves, as if I has just run a marathon, my cheeks are burning, and there is not a trace of hair styling.

Frantically, I pull tissues out of the wall holder and begin to clean the lipstick from my face. I rub to such an extent that my irritated skin turns red, and my eyes shine from overflowing emotions. Every part of my body, which Alexander's hands shamelessly explored, burns worse than several hours on the beach under the scorching sun.

"It was just a kiss, calm down," I say in a trembling voice to my reflection in the mirror.

I understand that returning to the party is out of the question. I am not able to show joy on my face and carry on conversations. All I want to do now is to be swallowed up by the earth so that no one will ever find me.

After rinsing my face with cold water and wiping off the cosmetics debris from the sink, I decisively leave my refuge with a deep exhalation. I try my best to maintain confidence in every step and pray that I won't meet familiar faces along the way.

Successfully bypassing the corridor, I pass through the hall, happily noticing that everyone has sat down in their places and turned their attention to what is happening on the opposite side. I easily recognize Alexander's voice. He stands, looking around at all the people with his heavy gaze and says some kind of toast, and then everyone starts applauding him and clinking glasses.

"Soph!" I hear Christine's voice. She is standing up to hug her father as she calls my name. The back of my head starts to ache. On a physical level, I feel exactly where Alexander's gaze is focused. I quicken my pace, pretending not to notice anything or anyone around.

I don't care what others think, but I'll explain myself to Christine tomorrow. I'll lie that I felt bad and didn't want to attract attention.

I literally stumble out of the restaurant and press the elevator button repeatedly, as if this would speed it up. Unfortunately, the screen above the sliding doors shows that it is stuck on one of the lower floors with no immediate intention to budge. Angrily, I slam my open palm against the metal sliding door.

"Sophie," the way my name comes out of his mouth sends shivers down my spine and concentrates in the depths of my stomach. Only this was not enough.

I don't want to turn around, I don't want to fall into the trap of his eyes again, from which it is impossible to tear myself away. It's not normal that a stranger has such power over me.

When I hear his boots on the marble floor of the hall, I can't stand it and take off, rushing towards the first door that I come across. My heels slip on the smooth surface, but that doesn't stop me. Having successfully reached my goal, I pull the doorknob and find myself on the stairs. Bingo! Somewhere, Mrs. Luck is on my side.

I run down several flights of stairs, and, finally, out of breath, I stop. The right side of my body throbs in pain, bringing me to tears, and my ankles hurt where the straps of my sandals rip at my skin. I try to listen and hear nothing but my heavy, hysterical breathing. No one seems to be following me.

I grin, imagining how broad-shouldered Alexander in his perfectly tailored suit running down the stairs on sparkling, polished boots. Silly dreamer.

I take off my heels and go down the stairs a little more calmly, still afraid to go out to the elevators. On the way, I call for a taxi. Finally on the street, I jump into the taxi, exhaling a sigh of relief. The driver looks at me like I'm crazy. Apparently surprised by the eccentric barefooted girl, but I don't care at all.

A sense of shame overtakes me later, when I stumble into the apartment, shutting the door before sliding my back down it until I'm sitting on the dirty entrance rug. I look around my small studio apartment and wince when Oliver, who has missed me, starts rubbing against my foot. An all-black shorthaired Brit with bright yellow eyes looks at me accusingly for leaving him home alone.

"Hi, baby," I coo over the cat, scratching behind his ear. "You won't believe how happy I am to see you."

He purrs lingeringly, poking his muzzle into my shoulder.

"Don't ask, it went horribly," I sigh, feeling the warmth of my beloved pet. This has a calming effect on me, and I relax a little, resting the back of my head against the door. "You just have a disgustingly shameless mom."

As if to confirm this, the cat purrs once more and settles down on my legs, wagging his tail.

In the darkness of the apartment, the invasive beep of my phone makes Oliver and I jump. The Brit squints angrily, then jumps off and walks away, leaving me alone with my problems and remorse.

I look at the blinding screen of my smartphone. There are several messages from Christine: she's worried about me, asking where I am, what happened to me and if I need help.

I lock my phone screen and leave her messages unanswered. Yes, it's selfish to leave a friend in the dark by running away from her party. But now, for the first time in my life, I want to listen to myself, what I want, and not be pleasant to everyone. So, I take a shower, trying to scrub HIS touches and looks with a washcloth, and then go to bed.

An episode of a funny series that does an excellent job of distracting me from bad thoughts, the cat curled up at the feet of a warm ball, and I fall into a dream, as if this evening did not exist at all. I'll have time to overthink and arrange brainwashing myself tomorrow with a fresh mind.

In the middle of the night, the melody of an incoming message interrupts my already ragged sleep. I open my heavy eyelids, trying to figure out what time it is, and look around the room. The laptop continues to play the already incomprehensible episode of the series, illuminating the apartment with the light of the screen. The annoying sound repeats again.

I reach for my phone on the nightstand, rubbing my eyes with my fingers. The dream lifts when I see that the message is from an unknown number. My finger freezes in uncertainty over the screen, which manages to fade to black. I stare into the darkness, and then tap the screen again. I unlock my phone and bite my lip until it bleeds, rereading each word several times.

> *You can't run away from me, Sophie.*

With a silent scream, I throw the phone away like a hot coal and roll over onto my stomach. I whip the pillow with my hands, imagining that it is Alexander's face and give him juicy slaps. But in my chest, for some reason I don't understand, a maddening warmth spread.

Chapter 6

Sophie

"You really don't look well," Christine frowns as I sit next to her on the couch.

Deciding to redeem myself for last night, I invited Christine to our favorite cafe that we used to go to almost every day after class. All morning I rehearsed in my head the excuses and reasons for my escape last night. I settled on the fact that my stomach was cramping due to it being "that time of the month". She definitely understands me.

"I'm sorry I had to run out last night," I begin to babble the memorized phrases, but I don't have time to say a word further, because she interrupts me.

"It's okay, I understand everything," she says suddenly.

I look up at her, feverishly going over in my head what exactly she understands. Did she me with Alexander? If so, why is she so calm? No, it's clearly something else.

"Come on, don't worry so much," Christine places her hand on top of mine on the table in a sympathetic gesture. What the hell is going on?

"I saw him," she stuns me and pats my arm. "I understand everything."

"I can explain everything. It happened by accident," I blurt out, looking at her in horror. That's it, our friendship is over. She's deliberately pretending to be calm, or maybe the reality of the whole situation hasn't dawned on her yet. But soon she'll realize, and then our relationship will be over.

"Soph, no need to explain anything," interrupts Christine once again. "When Liam came up to congratulate me, I understood everything. Don't worry about it. You can roll your eyes back into your head now," she smiles kindly.

"Liam?" I ask her confused. He wasn't even at the party.

"Well, yes, right after you left he came out of the restroom. I thought that you met there, talked and you ran away. So, what happened?"

It's like a black hole in my head: thoughts coming and passing through creating a chaotic, meaningless set of words. Was Liam at the restaurant then? In the men's room? Was he so close and I hadn't even noticed him? What if he saw me with Alexander?

I shake my head, trying to pull my thoughts together. It's hard to take control of myself, but I find a way out of the situation. I don't even have to come up with an excuse, Christine gave it to me on a silver platter. All I need to do is agree with her assumption. After all, I would be behaving in a similar way if I had met Liam. Perhaps a little calmer.

"Yes," I nod and try to keep my voice calm. "Liam surprised me, and I wasn't prepared to see him last night. I didn't even know he was coming."

Christine curves her lips into a sad smile and wraps her arms around my shoulders, pressing against my cheek.

"My dear, I need to apologize that he was at the party," she kisses me on the cheek. "My dad's assistant was in charge of the guest list, and she invited everyone she saw as friends on my social networks."

Did fate smile on me? I don't know. But if so, then I am grateful to her. I hate to lie.

"I told my dad everything, and I made a huge fuss at home that because of his stupid assistant, you were forced to leave the party."

I freeze, eyes wide. I stare thoughtlessly at every line on the opposite wall, trying to figure out what this information means to me. Alexander now knows who my ex is. So what? Who cares? I don't find anything wrong with answering these questions. So why is my stomach so unbearably reduced to nervous spasms?

"My dad gave me an apartment in the house where our favorite actress lives, can you imagine? I'm in shock," Christine finally releases me from her arms. "After the renovations, I can finally move out from my mom's place and live on my own."

"Oh, cool, congratulations," I say automatically, not actually hearing her words. They just pass my ears. I'm still trying to understand the cause for what I'm feeling. Feeling like Alexander caught me hot when he found out about the existence of Liam.

Christine continues to talk about how her birthday went. She shares the details of who was there and what each of them gifted her, and that her dad has famous friends that she did not even know about. She shows me an endless stream of photos of the guests and their gifts. I feign interest.

Christine, due to her upbringing, has always been very mercantile. She could easily determine the brand of any item worn by our classmates, determine a fake from an original. For the former, she would immediately, to put it mildly, condemn the person. And for the latter, she would envy. She probably developed this attitude from her mother. She also likes to count other people's money.

If her father had been raising her, would Christine be different now?

We end our meeting in the late afternoon. Throughout the conversation, I am mostly silent, staying somewhere deep in my thoughts and memories of Alexander's caresses.

My lips are sore and sting ruthlessly as I imagine his rough, greedy kisses over and over again. My cheeks flush with every glance from Christine. She tries to get my attention, and then she seems not to care, and enjoys her own monologue, listing the brands of jewelry and bags that she received as gifts yesterday.

"Dad's here," she says, answering a message on her phone.

Electrical impulses spread through my skin as I realize that I am about to see Alexander again.

"I thought you drove your car today," I swallow, gathering my things.

"It's in service," shrugs. "Dad insisted on picking me up."

Did he know that Christine was meeting me today? He must have. She told me that she was going to apologize to me today in order to continue humiliating her father for his reckless choice of guests. So very much like Christine. She never let's me down on the little things, like pointing out my mistakes over and over.

"You never told me that your father is like... This..."

"What? Successful businessman? Owner of a media company?" Christine lists with pride.

I shake my head. She could never understand that I don't care about the amount of money people have. If a person is good, then what difference does it make what kind of wealth he has?

"I meant he looks so young."

Christine laughs.

"Well, he's only forty-five, what else should he look like?"

Hearing Alexander age for the first time, I calculate our age difference. To my shock, I realize that I slept with a man who is twice my age. My cheekbones begin to tingle.

We leave the cafe just at the moment Alexander throws his cigarette butt into the street ashtray next to the entrance.

"Hey dad," Christine kisses him on the cheek. "Thanks for picking me up."

For the umpteenth time, I notice how dramatically she changed her attitude towards him. When he simply sent her money in a card, she was not particularly disposed to him, but as soon as he began to shower her with gifts, he immediately became the best father in the world. I involuntarily cringe at the sight of this.

"It's not difficult for me, I was nearby," Alexander says unemotionally, turning to me. "Good afternoon, Sophie. Good to see you. I hope last night wasn't too bad and no one bothered you?"

There is a subtext in his words that I immediately catch. It seems that my cheeks are about to become like hot coals.

"Good afternoon," I choke out, trying not to look at him. "No worries. Everything is fine."

"Soph, can we give you a ride?" Christine proposes unexpectedly.

I quickly start shaking my head. I dig my nails into my palm until they cut into my skin, using the pain to pull myself together and to calm down. I need to stop reacting so violently. I don't understand what is happening to me. The energy wave that emanates from Alexander, at each meeting, takes me out of my usual comfort zone, filling every cell of my body with awkwardness.

"No need," I try my best to speak calmly without breaking into a squeal. "I still have to do some things for work."

"Okay," Christine shrugs. "Let's go then, dad?"

Alexander gives me another heavy look from head to toe, and then nods in agreement. I say goodbye and turn around before they leave. From behind me, I feel the unrelenting stare of his dark eyes upon me, raising chilling goosebumps that run like a colony of ants down my spine.

Chapter 7

Sophie

It takes me an hour before I can start concentrating on work. I habitually keep checking my phone screen. Now that I know that Alexander has my number, I involuntarily wait for another unexpected message.

It's been a little over a week since our last meeting. And the longer I've been without his attention, the more I want to get from him. My hands are itching to grab the phone and, send him a message daring him, demanding him not to pursue or try to find me again. But no message comes from him anyway.

The whole Bailey family seems to have forgotten about me. Christine hasn't been in touch since "the apology". She is too busy with her new life. In her videos on social networks, she chronicles her many trips to furniture stores and hardware stores with a popular interior designer from the capital.

Christine and the designer act like they are old friends. They even go to restaurants and parties together. Before, Christine always invited me. At the sight of each new photo, jealousy eats me up inside. I'm used to being her only friend.

"Hold it." Stella drops a heavy folder, that lands on my desk with a loud thud. "Project "Black Pearl" just like you wanted."

Hearing the name, I look dumbfounded from the folder, on which the embossed emblem of our firm is displayed, to Stella. The workers

Elisabeth Baldwin - 35

who are sitting nearby in the open space are smiling happily. Of course, I brainwashed them all during lunches, that I want to finally take on something worthwhile, and not build barracks.

"I was assigned to handle this case?" I ask breathless with disbelief. I've waited so long to be given a major project! And I certainly did not expect that the first of them would be one of the most important for the company.

"Paired with Christopher," Stella nods towards the private office of one of the main architects. "He asked you to come by tomorrow and discuss all the details, but in the meantime, study all the descriptions, documents and drawings."

"Thank you!" I squeal and jump up from the table to hug my colleague. She pats me softly on the back and pulls away.

"Be prepared for hard work," Stella lowers her voice. "Christopher reprimands everyone for the smallest mistake, so I advise you to prepare to meet him like you have a university exam."

I whistle in the air-conditioned air through my nostrils. I've heard a lot about how interns flew out of the firm in batches after confusing an insignificant thing once. Christopher always says: "Today you made a typo in the document, and tomorrow you will forget about the load-bearing wall. An architect must always be focused." Every day I am surprised that I have not yet been fired for my absent-mindedness, that has become especially pronounced in recent days.

Time goes by quickly as I study the documents and drawings. At exactly eight in the evening, I tear myself away from the pages, noticing that the entire computer screen is covered with notes on multi-colored stickers. I smile proudly, satisfied with the work done.

I look around the office while I collect my things in a bag: everyone has long gone home, only Stella and I, as always, stay late. She, because she is a workaholic, and me because I can't lose this job, so I try to delve into every detail and show my industriousness to my superiors.

Warm air hits my face as I step out onto the office porch. I don't remember the last time it was so stuffy at the end of July. I take out my phone to check the balance on my card and whether there is room in my budget for one more taxi ride. I don't want to ride in a stuffy, crowded bus.

"Would you like a lift?" I flinch at the familiar voice, and my phone falls onto the cobblestones, face down. I swear loudly, not holding back the desire to say a couple of biting expressions.

"How ugly to say such things with such a beautiful mouth," Alexander grins, but I'm not laughing. My phone crashed and didn't survive. And I literally have my whole life in it, all my important contacts and memorable moments captured in the photo.

"Are you following me?" I blurt out in annoyance, at the same time forcing the power button. The smartphone finally turns on, and I breathe a sigh of relief. The screen, however, is shattered, but it can always be changed. So, no taxi today.

I understand that Alexander has been silent all this time and is carefully watching my movements. I look up at him. He's perfect, as always: coiffed black hair, neat stubble on his chin and cheeks, a white cotton shirt accentuates slightly tanned skin, and creased black trousers hanging provocatively over sculpted thighs.

He is leaning on the bumper of his navy-blue Bentley, a cigarette dangling between his fingers. I don't like smokers. Liam smoked and it really pissed me off, especially when he wanted to kiss me, and his mouth smelled like an ashtray. But for some reason, neither in the hotel nor in the restaurant, I did not sense the tobacco aroma on Alexander's breath.

"How did you know where I work?"

He watches me put my broken phone into my bag.

"Christine is too talkative. Just like her mother," he grins wryly. For a second, I think that discontent flashed in his eyes.

"Are you following me?" I repeat my question, folding my arms over my chest. "Aren't you afraid? I'm your daughter's friend."

Alexander throws the cigarette butt onto the pavement and extinguishes it with the sole of his shoe. Putting his hands in his pants pockets, he takes a step towards me, but stops a meter away.

"Maybe I like you?" He squints, never breaking eye contact.

"Do you like your blonde too?" I raise my eyebrow. Draw. I won't let you play with me.

"Lola? What does she have to do with it?" The expression on his face does not change, as if he absolutely does not care about this conversation.

I clench my fists because I am annoyed by his eternal calmness and the reaction of my body to his presence. My skin burns from the touch of his gaze, and warmth spreads in my lower abdomen. I'm turned on by the fact that this is the first time we've had a full conversation since the incident at the hotel.

"Listen," I exhale irritably. "I don't want to be like my ex's current girlfriend. I don't want to ruin someone's relationship and be the third wheel. I've been on the receiving end, and I know what it feels like."

Alexander cocks his head to the side, and the corners of his lips lift slightly, as if he's trying to suppress a smile.

"So that's the problem? The stupid teen who broke your heart? Is that why you're running from me?"

"That's not the point," I shake my head.

"What makes you think that Lola and I have anything in common?"

"The same too talkative girl told me that she walks around your apartment half-naked. And I saw how she looks at you," I put all my cards on the table.

"I should have worked on her upbringing," Alexander sighs. "For my part, everything is very clear: I am a free man and I love regular sex, she is a new actress in the industry and also pursues her own benefit. What's wrong with that if everything is by mutual agreement and everyone is happy?"

I am surprised at how easily he tells me about his disgusting relationship with Lola.

"Are you sure she's okay with that? From the outside it looks like she's in love with you."

"That's not my problem," Alexander shrugs calmly. "My obligations under this arrangement have long been fulfilled, and Lola will move out of my apartment soon, regardless of her feelings for me."

"Do you want to buy me too?" I look at him with a challenge.

"You can't be bought," he closes the distance between us and runs his fingers down my cheek. "That's your beauty."

"Well, what do you want from me?" I ask hoarsely, feeling my skin goosebumps at his every touch. It becomes unbearable. Alexander always fills all the space between us, no matter how spacious it may be.

"Right now, I want to give you a ride home, and then we'll see," his eyes sparkle brightly in the sunset.

"Then you'll know my address."

"That's my cunning plan," Alexander grins and winks at me.

I don't know why, but I agree to his proposal, admitting the possibility that I will later regret it very much.

A moment later, we are rushing through the evening twilight, cutting through the flow of city traffic. The inside of the car smells of leather and spicy men's cologne. Alexander drives calmly and smoothly, with relaxed steering and the changing of lanes. The sedan is filled with light jazz music, which surprises me. I expected to hear rap or deep house.

"How did you get my phone number?" I ask when he stops the car in front of my building.

"Nowadays, when everything about a person is online, it's not that hard to do," he replies cryptically.

"Checked on Christina's phone?" I'm trying to guess the right answer to my question.

"Yes," Alexander laughs. This is the first time I hear him laugh. Deep, low, and insanely pleasant. It caresses my ears and spreads through my body with a languishing vibration.

I unbuckle my seatbelt as he catches my wrist and starts stroking my skin with his fingers, leaving more burns on it.

"Will I see you tomorrow?" He asks, looking into my eyes. I'm confused by his proposal. Is he asking me out on a date?

"I'll only agree to a date with you if you stop following me."

"You make conditions? I like it," Alexander chuckles and grabs my chin. "See you tomorrow, then," he says directly into my lips, and then covers them in a light kiss.

"See you tomorrow," I whisper, unable to hide my smile.

When I get out of the car, I know that this is the day my world will be turned upside down. I still don't understand exactly how and what awaits me, but it will definitely never be the same ever again.

Chapter 8

Sophie

Cool air flows into the car through the passenger side window, and mixies with the light jazz as we slowly roll through the night streets of the city. Sticking my hand out the window, I catch its streams with my hand, and pretend to look intently at the sights rushing by.

At the pit of my stomach, it aches unbearably from Alexander being so close to me. He sits behind the wheel, occasionally casting sideways glances in my direction with a slight smile. I avoid eye contact with him at all costs, because I don't want him to see the reaction he brings out of me. It's enough that I couldn't help screaming with delight when he met me after work with an incredibly beautiful bouquet, which now lies on my lap. Liam never gave me flowers during our relationship. He always treated our relationship as something ordinary and taken for granted.

I instantly forget about the scolding Christopher gave me at today's meeting, pointing out that I did not study the project well enough. Although I had spent half the night going through the pages. Perhaps it was the fact that most of the time I sat with a stupid smile on my lips and stared at the wall, remembering Alexander's kiss and his invitation to a date.

"How was your day?" He breaks the silence, pulling the car alongside the curb and coming to a stop.

"Not bad," I answer, listening to my feelings from the ensuing dialogue. It's strange to me that we can just talk about everyday things like that. Is an adult man really interested in what is happening in the life of a student?

"Move your hand," Alexander suddenly orders, a little too abruptly, I think. I pull my hand inside and put it on the bouquet, nervously stroking the iris petals. The car window goes up, separating us from the outside world and leaving us alone with each other. The music stops.

"Just not bad? Christine told me that you are now doing an internship in a company that did not take her because of the big competition."

Forgetting all the awkwardness, I sharply turn to Alexander and look at his face, which is illuminated by the headlights of oncoming cars. I involuntarily admire his beautiful profile and neatly styled hair.

"Did Christine apply for an internship?"

"Yes, but no company accepted her, so she decided to focus on her master's degree."

The news shocks me so much that I don't know what to say. Christine never told me that she even wanted to do an internship, let alone that she had filled out applications. I remember her bravado she spoke about the benefits of not thinking about money and just enjoying her studies and student parties. Then, Christine still lived with her mother, and she fulfilled any of Christine's whims out of guilt for her alcoholism.

"Oh, yes, I completely forgot about it," I decide not to betray her.

There is silence in the car, interrupted only by the clicks of the turn signal. I notice how Alexander squeezes the steering wheel, which makes my skin begin to creak as he was squeezing my thigh. He's probably thinking that he is in the company of a forgetful fool and now considering how to interrupt this reckless date.

"And how was your day?" I decide to ask a question in return. So, as not to pass for an ill-mannered youngster and even out my impression of myself.

"Fine," Alexander cuts off any chance of continuing the conversation with his rough tone of voice, and pulls the car back onto the road.

I clench my fingers around the flowers, rustling the cellophane wrap and start looking at the pearl ribbon binding them together. *Fool, you need to control what you say and not give in to every emotional impulse.* I feel I've completely ruined the evening before it even starts.

We pull into the parking lot of one of the skyscrapers, continuing to listen to the silence. I frantically think about how to fix the situation, but I do not find a single solution. I'm physically close to Alexander, but for some reason, on a mental level, I cannot connect with him. I blame it on my embarrassment and self-doubt.

Having parked, Alexander is in no hurry to leave the car. Unfastening his belt, he turns to me. His penetrating gaze seems to get under my skin and scans every millimeter of my face. I feel my cheeks blush in a second, and I look down at the armrest between us.

"You can leave the bouquet here," he says a little softer and moves the flowers from my lap to the backseat. His fingers lightly touch the skin of my buttocks, which are exposed because my skirt has been pulled up from my fidgeting. My exposed skin begins to tingle immediately, and every negative thought leave my head.

Alexander leads me out of the elevator on the top floor of the tower. We find ourselves in a panoramic cafe, that, to my surprise, is completely empty. It's strange because at this hour the dining room is normally full of couples and groups of friends have dinner and the din of utensils on fine China fills the room.

A lone waiter promptly seats us at a table by the window and immediately brings a bottle of white wine, pouring it ceremonially into our glasses.

"Will they give us menus?" I whisper, afraid that in the penetrating silence the skeleton crew of wait staff will hear me.

"No," says Alexander and takes a sip of wine. "I made arrangements for our menu before our arrival."

I nod, trying to hide my shock. Did he take the time to arrange our date in advance? For me?

"It's beautiful here," I look around the elegant Art Nouveau room and fiddle with my glass, twisting it on the table by the stem.

Alexander does not answer, just looking at me with his calm and thoughtful gaze. His reticence makes me nervous, and I try to fill the oppressive silence with stories about my new project, which I was entrusted with at work. He patiently listens to everything I tell him. When appetizers finally arrive, I pause and dive into the tasting.

"Tell me something about yourself," I ask, when I realize that I can no longer do my monologue because I've run out of things to say.

"What do you want to know?" Alexander leans forward a little, his eyes flashing.

He seems to like it when people pay attention to him. The fact that he was quite narcissistic was clear from our first meeting, his egotism became more and more apparent as I showed increased interest in him after a couple cocktails. In the moment, it didn't frighten me at all because I only needed one thing from him. If our incomprehensible relationship should grow to a much deeper level, I begin to wonder if it will be acceptable to me.

"What do you do? What are your hobbies? How do you spend your free time?" I bombard Alexander with questions, but I don't have time to get everything out because his phone interrupts with a trill.

He raises his hand, indicating that I should stay put, and gets up from the table, looking at the screen. He moves to the far corner of the window, one hand in his pocket.

"Yes," he replies sharply. "I can't talk now." He pauses, looks back at me, and I turn away, pretending not to eavesdrop. "I'm in a business meeting. I'll call you back."

A business meeting. I chuckle. If all his business meetings are like this...

The idea pierces me like lightning. A restaurant closes for us; excuses given to an invisible caller. Of course, a successful businessman who knows half the city, if not the country, will not allow himself to appear in public with his mistress.

Mistress. How stupid and naive I am. I believed all his fairy tales about the aspiring actress. It must be Lola calling him asking where he is and whether to expect him for dinner.

The emptiness of the restaurant begins to press on me even more. My head is spinning from disappointing thoughts. Alexander is twice as old as me, he has had a stable life for a long time. He's my best friend's father. I soar in my dreams, allowing myself, even for a second, to think that he is really interested in me as a woman.

What the hell is his interest? What does he think about me? The girl who jumped into his bed without knowing his name. Agrees on a date, betraying his daughter, getting into his car, shamelessly telling him her address. In his eyes, I am an ordinary cheap girl with whom you can spend time, escaping from the everyday routine.

"So where did we stop?" Asks Alexander, returning to the table.

I sip my wine, justifying my silence. I see no reason to continue our date, but I don't know how to end it either.

The solution comes to mind when the waiter brings new plates, which I ignore.

" I need to go powder my nose," I smile tightly and get up, grabbing my purse. "I need to fix my lipstick." I mutter the first excuse that comes to mind.

I'm heading towards the restroom that is right next to the elevators. It seems that fleeing restaurants is becoming a bad habit of mine.

Chapter 9

Sophie

"Hello Soph!" Christine yells into her phone. She's been ringing my phone for the past few hours, causing the entire team at work to look annoyingly at me throughout the entire meeting. "It's impossible to get through to you. You're like a queen, now. Are you disappearing into your work?"

"Christine, did something happen? I just got out of the office, I couldn't answer before, sorry," I gasp, pulling the phone away from my ear as a shard of broken screen digs painfully into my skin.

I curse Alexander and remind myself that I need to get my phone to the repair shop soon.

"Yes, yes, I understand that. Listen, I was invited to a party. Do you want to go with me?"

I stop in the middle of the street. The man walking behind me swears loudly, scaring the hell out of me when he nearly runs into me from behind. I make my apologies for stopping so abruptly during rush hour near the subway station.

I have not talked to Christine for three weeks now. This is the longest break we've ever had. So, her offer to go to a party together comes as a complete surprise to me. I'm not sure I want to go to the party, but I don't want to miss the opportunity to hear about Alexander either.

I am a textbook example for all of the stereotypes about female logic: I run away from a date; blacklist his phone number; complaining that all men are womanizers and cheaters. Then I wonder why he does not pursue me and does not look for "casual" rendezvous.

No, I have drawn all the conclusions for myself, and I am going to stick to my position. I don't want to be like the girl who became the third wheel in my relationship with Liam, who he left me for. I am not a destroyer of families and not a stupid mistress who will wait for years for a man to leave his wife. But I also really want to know about Alexander. My curiosity does not allow me to live in peace.

"When is the party?" I ask Christine and write down the time and address in my notes.

I dressed to the nines for the club. I even bought a new dress with the last of my savings so as not to look worse than Christine's new, privileged friends.

Approaching the party location, I already regret that I agreed to this adventure. The club is too pretentious, and the visitors are way too arrogant.

"Honey!" Christine screams and kisses me on both cheeks. "I'm so glad to see you! It's wonderful that you were able to join."

There was something cutesy about her speech during our parting, and her gestures became more energetic.

"Don't be mad at me, but I invited you for a reason," Christine begins to mumble, handing me a cocktail. How could I have felt that she had invited me just because she missed me? I'm not sure she's even capable of that feeling.

"So, what happened?" I ask indifferently and take a generous sip of the alcohol. I need to quickly wash down the frustration caused by her behavior.

"The owner of this club is a guy I like," I can even see through the multi-colored spotlights how Christine's cheeks are blushing rapidly. "Well, actually... He's my dad's business partner and he's fucking old. But I fell for him like a stupid kid and now I have no idea what to do about it."

A nervous laugh escapes my lips. What I didn't expect was that Christine and I would switch places.

"Don't laugh at me!" Christine groans with an exhausted expression on her face. "He is so handsome! He came to our house a couple of times, to bring some documents for dad. Then I spent the next fifteen minutes trying to pick up my jaw up from the floor."

"So, how old is he?" I wonder as I nibble on a paper cocktail straw and look around the crowded club, trying to figure out who might be Christine's latest love interest.

"Thirty-eight. Can you imagine?!" Christina rolls her eyes and hangs on my shoulder, whimpering in my ear. "He's older than me by fifteen years, and he obviously likes girls more experienced than me."

I chuckle, thinking that she has no idea how old the man I like is.

"You slept with that stranger, according to you, he was also about that age," Christine looks hopefully at me. I try to hold back the cocktail that has risen in my throat. "What did you do to hook up with him? Help me! I need a plan of action now."

"Christine, I didn't do anything," I brush her off, trying to end this conversation, otherwise my heart will jump out of my chest with excitement. "He sat down with me at the bar and bought me a cocktail."

Christine stamps her foot in annoyance.

"You really are the world's best wingman, aren't you?" Christine snorts sarcastically, and then squeezes my elbow so hard that sparks fly from my eyes. "It's him, it's him!"

She points at one of the tables behind the railing. A slender, fit, blond in polo shirt and trousers sits there. He talks about something with the hostess, and then returns his attention to his companions. I do not find anything interesting or attractive in him. Maybe he's just not my type.

" Just go up to him and say hello," I suggest ingenuously, continuing to gnaw at the straw with my teeth.

"What?!" Christine screams and looks at me like I'm stupid. "Are you crazy? I can't do that!"

"Christine, how else can you do it?" I snort, not knowing how to please her. "You know him. He's seen you several times, and he probably remembers you. Just say that you saw him and want to say hello. Why don't you just start the conversation?"

Christine stares in the direction of her unsuspecting target for a minute, weighing all the pros and cons, and then nods confidently.

"You're right," she hands her glass to me and smooths her hair. "I'll just go right over there and introduce myself."

I watch as she squeezes through the crowd of dancing people, and then stands next to the railing, leaning over it with her leg up. I want to punch myself in the forehead. She pulls a lock of her hair with a finger and giggles stupidly. It seems that even through the roar of music I can hear her piercing voice.

The blonde's face is expressionless. Either he always smiles so politely at everyone, or Christine's company is annoying him, and he wants to get rid of her as soon as possible. He keeps looking in the direction of his friends, as if apologizing for this intrusion.

It's rather petty of me, but I get a perverse sense of pleasure from watching Christine's walk of shame back to me, her misery etched on her face. She is clearly unhappy with the outcome of the conversation. I even forget that I wanted to casually mention her father to find out at least something about Alexander.

"Well, how did it go?" I smile at her for the first time in the evening.

"Disgusting." She snatches her glass from my hands and gulps down the rest of the cocktail. "I tried to talk to him, but he only answers yes or no to questions."

"Maybe he has someone or you're not his type?" I guess swaying to the music.

"I'm not his type?" Christine is outraged. "Do you see me? I'm beautiful! I'm everyone's type."

I burst out laughing at her words. Sometimes I wonder how she can be so self-confident. Apparently, she gets it from her father. This thought makes me order another cocktail. This one stronger.

After the failed conversation, Christine gets so drunk that at midnight I have to drag her out of the club with me. Security personally wanted to escort us out, because Christine mustered up the liquid courage to do a strip tease on top of the table across from the table occupied by the blond man of her desire. I stopped her just in time and forced her to leave.

"Soph," Christine says drunkenly, leaning against the side of the building as I try to hail a taxi. "I can't go home."

I turn to her and just in time. She starts to slide down onto the sidewalk, but I manage to catch her.

"Dad will kill me," she wraps her arms around my neck, putting her full weight on me. "He doesn't like drunk people. He'll start shouting again that I'm like my mom." Christine breathes ribbons of alcohol vapor into my face that makes me wince involuntarily.

I sigh heavily and give the taxi driver my address. With a sixth sense, I feel that my kindness will come back to haunt me.

Chapter 10

Sophie

The disgusting rattle of the coffee machine pulls me out of a sweet dream, in which Alexander's burning hands explore my body, caressing and, fondling me in places I forgot I had. Even in my sleep, groan in uncontrolled pleasure. Once again, I awakening in a cold sweat and a another frustrated groan escapes my lips. Alexander has penetrated too deeply into my head, and I have absolutely no idea how to push him out of my mind.

He was supposed to be my pill for a bitter breakup, and as a result, I am now moving away from the side effects of the drug. Liam has already been forgotten. So, the antidote proved to be effective.

"Good morning," Christine squeaks happily, shouting over the noisy coffee machine. "I'm making coffee. Do you want it with or without milk?"

Her unexpected concern does not go unnoticed to me. Apparently, this morning she is suffering not only from a hangover, but also from a sense of guilt for yesterday's situation in at the club.

"With milk," I stretch in bed, considering the drawbacks of living in a studio when you do not live alone, and your schedule is not synchronized with your roommate.

The sun is already shining outside the window and its rays peek through the tulle. I still want to burrow under the blanket, but the presence of Christine does not allow me to completely relax. I can hardly tear myself from the bed under the gaze of the cat that obviously does not like guests. I look at the time: the green, LED numbers of the alarm clock display eight o'clock in the morning.

"Why are you up so early?" I rub my eyes with my fists. "I thought that after last night you would sleep until noon."

"Don't remind me of last night," Christine moans, bashfully covering her face with her hands. "Thank you for getting me out of there before I took my clothes off. I'd never be able to get over the shame. "

I don't know why, but now all her shameful moments fill me with a pleasant feeling of gloating.

I do not hold out any hope that my friendship with Christine will return to the way it had been all this had happened. She now has a new life that, in her opinion, I am completely unsuited. It happens. People change, and their circle of friends change. All that remains is an the unpleasant aftertaste of resentment because I believed that our friendship was higher than material status and envy. Even though I know how materialistic Christine really is.

"Come on," I wave her off and head for the bathroom. "You would do the same for me."

No, she wouldn't. Most likely, Christine would just laugh and mock me. But she doesn't need to know that I know how she treats me. If it is more pleasant for her to think that everyone around her are fools just to make herself feel important, then why not? I'm okay with that. Living without stress is so much healthier than constantly trying to change things that can't be changed anyway.

The doorbell rings just as I lather my face with foam. I freeze over the sink, wondering who it might be. We didn't order food, and I I'm not expecting any deliveries. Maybe the annoying neighbor is dropping by to talk about arranging the yard and planting flowers? She likes to do it early in the morning on weekends. Most of the time, I just ignore the knock on the door and pretend I'm not at home, cuddling with the cat in the corner of the room.

"I'll get the door," Christine yells, and I hear her bare feet slapping across the floor.

I hear the click of the turning lock, the rustling of the door knob and the door swinging open. And then complete silence. I stain to hear, trying to make sense of the unexpected silence.

"Well, well, well," Christine's shrill voice exclaims. I hear the clear notes of dissatisfaction boom throughout the small studio. "Soph, get out here and explain yourself."

I open my eyes so wide that foam gets into them, which begins to burn unbearably. Stunned by Christine's strange statement, I automatically begin to wash the foam from my face.

A million scenarios run through my head. What could have happened? Who's at the door? Why is Christine angry again? Could it be Liam? But what would he be doing here? He doesn't even know my new address. I moved here after we broke up, and I never told him my address.

An unthinkable idea crosses my mind so quickly that it starts to press into my throbbing temples, and my heart beats wildly. Alexander! He knows my address and probably suspects that Christine is spending time with me. Has he come to pick up his careless daughter?

I'm trying to imagine what it will be like if it really is Alexander standing at the door to my apartment. My stomach shrinks with excitement, and my head resists such thoughts. No, he can't be allowed into my apartment. This is my world, he does not belong here. Let him continue to have fun and arrange an adrenaline ride with someone else. I am above it. The memory of Lola's haughty face flashes before my eyes, and I get chills.

I dry my face with a towel and toss it into the laundry basket. Convinced that I don't look so bad, I straighten my shoulders belligerently and throw open the door. I don't know what I will do next, but the goal is to kick Alexander out of the apartment, and if necessary, his daughter along with him.

Chapter 11

Sophie

When I pull the bathroom door open, the scent of freshly brewed coffee wafts through me. A piercing cat screech distracts me from what I've planned to do. Instead of kicking out my uninvited guests, I pick up the cat and kiss his face. I mutter apologies for his battered psyche and his tail pinched by the door.

"Soph! Don't try to hide by pretending to be busy with the cat," Christine draws my attention, nervously tapping her nails on the kitchen countertop.

Reluctantly, as if in slow motion, I turn around to face her and freeze, squeezing the cat even tighter. Oliver, unable to withstand such pressure, clings to my skin with his claws and jumps out of my hands.

Rubbing the scratches, I carefully approach the giant bouquet of flowers. Irises. Just like the ones that Christine's father gave me the night I decided I didn't want to continue my relationship with him. And which I left in his car during the escape.

Unlike the previous small one, there are a hundred buds in this bouquet, no less. I was almost right in thinking that it was Alexander who had come.

""You definitely won't forget these flowers, and my number is not blocked in this phone." The card was signed simply, A." Christine read the note with expression. "Who is 'A'?"

I blush for several reasons: the first letter of her father's name is staring her in the face and there are too many intimate details that I do not want Christine to know. Next to the bouquet is a box with a new and insanely expensive smartphone.

"Sophie, what are you hiding from me? Your secret boyfriend?" She moves her eyebrows playfully and smirks, but envy comes through in her voice.

Why now, weeks later, is he sending gifts and a note with hints? And again, this inconsistency of emotions, which only Alexander can cause in me. I am bursting with the desire to throw the boxed phone at him (preferably right into his handsome face), but at the same time I go crazy with tenderness, because Alexander remembered that my phone is broken.

Or does he just not like being on my blacklist? In any case, no one has shown this much interest in me yet. And it turns out to be extremely enjoyable.

"Do I have to dig the dirt out of you with my claws?" Christine pulls me out of my thoughts and hands me a mug of hot coffee.

I don't know how to answer. I have no excuses or reasons prepared. I had no idea that men could make such gestures. I've only seen it in movies and on TV.

"Maybe it's Andy, from our university?" Christine speculates thoughtfully. "No, he is clearly not your type, and he doesn't have the money for gifts like these..."

Christine takes a sip of her coffee and then almost chokes on it, her eyes wide. I clutch the mug in my hands, afraid to move. My stomach tightens and I nervously nibble on the inside of my cheek. I'm afraid to hear her next guess. The letter is too easy to decipher...

"It's your stranger from the hotel, isn't it?" She blurts out and slams her hand on the table. "Oh my God, that's right! 'A'! ANONYMOUS!" She whispers the last word.

I almost faint from overexertion. The back of my head goes numb and my fingertips tingle with adrenaline. I sit down at the table so as not to betray my anxiety through trembling legs.

Christine is beating around the bush and it's only a matter of time before she puts all the facts together. Of course, maybe I'm overthinking it? Well, what does Christine know about my stranger? There are no real details, nothing that could point to Alexander. But, what about the letter on the note? There are many male names starting with the letter A.

All fears are only in my head because I know the secret, but I completely forget that others do not.

"Wait," she continues to reason. "If he sends you gifts, it means he knows your address. Are you starting a new relationship behind my back? What kind of friend are you?!"

Her annoyance makes me laugh. Is Christine telling me how a friend should behave? Her hypocrisy puts a quick end to my insecurities. At some point, I even want to point out her mistakes and ask why she lied to her father about the internship, but I stop myself in time.

"Christine," I sigh. "I really think I have the right not to tell..."

"Crap!" Christine interrupts me. "Wait! Dad is calling."

She clears her throat and quickly answers the phone.

"Yes, daddy," she chirps sweetly. "I was at home, but went out to take a walk. Yeah. Yes. Good. Well, okay, have a good flight. Bye-bye!"

The swarm of thoughts in my head begins to buzz unbearably as the information provided comes together. Alexander does not know that Christine spent the night away from home. So, he's not in town. But what about Lola? She would have given up Christine one hundred percent just to set her up.

"Are you lying to your dad?" I sip my coffee, pretending to be indifferent.

"I don't want him to know I'm hanging out at his business partner's club," Christine rolls her eyes. "It seems to me that he knows that I've fallen head over heels in love."

"But what about his lady?" I can't hide my sharp tone of voice.

"Lola?" Christine is surprised. "Didn't I tell you? Dad kicked her out of the house the other day. I saw her packing her clothes in tears. And before that, he was walking on egg shells for several days. I was afraid to approach him. I think they broke up," she smiles slyly. "I think it's because of me. Apparently, dad saw how she was treating me and said goodbye to that fool."

Time seems to stop and everything around me freezes. Christine is speaking, but I can't hear a single word that she's saying. Pain fills my heart, my lungs cannot take a breath, and my legs give way.

The events of that evening flash before my eyes: Alexander, leaning on the hood of the car, his slight smile, and a bouquet of irises, which are neatly held by strong hands.

So, he wasn't lying about Lola? But that doesn't explain his behavior in the restaurant. I want to talk to him until my knees tremble.

My hands find the box with the phone and open it. Without thinking about the logic of my action, or about the presence of Christine in my apartment, I turn on my brand-new phone to type a message to the only contact in the phone book.

Chapter 12

Sophie

I spend the rest of the day on pins and needles. Alexander's answer to my request to talk was not long in coming. He immediately replied that he would visit me this evening.

Christine leaves in the afternoon, wearing my T-shirt and shorts, with the promise that she will return them to me spotless and clean. Throughout our friendship, I have lost several items of clothing to her, so I mentally say goodbye to anything I lend her.

To fill the time, I clean my small apartment from floor to ceiling until it shines. And in horror I find myself sweaty, bent over a toilet with a brush when a message comes through the phone.

Alexander will be downstairs in thirty minutes.

I hurriedly put the cleaning supplies back under the sink, which continue to fall out one after another and do not allow me to close the cabinet doors. Finally, having dealt with the plastic bottles, I hurriedly take a shower using the most delicious-smelling gel.

An incoming call to my brand-new phone rings as I nervously rub my damp hair between the two ends of the towel.

"I'm downstairs," Alexander's voice comes from the speaker, and I silently nod, forgetting that he cannot see me. But I do not have time to voice my action in words, because Alexander has already disconnected the call.

With trembling hands, I pull on a sweatshirt and jeans, and frantically look around. For some reason, I take a bottle of perfume and do a couple of puffs in the direction of my neck and chest, which quickly rises from frequent breaths.

Coming out of the entrance, I look around the yard filled with cars parked way to close to each other, and some even blocking the sidewalk. This always happens because the building does not have organized parking, and there are a lot of residents.

Among all the beat-up cars, it is not difficult for me to find the dark blue Bentley polished to a shine that is under an overgrown apple tree next to the playground.

I take a deep breath and head towards him, feeling the cool August breeze chill the damp hair on top of my head.

"Hi," Alexander says as I slide into the passenger seat and close the door, but not all the way.

"Hi," I answer him quietly, looking at his tired face. There are small dark circles under his eyes, and his stubble has grown to the state of a short beard. "Is everything okay?"

"Yeah," he shrugged it off, adjusting the collar of his polo sweater. "Just solving some problems at the branch."

Christine's morning conversation with her father and her wishes for a good flight flash through my head.

"Did you just get back?" I ask and bite my lip. Why do I never think before I speak?

Alexander squints and looks at me for a few seconds, during which a whole waterfall of sweat flow down my back. I look away, pretending my attention was drawn to the leather-covered console.

"Christine was with you, right?" He asks and I just nod. There is no point in hiding the truth and lying. I'll let Christine deal with her own lies. I'm so tired of always covering for her, especially now that Christine's attitude towards me is quite clear.

"Little liar," Alexander chuckles. "Good thing you were with her."

The last sentence makes my head turn sharply towards him.

"Did you know she wasn't at home?"

"Of course. Christine forgot that the alarm system sends me alerts every time someone comes and goes," he chuckles. "So, you had fun yesterday?"

My foot begins to tap out the rhythm of the music pouring from the speakers. I feel like I'm back in my teens, and that I'm making excuses to my dad for a night out.

"We just went to the club. We're not little girls, and we wanted to take a break from a hard day at work," I bristle, remembering in time that I am no longer a child, and it is not my father sitting next to me.

"Hush, tigress," Alexander laughs wearily. "No one's blaming you. It's good that you know how to take a break from work."

I look anxiously at every inch of his face as he massages the bridge of his nose with his forefinger and thumb. I can see how exhausted he is.

"You haven't been home yet?" I soften a little.

"No, you said you need to talk urgently," Alexander catches my eye. My heart skips a beat and then begins to beat faster. Again, I'm walking on the edge between hitting him or hugging him tightly.

"I wanted to thank you for the flowers and the gift," I hold up my new phone and smile awkwardly. I don't know how to react to kind gestures from men. Maybe it was still worth not opening the gift and returning it?

Alexander smiles a little warmer and reaches for my cheek, but sharply moves his hand aside and touches my wet curl. He wraps it around his finger and then tucks it behind my ear. From his touch, a million small goosebumps rise on my skin, heat burning in my stomach.

All my organs are jumping with delight when he, frowning slightly, runs his fingers along my cheekbone.

"You've gone out of your mind going out with wet hair?" He says hoarsely, not letting go of my face.

"I was in a hurry to see you," I look away in embarrassment, because I'm telling the truth. I really was in a hurry to see him for the first time in a long time. It turned out that all the those days without him being around me has left me feeling unbearably ill and broken without his intense glances and the burning touch from his hands.

The phrase "you never really know what you're fighting for until you lose it" begins to take on real meaning to me. All these weeks I have been telling myself that I do not need his presence in my life, but for some inexplicable reason I am drawn to Alexander.

Only for him does my heart long to jump out of the shackles of my ribs, and my head is spinning at his slightest touch. Without these emotions, I'm turned inside out, and I am ready to do anything to feel them again.

If there is a dependence on people, then I've gotten myself into a big mess, and it seems that no attempt at rehabilitation will save me.

"Don't do that next time, I'll wait," he says in a hoarse voice. The corners of his lips lifting slightly. My heart makes another somersault, and I stop breathing.

His "next time" gives me hope. All questions about Lola and his attitude at the restaurant are forced out of my head, but I do not forget about them. I need to catch my breath and have some space to collect my thoughts.

"Do you want to come up for a cup of coffee?" I quickly blurt out before I get scared of my brazenness and change my mind.

Alexander takes a quick look at his watch, then nods wordlessly. I wanted to argue that if he does not have time, then it is okay, but he has already gotten out of the car, sprinted to the passenger side, and opens my door.

"Coffee won't hurt me now," he smiles as we walk to my entrance.

The inner voice in my head taunts me, remembering the promise I made myself this morning that I would never allow Alexander into my private space.

Chapter 13

Alexander

The doors of the old elevator swing open with a piercing screech on the tenth floor and we emerge from the metal box. Her building does not fail my imagination at all: it is just as shabby as it is outside.

Seeing it the first time — when I gave Sophie a lift — I thought that if it could, I would take this fragile girl away from here. I dread to imagine how many problems she faces every day due to old plumbing, annoying and loud neighbors, and her the long trip to and from work.

"Come in," Sophie says timidly, letting me through the open door ahead of her.

Surprisingly, the apartment looks fresh. The landlord obviously did his best: a major renovation, new appliances and furniture, restored parquet. It also smells clean. Just like the resident of this small studio herself.

The first time we met, I noticed that Sophie smelled insanely delicious. The scent of vanilla and berry followed her. At first, I thought it was perfume, but it turned out to be the fragrance of her skin. Her perfume only skillfully emphasized her aroma that blew my mind and stole my heart.

"Here, you can wash your hands," she points to the door to the right of the entrance.

Only now that I'm in the warmth and comfort of her apartment do I feel how completely exhausted I really am.

The business trip did not work out from the very first day. During the negotiations one of the branch managers categorically refused to provide premises for the filming of a new television show. I had to coax his married ass with trips to restaurants and strip clubs, and while he was drunk, get him to sign the contract I needed.

As I wash my hands, I feel something warm and soft rubbing against my leg. Lowering my eyes, I meet the gaze of golden cat eyes. The cat begins to purr and lays his muzzle on my foot.

"Oliver! Go away," Sophie tries to chase him away, but the cat gives her a lazy look and continues to use me as a pillow.

"I'm sorry, I'll take him away," she apologizes embarrassedly.

"Don't," I smile and bend down to take the cat in my arms. He, as if nothing had happened, calmly settles into my chest, and rubs his forehead against the collar of my sweater. I scratch the cat behind his ear. I have loved animals since childhood.

In the small village where I was born, stray cats constantly wandered onto my parents' property. Then we moved to the city because my father found another job, and pets were strictly forbidden to me.

I catch a startled look from Sophie, who looks at me like I'm an alien as I walk towards the dining table that is adorned with the bouquet of irises. The place of honor she has reserved for them makes me smile. I was sure Sophie would throw the flowers away.

"What's happened?" I grin as I sit down with my new friend on a chair.

I like to impress Sophie in all sorts of ways. Although she knows how to surprise no less than me. Especially when she runs away from restaurants. The last time, I stayed up for several nights, cursing her for jumping to conclusions, and myself for not discussing important points with Sophia in the first place.

"It's just that Oliver doesn't like strangers," she finally snaps out of her daze.

"So, I'm an exception. Aren't I, Baby?" I coo over the cat and stroke his head. My tenacious gaze does not hide the moment when Sophie starts at the affectionate nickname.

Her timidity and eternal embarrassment haunt me. When I met her in the hotel bar, I was convinced that she is a confident girl who knows what she wants. That's what attracted me to her: radiant femininity, flirtatious eyes, and interesting conversations about art.

I had no expectations of anything happening when I decided to invite her up to my hotel room, which I took for the night to relax and consider further plans for Christine and her mother. But Sophie, unexpectedly, agreed.

Only after we had sex did I realize just how unprepared she was for such experiences. This was clearly her first time with a stranger. Her trembling hands, embarrassed demeanor, and nervousness pleasantly excited me.

Usually, I'm the one who leaves right after making love, but this time I did not want to let her go. But, this time, the decision to stay or leave was had been hers. And she decided to leave.

This was expected, and I resigned myself to the losing her; although the phantom smell of her skin did not let me go until our next meeting. What I didn't exactly predict was that Sophie would turn out to be my daughter's best friend. A haze of mystery and prohibition hangs between us. And for some reason it turns me on even more.

"Do you want your coffee black or with milk?" Sophie asks as she inserts the capsule into the coffee machine.

"Black. I love a strong americano, Sophie," I savor her name on my lips. I like the way it tastes.

She sets the mug in front of me and takes the chair across the table from me, pulling the sleeves of her sweatshirt over her fingers. I really want to take her by the chin and make her look into my eyes, but she, as if anticipating my desire, raises her piercing blue whirlpools at me.

"Why Sophie?" She suddenly asks, and then explains. "Usually, people call me Soph. But you call me... it's too formal."

I wince at the idiotic contractions.

"I don't like when such a beautiful name is mangled, Sophie," I explain my opinion and take a sip of coffee.

Sophie nods silently and looks down at the mug in front of her. I sense the struggle raging inside her. She clearly wants to ask something but she doesn't dare.

"Sophie," I call her softly and release the cat to the floor. "What do you want to talk about?"

"About us," she blushes, nervously stroking the black polish on her nails. "Is it true that you kicked Lola out?"

I mentally chuckle, not allowing my emotions to show on my face. Christine blabbed. But, to be honest, I'm glad for her loose tongue. If it weren't for her, Sophie wouldn't have dared to send the message this morning.

"Yes," I nod to confirm my words. "As I told you, my arrangement with her had outlived its usefulness."

I'm a little cunning, not disclosing the true reasons. I asked Lola to move out immediately after Sophie left the restaurant. I realized that she is principled, and her experience will not allow her to accept some of my conditions. I didn't want to lose Sophie.

"You," she stammers, biting her lip in indecision. "You did it for me?"

"Yes," I say firmly, so as not to let a single shadow of doubt creep into her beautiful head.

Sophie finally looks up at me. Undisguised joy sparkles in her eyes.

I cover her cool hand with mine and stroke her fingers tenderly, trying to convey confidence through my touch. I need to find out everything that she's managed to think up and dispel all her fears and mistrust.

"Did you rent the entire restaurant so no one could see us?" She gets to the heart of the matter.

"Yes."

"Why?" She swallows nervously. Sophie did not like the answer, but she does not pull her hand back.

I'm setting myself up for a serious conversation. I must be extremely honest with her now to gain her trust.

"Sophie, I can't promise you a normal relationship. Especially now, that I just got my daughter back, and I don't want to lose her again. And I don't want to put you into an uncomfortable situation."

In an instant, her expression changes and moisture begin to shine in her eyes. I mentally reproach myself for bringing her to such a state. I can't bear to see a woman's tears.

"If she wasn't my friend, would things be different?" She asks in a whisper, closing her eyelids.

"Perhaps," I answer evasively. "None of us knows how it would be different. We have what we have, and we should should move forward based on what we have," I say a little harder to reason with Sophie.

My words do not affect her in the way I expected. Instead of agreeing, she jumps up from her chair, knocking over her mug. Coffee spreads over the table in a brown puddle.

Sophie stops by the window, and I see her wiping her face with the sleeves of her sweatshirt. There is an unpleasant itching in my chest.

I stand behind her, watching the flickering city lights against the night sky. I want to put my hands on her shoulders, but I pull myself back, afraid to frighten her and drive more fear and doubt into the far recesses of her mind.

"I will accept whatever you decide," I say softly, inhaling the berry scent of her hair, but I know that I won't. Even if she refuses, I will do everything I can to change her mind and make her mine. I can't let her go. I'm very used to letting go, but I will never let go of Sophie.

Chapter 14

Alexander

"Why is everything like this?" Sophie sniffled. "Exactly why were you in that damn bar? Why did I even go there?"

I would like to know the answer to this question. I ended up there completely by accident. I hadn't planned to leave the room that evening, but Laura's drunken call pissed me off, and I wanted to distract myself. Interestingly, I succeeded in being distracted. But now I clearly understand that I would not want to change anything. I'm addicted to my secret game with Sophie.

"Sophie," I say her name softly and wrap my hands around her shoulders. I try to calm her, but she immediately pushes me away and turns away from me.

Her eyes are red with tears, but they no longer run down her cheeks. Sophie composes herself, and her hopeless sadness is suddenly replaced with anger bright flames of fire blazes in her pupils.

"I just can't understand, why are you here? Why all these gifts for a girl who jumped into your bed without hesitation? I acted like a whore! How do you even allow Christine to talk to me? Why do you need a stupid twenty-two-year-old girl like me?" She questions endlessly.

Sophie's words evoke a kaleidoscope of emotions in me. I want to slap her and lecture her not to talk about herself despairingly, and at the same time hold her tightly in my arms.

My first impression of this girl was extremely erroneous. She has a lot of issues and fears. But at the same time, she has an inner core that just turned out to be broken due to previous experience.

I remember Liam's impudent face when Christine introduced me to him at her birthday, and Sophie's explanation that there was another girl and he had left her for the other woman.

My knuckles itch unbearably, how I want to smack this child. I'm not sure what it was that jumped in me: a sense of ownership for Sophie or anger that this guy once calmly caressed Sophie's body and then dared to hurt her so cruelly.

I feel how fatigue floods over me and black spots begin to dance before my eyes and a sharp pain shoots through my temples. I sit down on the bed behind me and squeeze my eyes shut, pinching the bridge of my nose to recover.

"Is everything okay?" I hear a worried voice from above. The knowledge that Sophie is worried about me makes my skin tingle pleasantly.

"Yes, I just haven't slept for a day, everything is fine," taking advantage of the moment, I pull her to me, wrapping my hands around her slender waist.

Sophie steps between my legs and shifts awkwardly, unsure of what to do. Then she gently places her hands on my head, running her fingers through my hair. From the proximity of her body and the tenderness of her skin, it begins to unbearably pull at my groin, but I try to ignore my feelings and concentrate on the seriousness of the conversation.

"So," I begin, clearing my throat. "I'm here because I really wanted to talk to you after you ran away, but I didn't want to pressure you. I gifted you the phone because I can't watch you prick your fingers on a broken phone screen. The flowers, because I saw how much you liked them, but you forgot the bouquet in the car. For me, age doesn't mean anything. Sometimes people in their fifties act like they're still in high school, and others in their twenties act like they've been through more than old people."

To some extent, I'm lying. I knew Sophie would be back sooner or later. I saw that I had managed to hook her. She doesn't know how to hide her feelings. And with the gift I wanted to push her to communicate, to create an excuse to see her, whether it was out of gratitude for the phone or an attempt to return it.

"And most importantly: you are not a whore. They take money for sex or fuck everyone indiscriminately, and you just wanted to experiment. I don't see anything criminal in this."

"Especially since you decided to choose me," I mentally add to myself.

I feel her body tense and her fingers freeze between the strands of my hair.

"I didn't want to experiment, I was trying to forget Liam," Sophie admits quietly. My jaw cramps from the verbal slap in the face. Her confession stings my ego.

"And... Did it help?" I ask breathlessly, not taking my eyes off her.

Sophie gives a slight shrug and bites her lip. The corners of her mouth twitch upward, but she stops herself just in time. I will consider this reaction as consent because I do not have the strength to discuss this situation further.

"Is there anything else you would like to talk about?" I shake the watch on my wrist to see what time it is.

"I don't think you need to worry about Christine," Sophie surprises me and makes me frown. "She and I are not close friends anymore. Christine, she... hasn't been talking to me lately. She has a new circle of friends with money and beautiful cars. She doesn't need a friend like me. That's why I wonder why you are here."

I rest my forehead against her chest and exhale noisily. I would never have thought that such a beautiful girl has so many unnecessary complexes. I'm used to having a bunch of models and actresses spinning next to me, who are confident in their beauty and attractiveness.

"I'm sorry you judge me by my daughter. Unfortunately, I didn't raise her, and, in that regard, she took after her mother," my words are streaked with annoyance, not because of Sophie's stupid assumptions, but because of Laura, who raised our daughter in her own way. "Christine talks about you all the time. It made me crazy after you ran away from our date."

Sophie's chest rises with a surprised gasp. She has no idea what influence she has on my daughter. She is like an idol for Christine, whom she looks up to. My ears were buzzing about what a good, hardworking and most understanding and supportive friend Sophia is.

"What happened between you and Laura?" She breaks the silence between us. It seems to me that I can even hear her thoughts convulsively spinning in my head.

"Can we not go into all that right now?" I ask her, realizing that she will most likely try to figure everything out on her own. "I'm not in the best frame of mind to talk about this right now."

I wonder who she thinks I am. An amoral bastard who abandoned his unborn daughter? I would really like to refute this image, I have something to say, but not today. I won't do another hard heart-to-heart talk.

I pull away from Sophie, stroking her thighs with my fingers. Her thoughtful expression does not show a single emotion by which I could understand what decision she made.

"If you don't mind, then I'll go home. I need to sleep. I have an important meeting tomorrow."

She looks at me and focuses on my eyes, fiddling nervously with the hem of her sweatshirt.

"So what? We'll just have a secret relationship?" Sophie asks as I cross the threshold into the building's hallway.

"Yes."

She is silent, looking at the shabby wall of the corridor.

"I'm not sure if that's for me," Sophie declares quietly. "I'm not ready for this."

I expected that she might answer like this. I silently nod and turn towards the elevator, creating a distance between us.

I count to three before hearing the sound of her bare feet on the concrete floor of the corridor, and then cool fingers wrap around my wrist, forcing me to stop.

"Just give me time to think," Sophie gasps uneasily, but I already know her final decision.

Holding back a victorious smile, I get into the car and start the engine, contemplating my next steps.

Chapter 15

Sophie

"Sophie, are you listening to me?" Christopher's irritated voice reaches me. I shake my head, leaving my world of illusory fantasies, where Alexander leads me by the arm to the restaurant, tacitly declaring us a couple.

"Yes, Mr. Harrison, I understood everything, I need to check with the district committee about the number of floors permitted in the building," I repeat the last words that I remember from the meeting.

My boss wearily rubs his face with his palms and looks at me like he's about to kill me. He is clearly angry.

"Sophie, we discussed this twenty minutes ago. Get your head out of the clouds, or I'll remove you as my assistant and put you back designing barracks."

"Sorry," I mumble under my breath in embarrassment, and start sorting through the papers in front of me. I notice with horror that on some of them I wrote the letter "A" in different fonts.

For the rest of the meeting, I carefully concentrate on Christopher's words and take important notes in a notebook. I urgently need to come to my senses, otherwise I will not get a permanent position. I have already received two verbal warnings this week. As a rule, the third becomes the last.

All day long I walk around like I'm sleepwalking, forcing myself to stick to my daily schedule. Wake up, cup of coffee, work, lunch, work, subway, bed. Sometimes I even set an alarm so as not to forget to eat and again not fall into hungry pangs, as happened a couple of days ago. The whole office was concerned about me.

Sitting in the subway, I read the messages that Christine had sent me earlier today. After Alexander's words, I began to talk more actively with her again, not being afraid to send her little stories that happened to me during the day. I would really like to have a heart-to-heart talk with her, but I understand that I can't do it without mentioning Alexander's words about her attitude towards me.

Today, while having lunch with her father, Christine saw the man of her dreams again. She made a video while there, which "accidentally" captured her chosen one in the background.

I pause the video when Alexander appears on the screen. He is enthusiastically discussing something with a business partner, holding a cup of coffee that looks too small in his powerful palms.

I remember how those hands stroked my thighs soothingly during our last conversation. My body immediately responds, covered with goosebumps, and my heart begins to beat quickly.

I want to be with Alexander, but I'm scared. Nothing like this has ever happened to me before. Everything is cutting edge with him: sex, where only he dominates; relationship on its own terms; his presence with me in the same room, when my lungs burn from the excessively electrified air, and my lower abdomen pulsates with pleasant warmth.

It's also scary to destroy my friendship with Christine, whom I gave a second chance.

She started calling me, wanting to spend time together again. I constantly refuse, blaming my work load at the office. But the truth is that starting to meet with her again, for some reason, seems to me to be the moment when I will have to make the important decision about my relationship with Alexander.

Approaching my house, I immediately notice a familiar car. It is impossible not to notice it, it stands out as a bright turquoise spot within the mass of gray.

"Surprise!" Christine jumps out from the driver's door and throws herself at me with a big hug. She waves a paper bag with the logo of our favorite restaurant. "Will you let me in? I've got your favorite salad here," she makes pleading eyes, just like a cat from a famous cartoon.

I smile widely, not bothering to hide my joy from seeing Christine. All prejudices evaporate immediately when I see the outgoing initiative from my estranged friend. It's so obvious that she has missed our conversations.

"Of course," I nod to her in the direction of the entrance. "Let's go, since you have such a large bribe."

Christine chirps merrily about her meeting the man of her dreams as she places boxes of food from a bag onto the dining table. I finally find out that his name is Jeff, and he works as a producer on one of Alexander's television shows.

"Today he pulled out a chair for me and recommended his favorite dish," Christine says dreamily, chewing on a piece of bread.

"First chew, I can't understand you," I grin at her emotionality. "What did he do to you?"

Christine rolls her eyes and chews vigorously before uttering a phrase that makes me blush to the tips of my ears.

"You're just like my dad," she laments. "Same grumble."

I leave this remark without comment, pretending that I am too engrossed in eating my dinner.

"By the way, my apartment will be ready soon," says Christine. "I want to have a housewarming party. Can you help me with the organization?"

"Of course," I immediately agree, pleased that she needs me again and is asking me for help, and not her famous interior designer.

Our spontaneous evening gives me strength and confidence in returning trust between us. Now all the doubts about Christine that have been tormenting me lately seem to be sheer stupidity. She has her own cockroaches in her head, but, as before, I can ignore them, and just enjoy talking with Christine.

Having finished an endless conversation about the latest gossip from the lives of our classmates, Christine is hurriedly going home. She still has to go to the dry cleaner's to get her dress, and we, as usual, chatted until late.

"Soph, I almost forgot," she straightens up from putting on her sneakers. "My dad invited us to a party. Let's celebrate the launch of his new TV show. There will be only our own people, a lot of stars and everyone who works on the show. Well, you know, all the cinema bohemia."

I do not hear her enthusiastic words about who will be at the party and the list of big names who will be there. They are drowned out by the ringing in my ears and the information that I have been invited.

"Us? Me and you?" I am clarifying to see if I misheard.

"Well, yeah. He seems to like you," she winks, and my cheeks instantly turn crimson. "He brainwashed me that starting a new stage in life, I should not give up on the people who were with me in the past at the most difficult moments. I don't know why he thinks that I was giving up someone, but he clearly was hinting about you, saying that he noticed that I began to talk less with my old friends."

Something inside me turns over after these words. I bite my lip nervously, so hard I can taste the metallic taste of blood on my tongue.

"So, are you going to come?" Christine clarifies, pulling her car keys out of her bag.

I nod mechanically and walk her to the elevator, automatically asking her to text me when she gets home.

I lock the door behind me and mindlessly watch my cat lick his front paw, settling in the chair where Christine was sitting a few minutes ago. Warmth spreads throughout my body when it dawns on me that Alexander is not indifferent to my relationship with my friend.

Chapter 16

Sophie

I agree with Christine that she will pick me up before the party to do our hair and makeup together. She's hired a famous makeup artist to get us presentable. But Christine is late.

Forty minutes later, when I had already reconciled with the fact that we would not be going to the party, I receive a message from Christine in response to a dozen missed calls from me.

"I'm sorry it took so long. I met my mother, and she threw a tantrum when I told her that I would be living alone soon. She begged me not to trust dad and said that he is deliberately alienating me from her," she rolls her eyes as I get into her car. "Her usual drunken raving."

"You never really told me why they broke up," I make an attempt to pull the answer out of her that has long been of interest to me.

"I don't know. According to mom, he left her as soon as he found out that she was pregnant, and dad doesn't want to talk about it," Christine shrugs.

"Why doesn't he want to?" I continue to prod as I fasten my seat belt, remembering how well my friend drives.

"I don't know. I think it's an uncomfortable topic for him," Christine pauses, checking for passing cars, then changes lanes. "Either he doesn't want me to know some dirty details that will tarnish his honor," she chuckles.

I ponder her words as we silently drive down the road towards the center. Perhaps Alexander does not want their shaky relationship between new, full-time father and newfound daughter to completely collapse.

For some reason, Alexander's past stopped bothering me as much as when I accused him of abandoning his daughter. I didn't know him at all then, and now I have before me the image of a strong man who knows what he wants and is sincerely trying to improve the relationship with his own daughter and correct the mistakes he made. Even if it means that he will have to give up his personal life. This is how he earned my respect for him.

"The dress is just drop dead!" Christine admires, after three hours on a chair under the close attention of a makeup artist and one bottle of champagne, that had been meant for two.

I really tried hard today. I chose the most beautiful and revealing dress in my wardrobe: a short black dress with small glitter and thin straps. I want to make a great impression in front of Alexander and not lose face in front of the "cinema bohemia".

"My Rosalies are perfect for you," Christine hands me a pair of her signature black leather high-heeled sandals with red soles.

"But what about you?" I ask as I try on the shoes. Thanks to a comfortable last, they sit on my feet like slippers, and my fresh scarlet pedicure looks even more elegant. Well, expensive shoes make women's legs even more beautiful.

"I brought a few pairs with me," she dismisses, showing off neon pumps from the same brand.

We are a little late to the party, having missed the introductory part and words of gratitude to the film crew. All the people present have already begun to have fun, dispersing through the spacious banquet hall of the restaurant, located in an old building, its interior decorated in neoclassical lavishness. In one word — pompous.

Christine begins to greet her acquaintances, to whom she happily introduces me as her best friend and future successful architect. I blush in embarrassment at her praise and take sips of champagne as often as I can, trying to calm my frayed nerves.

My gaze drifts through the crowd and people passing by, hoping to stumble upon a familiar male face. But Alexander does not seem to be here.

I go to the bar to grab a fresh glass of champagne and catch my breath from too much socializing. I haven't made so many new acquaintances in a long time and my introvert personality needs a recharge.

"Did you forget the outfit, or was that intended?" The languid whisper of a husky male voice triggers electrical impulses across the entire surface of my skin. His stubble, pricking his ear, spreads a gaggle of goosebumps.

I can't help but smile when I turn to face Alexander and catch his darkened gaze on me.

"You don't like my dress?" I playfully raise an eyebrow, surprised at my own courage.

"Is this a dress?" Alexander smiles. "In this, I would only let you walk around the house."

I want to be angry, but I can't. I like his possessive reaction to me. Coupled with a long time without meetings, this gives a stormy mixture that blows away with a wave of excitement.

For a moment, time around us slows down, and I see nothing but his dark eyes, which are drawn in like two whirlpools.

"I'll be waiting for you in fifteen minutes," he hands me a white plastic card. "Second door around the corner after the restrooms."

***

I grip the card key tightly with frozen fingers as I turn into the corridor I need and count up to the entrance I need. I look around and, making sure that there is no one around, I put the piece of plastic on the reader. The light turns green, and I press down on the metal knob, taking a deep breath, trying to calm my nervous trembling.

"Storage room? Seriously?" I chuckle, looking around the small room with the shelves, among which Alexander, in his perfectly tailored suit, looks as ridiculous as in my small, simple apartment or me in frayed jeans and a sweatshirt in his expensive Bentley.

"What's wrong with back rooms?" Alexander grins, putting his hands in pants pockets.

"You work on TV. Isn't this a bit of a cliché?"

"Perhaps," he tilts his head and squints at me from head to toe. "But it's quiet here and we can talk."

"Are you trying to force me to make a decision about our relationship?"

"I'm not trying," he shakes his head. "I just think enough time has passed to discuss the pros and cons of our... relationship."

I lean with my back against the door, giving my sandaled feet a rest, and at the same time keeping a bit of distance between Alexander and me. He already fills all the space around me, and I'm afraid that I won't be able to discuss anything sanely if I come closer to him. But I have been setting myself up for this conversation for too long.

"So, what did you decide?" He asks again.

I am silent, collecting my thoughts, which are bouncing around in my head because of his gaze.

"I'm ready to try," I stop Alexander with a wave of my hand as he takes a bold step towards me. "But I have conditions: Christine cannot find out about us, and I don't want to hide in apartments and hotels, I want to be able to go out with you in public but how do we make sure that no one finds out about us? You need to figure that out."

Adrenaline surges in my blood and my heart beats in my temples. My newfound self-confidence is shattered by the fear that Alexander might refuse me or send me to hell with dictating such rules.

"The cat has released her claws!" He grins and overcomes the distance between us, freezing a couple of inches from my face. "I don't like it when conditions are put on me, but I'm ready to listen to your wishes."

"I hope you do," is all I can say before Alexander's lips meet mine in a greedy kiss. Our teeth slam against each other, and his hands impatiently lift the hem of my dress and wrap around my buttocks, lifting me into the air in one motion and pressing me against the door.

I wrap my legs around his waist and finally lose my mind when I hear Alexander's quiet moaning through the kiss.

"Do you have any idea how many times I wanted to do this?"

Chapter 17

Sophie

Alexander's hands roam my body as his mouth sucks all the energy out of me. Our never-ending kiss takes my breath away. The arousal hits my head and fills every cell, so much that I forget that we are in a public place, and there are several dozen people outside the door, including my best friend and his colleagues.

I had no idea how much I needed his touch. I slide my hands under Alexander's shirt, feeling his collarbones and shoulders, digging into his skin with my nails every time he bites my tongue and lips.

I like that I can be crazy with him. He lets me be that way around him. Unlike other people, in front of whom I must be a cultured and decent girl, the way my parents raised me.

My moans are more like sobs as Alexander descends lower, his kisses trailing down my neck to the neckline of my dress. The fabric is so close to my body that it is impossible to move it, which is why he curses through his teeth.

"Don't rip it," I beg him as the voice of commonsense breaks through my hazy mind, screaming that I still must go back to the party.

Alexander grins, but leaves the dress alone, kneeling in front of me. He lifts the already too high hem and runs his hands from my waist to my buttocks. My skin instantly responds to his touch, covered with chills.

Rough fingers hook the lace of the panty and slide them over my thighs. I move my feet, allowing Alexander to take them off me. The clatter of my heels echoing in my ears.

He spreads my legs wider and covers the place that was hidden under the fabric just a moment ago with his lips. The air leaves my lungs and I throw my head back, banging the back of my head against the door frame. My skin prickles from the direct contact of his stubble and a rolling wave of desire pulses through me.

It doesn't take long for Alexander to make streaks of lightning flash before my eyes. I was madly hungry for his caresses. I bite my lip, stifling a loud moan, and cover my mouth with my hand to hold back the sound of passion.

He rises to his feet, crumpling my lace panties in his hand and stuffing it into his suit jacket pocket. He carefully straightens my dress and tucks a stray strand of hair behind my ear as I recover.

"I want you to walk like this all evening and remember what happened here," he whispers next to my lips, and then gives me a light kiss.

Adrenaline pumps through my veins as I step out of the bathroom after finishing my make-up. "Down there" is unusually free and cool. Before, I never even thought I could afford to go without underwear, especially in such a short dress.

"Where were you!" Christine runs up to me as soon as I go to the bar to take a glass of champagne. My throat is unbearably dry. "I've been looking for you everywhere, where have you been?"

"In the closet," I smile tautly as I take a sip. The bubbles pleasantly tickle my palate and immediately make me lightheaded.

"It's strange, I went there and called you, but you didn't answer," Christine narrows her eyes.

"Probably didn't hear you," I shrug my shoulders and wonder at how easy it is for me to lie to Christine straight to her face. "I was wearing headphones, trying to catch my breath. You know me, I'm not really used to this amount of attention."

"Exactly," she smiles. "You really are a home body, girl; you would prefer chamomile tea to parties."

Christine wraps her arms around my shoulders and reaches for my ear.

"Jeff is here," she whispers hotly, nodding toward the tables. "I want to introduce you to him and get your opinion."

I easily find the blond guy sitting in the company of Christine's father. They are talking about something intensely and drinking whiskey. As if sensing my gaze, Alexander turns his head in our direction and looks straight in my eyes. The corner of his lip lifts slightly, and he gives me a tiny wink, his hand clutching the silk and lace hidden in his suit pocket.

My lower abdomen begins to blaze with fire, and my cheeks flush a dark pink. I gulp down the remains of the cold champagne to cool myself. Water from the sweating flute glass runs down my fingers and it seems to me that it instantly evaporates when it meets my heated skin.

Christine leads me by the hand through the crowd, which is already wriggling in drunken ecstasy to the sensational music hits of this summer.

"Jeff," Christine calls him too enthusiastically as she walks over to the table, "this is my best friend, Soph. Soph, this is Jeff, my dad's business partner."

I pretend to see Jeff for the first time and that Christine hasn't told me everything about him already.

"Nice to meet you," I nod in response to his handshake.

"It's mutual," Jeff says disinterestedly and turns back to Alexander.

"Daddy, well, you already know Soph. I won't introduce you," Christine laughs nervously, clearly annoyed by the reaction of the object of her dreams.

"Good evening, Sophie," Alexander narrows his eyes. "I hope you're enjoying the party."

"More than that," I answer, bringing my knees together. "The party is amazingly organized."

"I'm glad to hear it," he smiles slyly, and lightning strikes my body. Because of our secret, this dialogue becomes ambiguous, and I turn on once again, dreaming of feeling Alexander's hands on my skin. It seems that I will never get enough of his closeness.

"Well, let's go," Christine purses her lips, keeping her eyes on Jeff. I don't even have to worry about the fact that she could notice our exchange of glances with Alexander, Christine is so passionate about looking at the blonde.

"Go dance," her father suggests, and I can hear the commanding note in his voice. "One of the best DJs in the country is playing tonight."

Christine takes me to the dance floor with a quick step, trying to match the beats of the music. She is clearly worried about Jeff's indifference.

"He doesn't like me at all," she breathes sadly.

"Why do you think so?"

"Did you see how he acted? Like an iceberg," she literally spits out the last word.

I can't help laughing as I watch Christine's comical anger.

"How should he behave when your dad is around? Throw himself around your neck with a boner?" I make assumptions without thinking about my words.

"Ugh, when did you get so vulgar?" she wrinkles her nose.

"It's the champagne," I shrug. I don't know when I became like this either.

"A man is known by the company he keeps," an inner voice chuckles, making me smile.

"You're probably right," Christine says thoughtfully. "We'll have to catch him when he's alone."

We laugh merrily. Christine noticeably calms down after my words, and we finally surrender to the power of music and alcohol seething in the blood.

Chapter 18

Sophie

Throughout the time spent on the dance floor, I feel Alexander's tenacious gaze on me. He shamelessly looks at me from head to toe. His overt attention gives me courage, and I begin to actively write eights with my hips, not caring about how it looks to anyone watching.

Apparently, not only the person that my gyrations are intended for draws attention from others to my splashing femininity and sexual message. At some point, a handsome dark-haired man is at my side, looking at me with interest and asking to dance.

I ignore his enticing hints, turning away to Christine, who sways to the beat of the music with her eyes closed. I feel someone persistently tapping my bare shoulder with fingers, but I don't have time to do anything, because an angry Alexander rushes past me like a whirlwind.

"Get away from girl, now," he hisses, effortlessly wringing the arm of my failed dance partner, who is staring in horror at his opponent.

"Dad, what are you doing?" squeaks Christine, who stops dancing, attracted by the scandal unfolding in front of us.

"Didn't your parents teach you not to hit on girls if they aren't interested in your company?" Alexander shakes opponent's shoulders aggressively.

"She asked me," he tries to justify himself.

"That's not the way I saw it," Christine's father chimes and pushes the man away from him. "Make sure I never see you again."

With eyes wide with horror, I watch Alexander adjust the cuffs on the sleeves of his shirt.

"And you," he says to Christine and me, "get out of here and go home. Now! Take my driver."

Christine tugs on my arm, but I can't move, watching Alexander as he returns to the table with Jeff. What the hell just happened?

"Soph, let's go," Christine looks at me worriedly. "Better not to argue with dad."

I let her lead me out of the restaurant. A cold wind blows my hair in different directions, but I don't understand what makes me shake more: the autumn weather or my nervous trembling. An evening that started so well has ended in complete failure. There is no trace left of the former excitement.

My teeth keep chattering even as we find ourselves in the back seat of the Mercedes that whisks us away through the night streets of the city.

"Turn up the heater," Christine asks the driver, stroking my arm. "Are you cold?"

I nod silently, not knowing what else to say. I don't want to start a full conversation, because I'm afraid that Christine might start asking questions that I'm unwilling to answer. I understand perfectly why Alexander got angry, but she doesn't. What did she think at that moment? How quickly will she begin to wonder about the reasons for her father's behavior?

I manage to come to my senses only when our car stops in front of a house that I'm unfamiliar with. I look around the street, trying to figure out where we are.

"You're staying with me tonight," Christine declares in an authoritative tone. There is something dictatorial in her, inherited from her father. "I won't let this evening end on a sad note," she softens, seeing my bewilderment.

We ascend to a spacious penthouse furnished in a contemporary style. The space is so sterile and clean, as if no one lives here. I would have thought that this is Christine's unfinished apartment, but we are in a completely different area of the city. The conclusion is obvious — this is Alexander's apartment.

This is my first time in his territory. His scent permeates the space confirming that this is his domain. It seems wrong that I am in this home without the owner.

"Come in, make yourself at home," Christine says, heading towards one of the doors, leaving me in the middle of a large living room complete with fireplace and access to a terrace filled with large planters with trees.

Half an hour later, we're sitting at the kitchen island on bar chairs eating honey and drinking herbal tea. The soft cotton pajamas that Christine loaned me finally warm me up and I relax a little.

"Forgive my dad's behavior," she apologizes. "He's too protective of me."

I shift my gaze to her. I completely forgot how self-absorbed she is. I would resent such an assumption, but now her selfishness and inability to see anything beyond her own nose works for me, so I shove my displeasure aside.

"Don't worry, it's okay," I reassure her.

"You know," Christine says seriously, putting the spoon back on her saucer. "I would probably tell dad that I'm attracted to Jeff and ask him to help me if it weren't for his tough character. I'm even afraid to mention it, knowing how he'll probably react."

"I understand," I nod, mindlessly stirring my tea. Today, for the first time, I experienced Alexander's fury and never want to see him in such a state again.

Christine puts me to bed in her room on the second floor. Her spacious bed could easily accommodate four. I try to adjust to her even breathing and fall asleep, but the thoughts of the past evening do not let me go, scrolling endlessly in my head.

The ardor of Alexander's strong character is both fascinating and frightening. I'm just now beginning to realize how unknown he is to me. I still have so much to learn about him, but I have already trusted him and there is no turning back. I know for sure that if I turn back now, I will greatly regret it in the future, and Alexander is unlikely to let me go so easily.

Chapter 19

Sophie

I wake up early in the morning, awakened by the rays of the dawn sun. Christine snores peacefully next to me. I try to force myself to sleep for a couple more hours, but nothing works. The dream was shattered as the events of the previous evening were torn from my memory.

Alexander's furious gaze, his tight grip on the shirt of the man who just wanted to dance with me. But suddenly the pictures from the back room break through and my feelings of his proximity. His jealousy and passion excite me. I have always been against solving problems through a fight, it seemed to me that a more civilized way to resolve misunderstandings is a conversation. But in the case of Alexander and testosterone bursting from him, everything is completely different. I was glad that he stood up for me. Especially in the presence of other people.

I close the curtains so as not to wake Christine and go out into the corridor, intending to go into the bathroom, but I stop at the railing of the balcony on the second floor, which overlooks the living room with the kitchen. From below comes the pleasant aroma of coffee, which Alexander is brewing.

He is standing with his back to me wearing only gray sweatpants, and I can easily see the snake tattoo that wraps around his torso. I bite my lip dreamily, remembering how my nails scratched into the ink.

Without thinking a second more, I tiptoe down to the first floor and approach Alexander from behind. I run my fingers around his waist, arranging my palms on his bulging abs. I expect him to flinch at the sudden touch, but he calmly continues to brew coffee in the cezve.

"Good morning," I kiss him on the shoulder blade. Christine usually sleeps long and hard, so I'm not afraid that she will suddenly leave the room and find us in an embrace.

"Good morning," Alexander says hoarsely. The vibration from his voice spreads throughout my body, concentrated in my lower abdomen. Next to him, I quickly become sexually aroused. He is the first man with whom I feel so feminine and desirable.

I pull away from him and lean on the kitchen sink. I want to talk to him about yesterday and it is important for me to see his face.

"Why did you do it?" I ask without any preamble because I know that he will understand me.

"I don't like it when people touch what belongs to me," his face, as always, is calm and does not express any emotions.

"So, I already belong to you?" I ask and am surprised at my playful intonation in my voice.

"Yesterday you gave a very clear answer," he grins, pulling his trophy out of his pants pocket and putting it back. I can't help but smile and blush, which instantly paints my cheekbones.

"Will you always carry them with you now?"

"Yes," Alexander removes the cezve from the stove and smears me with his eyes. "For good luck."

I put my cool palms on my burning cheeks. Euphoria flows through my veins from the fact that I have such an influence on this man. Thoughts and feelings that I am just a lover and a toy for him now seem simply ridiculous. Lola is no longer present in his life, he chose me, and also agreed to the conditions that I set him. There is no doubt that for him I am not just fleeting fun and entertainment for one night.

"Do you need help? I can make breakfast," I look around the kitchen for a frying pan, wondering if he has the ingredients for my signature French toast. I want to surprise him with my culinary talent.

"Better help me with this," Alexander raises his eyebrow, adjusting his pants at the bulging spot.

I quickly look towards the balcony of the second floor.

"What if Christine wakes up?" I whisper worriedly.

He follows my gaze and then suddenly tosses me over his shoulder as if I weigh nothing. I resist the urge to yelp, biting my fingers.

"What are you doing?" I am quietly indignant, looking at the parquet floating before my eyes below.

Alexander slaps my ass and then kicks open the door, and the dark brown wood is replaced by marble tiles. He puts me down on the counter next to the bathroom sink and locks the door behind us.

"I do what I want. It is my house," he says hoarsely, kissing my lips. His noticeably regrown stubble torments my skin, and his fingers unbutton my pajama shirt, caress my breasts.

A long groan sinks into his throat. His fingers tuck into the waistband of my pajama bottoms leaving me completely naked. Alexander takes two steps back, looking at every inch of my body with darkened eyes.

The lust that sparkles from him gives me courage, and I spread my legs, giving him a full view. In one second, he gets rid of his pants, allowing me to admire his powerful body. I run my tongue over dry lips, breathing heavily. I want Alexander right here and now, and the presence of Christine sleeping in the apartment triggers adrenaline into my bloodstream, kindling desire with a bright fire.

Everything happens in complete silence. Alexander takes a condom out of the closet and then breaks into my body, covering my mouth with his hand. I slam the back of my head into the mirror, leaning forward to close the distance between us and get even closer. I act intuitively, fulfilling the prayer of my body.

My hands wander across the surface of the countertop, and I accidentally knock off a glass bottle that falls to the floor with the sound of the tinkling shards spreading across the floor. The aroma of cologne immediately penetrates my nose. His cologne. The smell of it creates a bright flash that explodes in my head, and my body instantly responds to Alexander's assertiveness. My mind finally becomes hazy, and I scream into his palm, which extinguishes my cries of extasy.

"If I knew you are such a risk taker, I wouldn't have waited so long," he chuckles, pulling on his sweatpants as I button my pajamas with trembling hands.

I try to jump off the countertop, but Alexander stops me, grabbing my waist and carrying me to the door.

"Careful, there are glass shards everywhere," he frowns and straightens my hair. "Blushing suits you."

I smile at his compliment and watch him leave the bathroom. I count to ten, take a deep breath, and head to the kitchen, where a mug of fresh coffee is already waiting for me.

Alexander sits next to me at the kitchen island and slowly drinks his coffee, scrolling through the news feed on the phone. I lean against his forearm with mine and enjoy this simple closeness and warmth of his skin.

If I had my way, I would spend every morning like this. But it's still too early for that, even if his daughter lived in a separate apartment. I don't want to rush things. My plan is to enjoy this sweet period of our budding relationship for as long as possible. I had rushed the relationship with Liam, and it did not lead to anything good.

"Why are you both awake already?" Christine's voice comes from behind. She stands on the stairs and sleepily rubs her eyes with her fists.

I jump away from Alexander, the legs of the bar chair creaking on the floor. It is good that we are sitting sideways, minimizing her view, and my momentary weakness went unnoticed.

"Good morning," I smile nervously, raising my coffee mug in greeting.

"Morning," Alexander nods, returning to his phone. Someone calls him, and he leaves the room, leaving Christine and me alone.

"How did you sleep?" She asks, yawning sweetly.

"Very well, thanks," I look at her face and grin. "You've got toothpaste right here," I point to her cheek.

"Oops," Christine laughs and leaves. I am distracted by the message on my phone.

> *I'll pick you up from work the day after tomorrow. Dress warmly.*

I smile stupidly as I reread the message, and my stomach tightens in anticipation. I wonder what he is up to.

"So-o-oph," I hear Christine's voice. "Come here."

Chills seize my body as Christine screams from the bathroom where Alexander and I have just been. God, I hope he covered all traces of our little escapade.

"Is that yours?" She points her finger when I appear on the threshold. My panties are on the floor. Hell, they must have fallen out of Alexander's pants pocket.

I smile embarrassedly and pick up the black lace, inhaling the scent of the spilled cologne. I look at the piece with the label and commit the brand name to memory. Now I know what to give as a gift to Alexander.

88 -Forbidden secret

"Yes, apparently I accidentally left it here yesterday when I washed my face."

Christine laughs loudly.

"You have to be careful, otherwise it looks like my dad dropped his cologne when he saw them."

I nervously support her laugh, blushing to the tips of my nails. Going forward, I MUST be more careful.

Chapter 20

Alexander

The ringing of an incoming call fills the car, the illumination, like a candle in the dark dispelling the darkness. I take a quick look at the entrance to the offices — Sophie hasn't come out yet. Her colleagues leave the building in a slender line, some stop for a smoke break, while others go towards the parking lot or the subway. I pick up the phone from the console and see the name of my assistant.

"Yes," I answer shortly turning the music down. I don't like long greetings and small talk. Everything should be clear and to the point.

"Mr. Bailey," her hesitant tone does not bode well, I know Natalie too well. "Stevenson's manager called..." She makes a long pause, which starts to annoy me.

"Natalie," I bark, "stop beating around the bush. Tell me what happened."

"Well, after that incident at the party, he refuses to work with us," she says quickly.

"He has a contract signed for the main role in the series, he can't just leave, remind both him and his manager about that."

"I already reminded that to him, but he says he doesn't care."

I swear through my teeth and hang up the call, wearily rubbing the bridge of my nose with my fingers. How I hate these arrogant, over-conceited actors who think they are the center of the universe. They think they are allowed to do everything: touch other people's women, refuse roles, break contracts unilaterally. But they forget who believed in them from the very start and invested in their career, making them who they are now.

Cold air rushes into the car through the open door. I quickly take my hand off my face, force myself to smile and forget about the problem for a while. If we cannot persuade Stevenson to return to the project, then we will have to look for a new actor, which will be problematic, since there is currently no second star of this level suitable for this role.

"Hello," chirps the reason of my current problem and lands lighly in the passenger seat.

"Good evening, Sophie," I lean in and kiss her soft, caramel-flavored lips. I really want to deepen the kiss, especially after the little hassle, but I control myself, realizing that this is not the right place. There are too many witnesses who are already throwing curious glances in the direction of my car.

"Where are we going?" Sophie asks excitedly as she fastens her seatbelt.

"You'll see," I smile slyly. I turn onto the road and as my tongue runs over my lips, tasting the residue of her lip gloss that has transferred to my lips from hers.

As we drive to our destination, Natalie calls a few more times, and I turn the phone off in annoyance. Everything can wait for tomorrow, I still have time to fix Stevenson's brains. Tonight, I have a wonderful evening planned, and nothing can spoil it for me.

Along the way, Sophie talks about her new project at work, which she has only dreamed about in her wildest dreams. Today, her boss even praised her for a job well done, which, she says, he rarely does.

I would never have thought that such a fragile and petite girl like her wants to become an architect. I see her as an actress, artist or writer, but not leaning over a drafting table and calculating what kind of materials and type of foundation is best. She breaks all the stereotypes about pretty girls that have lined up in my head over decades of working in the entertainment industry.

We reach our destination, a country house, which contains the largest private collection of wine in the capital. An odd choice for someone who doesn't like to drink alcohol in excess, but completely predictable for someone who collects alcohol and prefers the story behind the label.

"We agreed that we wouldn't hide in rented houses," Sophie pouts, looking at the mansion through the window.

"Well, first of all, *we* didn't agree. I said that I would *consider* your request," I smirk, seeing her displeased face. "And, secondly, this is not a rented house, it's a country restaurant with its own twist."

"And what is this twist?" It is clearly visible in her eyes that what I've said brings her relief. I have noticed that Sophie does not know how to hide her emotions. And I really like it.

"You'll know if you stop questioning me and get out of the car."

Sophie rolls her eyes and snorts.

"You know, I trust you. I don't know why, but I do. I wouldn't be here if I didn't."

Her words ripple through my body. Despite my bad temper, she sincerely believes my every word.

After my relationship with Laura, I completely forgot what it is like when people believe and trust in me, completely surrendering to my power. It never happened to my ex. This is probably why I deliberately did not enter another serious relationship, thinking that women would manipulate me again.

"Tell me honestly: did you book the entire restaurant again so others would not see us, or are there no more connoisseurs of country taverns besides us?" She glances around the empty chalet-style space as the manager lead us to a table on the first floor.

Sophie makes me laugh again this evening. Knowing her bad habit of running away from restaurants. Choosing a secluded place will keep her from running away from me again.

"Not many people know about this place," I shrug. "That's the beauty of it."

"Is this like a private country club? Are we going to play golf later? Is that why you asked me to dress warmly?" She spews questions, pulling at the neck of her sweater.

"Patience, Sophie," I wink at her, enjoying the bewilderment on her face.

I choose my favorite wines from the menu brought by the manager, and after a few minutes he brings two glasses, and the sommelier tells the history of the French winery and interesting facts about the year of production of this particular bottle.

"You don't have to drink alcohol to lose control of your body," I stop Sophie from taking another big sip of dry red. "You savor noble drinks, feel their history. Each wine is a certain year of harvest. Find out more about it. Whether it was a dry summer, or, on the contrary, very rainy. It all affects the whole experience."

Under the pleasant crackling of the fireplace, she looks at me as if I were an exotic animal that she's never seen before. Once again, I've managed to surprise her.

"Jazz, history and wine tasting," Sophie lists, narrowing her eyes. "Who are you, Alexander?"

"A simple man with his weaknesses," I set my glass of wine down on the table. "Next time, let's go to the gallery."

"Are you also an art lover?" She raises an eyebrow.

"Yes, by the way, I sponsor exhibitions all over the world. Sculpture, antiques, paintings — I have great appreciation for the art world."

"Van Gogh, Munch, Picasso, Kandinsky, Monet, Manet, Chagall, Klimt?" She lists the names of artists. Now it's my turn to marvel at her knowledge.

"Don't look at me like that," Sophie rolls her eyes and takes a small sip of her wine, savoring it on her tongue as I had instructed her. I am pleased that she listens to my advice. "By the way, I graduated from art school. Without it I would not have been admitted to the architectural university. And just so you know: I had the highest mark in my art history class."

The expenses for my daughter's art education immediately pop up in my memory. Now I understand why Laura brainwashed me when she begged for money for Christine.

I take Sophie's hand in mine and pull it to my lips and place a kiss on her fingers, making her cheekbones blush simultaneously. Once again, I find myself thinking that our meeting was not accidental.

All my ex-girlfriends looked at me stupidly with open mouths and devoted eyes when I talked about artists. I liked to impress them and build a certain image about me. With Sophie, I can behave naturally and even argue about the contributions made to the development of the fine art of certain figures.

"Mr. Bailey!" The shrill voice of my assistant breaks into our cozy evening.

I turn to Natalie, intending to incinerate her with a glance for interrupting the solitude of the moment, but the sight of her makes me put on a mask of seriousness. Tousled hair, an untied bow on a blouse and heavy breathing, suggests that she rushed here for a reason.

"Be quick and to the point," I command, letting go of Sophie's hand.

"The writers found out about Stevenson's refusal and are threatening to go on strike. I called you, but you didn't answer!" Natalie screams in panic. "It's a mutiny!"

I take a deep breath and get up from the table. This fucking actor has ruined my evening with Sophie. There is no question of any walk through the beautiful surroundings of the mansion. I have no choice but to deal with this situation now.

"Understood," I nod to her, scrolling through the options. "Go back to the office. I'll be there in forty minutes. Call Stevenson and his manager."

"But..."

"I don't give a shit if he's sleeping or drinking at a bar. He must be in my office in an hour," I say every word clearly.

Natalie nods curtly and rushes out of the building, phone glued to her ear.

"Is something seriously wrong?" Sophie asks worriedly, standing next to me and touching my elbow.

"Nothing irreparable," I put my arms around her shoulders and kiss the top of her head. "I'll take you home. We'll have to reschedule our evening."

Before getting out of the car, Sophie gives me a deep and sensual goodbye kiss that makes me want to drop everything and stay with her for the night. And then she suddenly pulls out crumpled black lace from her bag and hands it to me.

"For good luck," Sophie winks and closes the car door as she heads for her building. I can only smile and shake my head in amusement. I'm a bad influence on her, but now I know for sure that the meeting with Stevenson will end well.

Chapter 21

Sophie

"Ta-da," I proudly demonstrate the set table that Christine and I carried from the kitchen to the living room, breaking a couple of nails and scuffing the freshly painted wall.

"Perfect, Soph!" She claps her hands. "Thank you for your help!"

I brush off her praise and adjust the bundle of balloons that are attached to a weighted bag on the floor. The spacious living room in Empire style, with high ceilings is lined with balls, tinsel, tables with snacks and drinks. The surroundings, excluding the decorations and food, are Christine's childhood dream of a castle finally come true.

Christine and I did our best to organize a housewarming party of the highest standard. The food was ordered from an expensive restaurant, and for every bottle of wine and champagne, Christine (or rather her father) had to fork out a lot of dough. Alexander would be proud of me, because I personally chose the wine under the surprised expressions of the sales clerk and Christine.

"Since when did you become a wine sommelier?" she asks, taking a sip of rosé. "This wine is really delicious!"

"You didn't believe me?" I snort in mock insult, suppressing a smile on my face.

"Just never suspected your wine abilities," Christine shrugs and hands me a second glass. I take a sip with her and chuckle. Exactly the soft and berry flavor, as that I expected.

After the interrupted trip to the country restaurant, I wanted to study all the information available on the Internet about wine in order to match Alexander's knowledge and be worthy of him in everything. I have watched dozens, if not hundreds, of videos of winemakers and sommeliers. And later I was able to surprise him when he came to my house for dinner, and a bottle of red dry was waiting for him on the table. A bottle that I had spent most of my budget on.

On the morning after this incident, Alexander left for work early, leaving several bills on the kitchen table. I wanted to be indignant, because I felt like a call girl whose payment is left on the nightstand. But I was smart enough not to fall into hysterics, but to judge sensibly and understand that Alexander simply appreciated my efforts with the wine and perfectly understood how much the bottle had cost. So he returned the money and added a bit more just to be sure he had covered the expense.

Since then, he started leaving me expense money, and when he got tired of constantly withdrawing cash from the ATM, he asked for my bank account number. At first, I resisted because I was uncomfortable. But Alexander, as always, managed to convince me that he was only making sure that I was being properly compensated for my expenses.

"Riding the subway is not safe. Order a car service for yourself, no taxis."

"You always cook dinner for me, but I can't eat you out of house and home. Buy groceries."

"Remember those shoes you saw in the photo? Buy them for yourself. I want to see you tonight. Wearing only the shoes," he smiled provocatively.

I blush deeply when I remember what we did that night. Christine had left to collect her remaining things at her mother's apartment and stayed overnight. It seems to me that every surface in Alexander's house was marked by us. Even the railing of the second floor and sofa on the terrace. Although it was a cold autumn evening, the heat of our passion warmed us to the point of burning.

"By the way," Christine snaps me out of my thoughts. "Great dress. Is that Dolce?"

She narrows her eyes intently. And I know her appraising look. She's mentally calculating the cost of my dress and trying to understand how I could afford it.

"Thank you," I spin around, showing off my new wardrobe in all its glory. "I decided to spend all my savings for you and your party."

It seems that this answer suits her quite well and the wrinkle on her forehead smooths. Christine mutters something like "you shouldn't have" and goes to open the door, where the first guests are already ringing the doorbell.

Gradually, the apartment is filled to capacity with people I know and don't know. Guests include our former classmates from university, and Christine's new friends from a fashionable company of privileged youth. She's enjoying the continuous attention and gladly accepts each housewarming gift. Especially the Baccarat crystal vase and "Christofle" egg with cutlery.

I take a sip of wine and watch Christine in her usual habitat. Today, nothing should overshadow her and the fresh, fashionable renovation of her new apartment in the expensive, uptown area of the city. I'm willing to bet that she would be at the throat of anyone who would dare to pull the blanket of attention from her.

"Hello," a familiar voice says in my ear, and I turn too abruptly, spilling wine all over myself.

I swear through my teeth (another habit I seem to have acquired from Alexander), wiping the spilled wine from the fabric with my palm, and angrily looking at the person who dared to sneak up on me.

"What the hell are you doing here?" I blurt out in low tones.

Christine did not invite him; I know that for sure. From the very beginning, we discussed the guest list, in which even Jeff appeared. Although, I doubt he will be here, unlike my ex.

"Aren't you glad to see me?" Liam runs his fingers nervously through his light brown hair and looks at me uncertainly.

"You weren't invited," I cut off any of his attempts to get through to me, not too kindly. I have suffered too long and I don't want to plunge into that icy whirlpool again.

"I just want to talk to you," he tries again.

"Do you really think that I have something to talk about with a man who betrayed me and left me for another woman after several years together?" I lose my patience and utter everything that has bothered me all this time.

Liam drops his head guiltily and then grabs my hand, clenching his fingers. Breaking out of his grip is not difficult. He is not as assertive and domineering as Alexander. Liam always went with the flow and if he didn't succeed in something, he didn't really get upset.

"Just give me five minutes," he looks up pleadingly. "That's all I need."

Throughout our relationship, I hadn't noticed what a bastard I had attached myself to. It's true what they say that you don't know what you don't know. Liam has no confidents and is weak. Comparing him to Alexander who is self-confident and tough, who knows what he wants and never bustles, I can't believe that I ever saw anything in Liam.

"Just five minutes," I give in and let myself be led into the corridor for our first tête-à-tête after parting. On the way, I catch Christine's surprised look, her lips mouth the words, "what is he doing here?". I shrug in frustration.

"Soph," Liam begins uncertainly, shifting from foot to foot as we find ourselves in a secluded corner of the hallway, "I broke up with Mary."

"And what?" My eyebrows instantly fly up. I don't want to know anything about this. I would rather live in the illusion that he left me for her, and they are living their happiest life with a bunch of small children.

"I realized that I can't live without you," his voice trembles. "She is not you and never will be. She can't replace you."

A hysterical laugh escapes my lips.

"Is that why you left me for her? Because she can't replace me?"

"I didn't know then..."

This conversation is getting even more absurd than I thought.

I roll my eyes, covering them with my fingers. When I open them, I see Alexander's head looming over Liam's shoulder, looking straight at us. I swallow hard because I didn't expect to see him here either. Christine said that her father would not be able to come because of work.

His jaw moves in different directions, and his hands are clenched into fists. He is clearly angry. Guests cautiously walk past him, lowering their eyes, as if water is flowing around an obstacle.

Not a trace of my former bravado remains.

Chapter 22

Sophie

"Baby," Liam mumbles. His voice breaks through the swirling water in my head. I focus my gaze on the pale face of my ex, who is frantically tugging at his hair. "My darling."

I wince at the once pleasant nicknames. Why didn't I notice before how disgusting they sound from him?

"I screwed up," he breathes heavily. "I'm an idiot, I know. If you want — hit me, if you want — yell at me. Do whatever you want, I'll accept and understand everything."

"Liam," I almost moan with hopelessness. "I don't want to hit or yell at you. And *I don't want* our relationship back either."

Liam grabs my shoulders and looks compassionately into my eyes, blocking my entire view. I'm trying to make out a person whose glance will give me strength, but my ex doesn't allow me to do it, holding me tightly in place.

"Baby," he begins again, softly stroking my cheek with his fingers. I shudder at his every movement, imagining with horror how Alexander will react and what he might come up with. "Do you remember how we checked every shop in the area one night and looked for the cake that you saw in the movie, and you wanted to try it? Do you remember how we went to the movie theater every Friday after classes? I always brought you your favorite salty popcorn and iced tea. Remember how we lived in your dorm? We didn't care about all *this*," he looks around Christine's luxurious apartment.

I hug myself tightly, resisting the urge to cover my ears with my hands and start singing rather than hearing Liam's words. Each shared memory is like a backhanded blow. He is not a stranger to me; we have been through a lot. Despite his betrayal, he is still shares a close connection to me. But now, it physically hurts me to hear him reminisce about our past.

I am happy with Alexander; he opens up a side of me that I wasn't even aware existed. Yes, we have our difficulties, but I am sure that this is a matter of time. Sooner or later, the situation with Christine and our secret relationship will be resolved. But the wounds of the past, as it turns out, are not completely healed. And now Liam is picking at the scabs, opening up the pain that I had forgotten.

I rise on my toes to meet Alexander's gaze, but there is no one in the hall. It was as if the wind had blown him away. Maybe I'm hallucinating?

"Who are you all looking for?" Liam asks irritably and looks around. "Did you even hear a word I said?"

His sudden mood swing scare me. I take a step back and run into the wall. There is not much space, but this allows me to increase the distance between us and gives me some room to maneuver.

"Liam," I say his name calmly, choosing my words carefully. "I heard every word, but I don't want to be in a relationship with you again. Yes, we were good together. Until, of course, it turned out that you were cheating on me. I don't trust people like you anymore. You betrayed me once and you'd betray me again as soon as the opportunity came around. I'm not ready to live that way, and I feel it's better for us to stay friends."

Liam's face instantly turns red and his hands clench into fists.

"You have someone, right?" He hisses. "Is he here? Are you looking for him? Let me meet him! I'll talk to him!"

His words make me laugh. Imagination throws up a funny picture: Liam approaches Alexander, who is a head taller than him and twice as wide, and Liam squeaks something to him, like a mouse to an elephant.

"Liam, yes, I'm not alone, but I don't have to answer to you. We broke up. Deal with it. Somehow I did it."

My words clearly hit him painfully. He looks at me as if he's seeing me for the first time.

"I didn't expect this from you," he says. "And your dress is ugly! Money doesn't suit you! You're too gray for such bright and expensive clothes! And you definitely don't belong in the company of your silver spooned friend! You're too different from her. You're a peasant!"

My patience runs out the moment he finishes his monologue. The rage that has been building since the moment I found out that Liam cheated on me bursts out.

"Fuck you," I say and raise my hand. A sharp and ringing slap lands directly on his right cheek. My hand hurts unbearably, but it was worth it. The shock on his face gives me incomparable delight. All these months, I was completely unaware that I dreamed of doing this.

I expect to hear something vile in response, but Liam quickly turns around and runs out of the apartment, huffing and muttering something under his breath, while rubbing his reddened cheek.

In a triumphant gesture, I straighten my hair and chic dress, fighting back against my nervous tremors. Although I emerged victorious from this situation, the victory does little to boost my confidence. His words remain a deep thorn in my subconscious.

"I didn't invite him, honestly! I have no idea how he ended up here," Christine blurts out immediately as I approach her and take the glass of wine from her hands.

All I want now is to fall into Alexander's arms and absorb the warmth and strength that emanate from him.

"Forget it, I slapped him, and he ran away squealing like a scared pig," I answer as Christine chokes on her drink while I peer into the crowd to see the face that matters to me. "I saw your dad. Has he left?"

Because of the sudden change of topic, Christine does not have time to comprehend everything that has been said and to adjust to my question. She looks at me for a few more seconds, batting her eyelashes, and then finally nods.

"Yes, he brought a gift and left. It seems he has some problems with Stevenson again. If he hadn't attacked him at that party, he wouldn't have been on the verge of losing the main actor of the show," Christine stomps her foot and then shrugs her shoulders. "Or he's spending time with his new girlfriend again."

I freeze with the glass in my hand and carefully examine Christine, trying to grasp the meaning of what she just said. A whirlpool of thoughts spins in my head, and I try to grab at least one. Stevenson? Party? Attacked?

So, the man who hit on me at the party is the actor the whole country is talking about? I was so absorbed in my emotions and feelings for Christine's father that evening that I didn't even notice that a famous actor was approaching me. And now Alexander has problems with him because of me. He had decided to stand up for me...

My next thought completely overlaps the other. Because Christine's words "with his new girlfriend" are starting to reverberate loudly in my ears and throb in my temples.

"New girlfriend?" I think I'm asking this question out loud.

"Yes, he constantly disappears somewhere at night, doesn't come to dinners, or spend the night at home. He's probably got himself a new slut."

With difficulty and the grinding of gears in my head, it dawns on me that I am that slut. Alexander spends all his nights with me.

"Can you imagine! I wanted to go to his house the other day because I forgot my laptop there," she switches to a hot whisper, looking around warily. "So I go into the apartment, and there are moans! I thought all the neighbors would complain about noise. I didn't even take the laptop; I just ran out of there as quickly as possible. What a shame!"

It seems to me that I stopped breathing, and my face turned to the color of paper. That evening Christine could have caught Alexander and me in such a state that no excuses would have worked. It's good that she came in at a time when we were not on the first floor, otherwise we definitely would have been caught.

Once again, we walked along the edge, but managed not to fall over the precipice. If this isn't fate pointing me to the right path, then I don't know what it is.

"Oh, I'm sorry," Christine misreads my paleness. "You probably feel uncomfortable hearing such personal things about my dad. I would feel uncomfortable too if you talked about your parents."

I nod my stiff neck and down the glass of wine in one fell swoop.

"So, what happened with Liam? Did you tell him that you have a mysterious admirer?" Christine is curious, playfully moving her eyebrows.

Chapter 23

Sophie

"Am I really that bad?" Christine sniffles, wiping her nose with a napkin.

She looks very comical, sitting in a fluffy dress on the floor in her new bedroom. Tears streaming from her eyes, turning her bright makeup into blurry spots on her face.

I'm probably the worst friend if Christine's tears bring a smile to my lips. She laments the fact that Jeff ignored her housewarming invitation and didn't even send a card. Her infatuation for him is already beyond reasonable boundaries and is now more like an obsession.

"Well, why are you so upset?" I sit down next to her, handing her a fresh napkin. "You had a great party, no worse than the local socialites. And the fact that he didn't come is just his loss. He probably spent a long, boring evening alone at home, and as soon as the news about the new party queen spreads throughout the Internet, he will bite his elbows for being such an idiot."

Christine laughs through her tears and looks at me with gratitude. All the guests had left, but I stayed to help her clean up. But the cleaning did not go as planned because of the hysteria that washed over her.

"Why are you so good to me? What did I ever do to deserve a friend like you?" She blows her nose loudly and hugs me with damp arms.

I feel ashamed because I'm not really that good of a friend. I can't even share my new relationship with her. And I would really like to ask Christine for advice and an outside perspective on why Alexander left the party without even saying hello to me. I want to express my concerns that he might have gotten the wrong idea when he saw me in a secluded corner with Liam.

"Silly," I run through her smooth black hair. "You know I love you like a sister."

"I never told you," Christine pulls away from me, wiping her cheeks with the back of her hand. "But it has always seemed to me like you are my sister. Like we were separated at birth."

There is an unpleasant pain in my chest. If she knew that I was meeting her father behind her back, what would she say then? If my relationship with Alexander goes further, then who will I become to her? Stepmother? I hadn't thought about this before... But I probably should have.

In the silence of the apartment, the ringing of my phone hits us like thunder. I immediately jump to my bag because I only have this ringtone for one person.

> *I'll be waiting for you in half an hour around the corner.*

I bite my lip, trying to muffle the delight that is swirling my insides like a whirlwind. After what happened, I didn't expect to receive a message from him today.

"That mysterious "A" again?" Asks Christine, who has materialized behind my shoulder. I quickly lock the screen, thanking my resourcefulness for not putting Alexander's full name in my phone's contact list.

"Are you dating him?" She smiles, squinting her eyes slyly. There is no trace of her former sadness left on her face. Christine was always more interested in other people's relationships than her own. Especially when they were working out better. She always stuck her nose into everything and said that I suck at choosing men. It was the same with Liam.

"Something like that," I answer evasively. My whole body is tense, and my fingers are trembling, clutching the phone with a death grip.

"That's so cool," she is quite sincerely happy. I can't hear any deceit in her voice, and this fact pushes me to do a rash act.

"He knows about Liam and why we slept in the hotel back then," I blurt out before I change my mind. "And now I'm afraid that he might get jealous, seeing that Liam wants to make things work again. I'm afraid that... That it might ruin our relationship."

Christine is silent, humbling me with a thoughtful look. Now she looks like her father more than ever. I already regret what I said and swear off having a heart-to-heart talk with her, but she suddenly says something that I never expected.

"You know, if this is true love, then he trusts you and won't let anything that Liam does ruin what's between you."

I arrive fifteen minutes before the appointed time and hide in the arch of a neighboring house, afraid that Christine will accidentally discover my lie. I told her a false story about how "Mysterious A" is always waiting for me around the corner of MY house, and therefore I had to hurry. She almost pushed me out the door, wishing me to have a good night and to finally send her a photo of my stranger.

Alexander arrives, as always, on time.

"Hello," I close the door behind me and inhale the aroma of musk and bergamot. The smell of Alexander has already become calming for me.

"Good evening, Sophie," he greets casually. The hoarseness in his voice sends sparks flying under my skin, instantly warming my frozen in the wind body.

"I saw you today. Why didn't you say hello?"

"Right off the bat," Alexander chuckles. "You don't know any other way."

I don't know whether to take that as praise and a compliment or reproach and dissatisfaction. I peer into his face, which is illuminated by the dashboard of his car, but it expresses nothing but calm.

"I just want to explain what you saw today: yes, Liam tried to talk to me and wants get back together," I say my piece, which I rehearsed while I waiting for Alexander. "But I sent him packing. If you had stayed longer, you would have seen how he ran shamefully out of the apartment after I slapped his face. By the way, my hand still hurts."

I demonstrate raising my right palm; which, of course, had stopped hurting hours ago.

Alexander looks at me for a long time in the darkness of the car, and then turns to the windshield and releases the hand brake.

"Fasten your seat belt," he says and drives off.

I flutter my eyelashes in confusion and automatically tug on my seat belt. I don't understand his reaction. Did I say everything correctly? Maybe I shouldn't have raised this topic? But I felt I needed to explain myself so there would be no misunderstandings between us. Especially after my honest confession about our first sexual encounter.

Mom was right when she said that sometimes I should keep my mouth shut.

"Where are we going?" I raise my voice, which dissolves in the melody of jazz flowing from the speakers.

Alexander is silent as he drives out onto the main street. The silence begins to press on me, compressing the whole world down to the inches that separate me and Alexander. My thoughts beat chaotically against my skull.

We are not heading towards my apartment, which means he has no plans to take me home and say goodbye forever. But that doesn't give me much confidence. I'm afraid to start filling the silence with stupid and meaningless conversations, and frightening away the fragile things that remain between us.

Unbidden tears well up in my eyes. I look down, examining my fingers and nervously rubbing my glossy manicure. I don't want this relationship to end, because of an idiotic accident.

"I love driving around the city at night," Alexander suddenly says as we rush past the square. "There is something soothing about it. The darkness hides all the flaws, and the lights transform the city and turn it into a magical place where all, even the wildest, dreams can come true."

His heavy palm rests on my bare leg and squeezes lightly, forcing me to look up at him. I have never seen Alexander in such a romantic mood. It seemed to me that this was out of character for him, so eternally serious.

Alexander frowns when he sees my wet eyes. We stop at the next traffic light, and his hand moves from my knee to my cheek. His fingers erase salty tracks, gently stroking the skin of my face.

"Why are you crying?"

I chuckle nervously and run the back of my hand over my face.

"I was just thinking..."

"That I'd leave you because of such stupidity?" His eyebrows rise in surprise, and my body goes limp with relief. "Don't be stupid. You're a smart girl."

"Sorry," I mutter, lowering my gaze to the armrest and covering his hand with my palm.

The traffic light turns green, and Alexander smoothly presses on the gas. I kiss his fingers, salty from my tears, and intertwine them with mine, promising myself that, this evening, I will never let go of his hand.

Chapter 24

Sophie

"I love this place," says Alexander, helping me out of the car.

After several circles around the city center, we stop on a pedestrian street. In the darkness of the night, it shimmers with the lights of signs, elegant lanterns and beautiful garlands that arc down between the houses, imitating the starry sky.

It's quieter than ever here at night. Only a few loving couples stroll along the sidewalk slabs, and bar patrons smoke near the entrances.

"Did you really slap your ex?" Alexander grins as we pass by the terrace of an Italian restaurant.

The memory of Liam's shocked face makes me laugh.

"Yes, for the first time in my life I slapped a person in the face," I look at my palm, as if there were still prints from my ex's cheek on it.

"I'm proud of you," Alexander hugs me by my shoulders and kisses the top of my head. A happy smile spreads across my face. Only he can turn my mood one hundred and eighty degrees with just one phrase.

Alexander continues to hug me, moving forward and talking about moments in his life that happened to him on this very street. For the first time I learn that he has two best friends. They often spend time together after work, drinking a glass of wine or whiskey, and discussing "boring male topics."

I ask if Jeff is one of them, to which I receive a negative answer. When I said his name, Alexander noticeably tenses up, and I hasten to assure him (knowing his jealous nature) that I was just asking, since he was the only one I saw in his company. I almost blurt out too much about Christine, but I bite my tongue just in time. In the end she trusted me, and I don't want to let her down.

We are already returning to the car when a man walking in the opposite direction to us stops abruptly.

"Bailey!" He shouts and quickly walks towards us. Alexander curses through his teeth and removes his hand from my shoulders.

"Duncan, long time no see," Alexander greets him, and they shake hands.

The name immediately pops into my head, only in Lola's squeaky voice. She asked Alexander to say hello to him at Christine's birthday.

I shift from foot to foot as they exchange pleasantries. I try to stand far away, praying that Duncan won't pay attention to me. At some point, I even think about running to Alexander's car and waiting for him there, but I force myself to stand calmly.

"How's Lola doing? Still giving head for roles in your TV shows?" Duncan bursts into vile laughter. It makes me cringe. I knew the specifics of the relationship between Alexander and Lola, he never hid it from me, but Duncan's words still resonate with an unpleasant feeling in my chest.

"No," Alexander answers coldly. "We broke up."

"Come on! Why? Have you found yourself a new actress?" Duncan looks over Alexander's shoulder straight at me. My cheeks instantly flush and the tips of my ears begin to itch. I had to run away.

"None of your business, Duncan," Alexander bristles. I see his fists clenching and he hastily hides them in his trouser pockets. "I have to go, but let's stay in touch."

Without waiting for his answer, Alexander turns around and nods towards his car. An unpleasant chill runs down my spine. I've already seen him in this state.

When we are finally alone in the car, Alexander exhales. But on the contrary, I'm freaking out more. My anger grows as he silently drives out onto the roadway.

"Just how many actresses do you have?" I spit out in irritation, clicking my seat belt.

"Stop it," Alexander snaps, focusing on the road.

"It seems to me that I have the right to know, since I'm being compared to women like Lola," I'm angry at his reaction. "I can imagine what your friend thinks about me now."

"Does it matter so much what other people think about you?"

"Certainly!" I wave my hands. "Can you imagine the rumors that will spread?! What if they reach Christine and she finds out that it's me? What will she think of me?"

"She won't find out."

His words cut into my heart like a sharp knife, carving it into pieces. Just like that, for the second time in a day, a gap forms between us, which I tried not to notice all this time.

"You don't plan to tell her about our relationship? Why? Because it's not serious to you?" My voice goes up an octave.

"That's not what I meant," Alexander mutters irritably, squeezing the wheel with his fingers until it creaks.

"Tell me honestly, am I just another toy for you? Is that why you want to hide what's happening between us from everyone?" I point my index finger at his shoulder. "You never took me seriously!"

"Stop it!" Alexander barks and sharply presses the brake, turning into the nearest gateway. The car stops in the dark arch of a building, hiding us from prying eyes.

The seat belt cuts into my chest and Alexander's angry gaze bring me to my senses. The red veil of rage subsides a little. I don't know what came over me. The uncertainty of our relationship and the secrecy we keep worrys me every time I think about the future. I want clarity, not illusory hopes.

"If I don't fucking take you seriously, then what is this?" He takes papers out of the glove compartment and throws them on my laps.

"What is this?" I mutter, straightening out the sheets of paper folded in half with trembling hands.

"Tickets," Alexander pinches the bridge of his nose with his fingers. "I wanted to surprise you today, damn it."

My eyes do not want to read the letters on the paper. I can't concentrate on anything. Alexander wanted to surprise me, and I threw him a tantrum in the middle of a romantic evening. I feel like a complete fool.

"You told me that you always wanted to see the sea," he exhales, leaning back in his seat. "I decided the ocean would surprise you more."

I put the tickets away and rub what's left of my makeup with my palms. I force myself to swallow back my tears. How stupid I am. Half an hour ago, Alexander was proud of me and said that I was smart. With just one action and constant rumination in my head, I trampled his entire idea of me.

"I'm sorry. Please forgive me," I whisper, repeating the apology. I don't know how many times I need to apologize to him to smooth out the nasty aftertaste of this evening. "Just Duncan's words and your reaction to them... Also, our secret and all the prohibitions around it. I know what I'm doing. It's just difficult for me. I thought it would be easier."

I feel Alexander's hot palm stroking my back.

"I thought it would be simple too," he says soothingly. "You wouldn't believe how often I want you next to me at boring events, to listen to your jokes and laughter, that would make the eternal conversations about work more bearable. Or when I meet with friends, and they bring their girlfriends."

I take my palms off my face and turn to Alexander. There is sincerity in his eyes. My heart skips a beat because I experience the same feelings every time. I miss him like air. Without him I'm suffocating.

Without thinking for another minute, I free myself from the seat belt and with difficulty climb over the armrest, sitting on Alexander's lap. I cup his face with my palms as if it were the most precious thing I have.

"I believe it," I whisper. "Because I want it too."

I cover his lips with a greedy kiss, to which Alexander instantly responds. His palms cup my buttocks and squeeze them. The dress is inexorably creeping up because of my widely spread legs.

"You're burning me to the ground like a damn crematorium," Alexander gasps through the kiss, interrupted by his heavy breathing and my moans.

His words motivate me to act decisively. With shaking hands, I unbutton his pants and lower his boxers, releasing his hard erection. I rub it with my palm, feeling the sticky lubricant between my fingers.

Alexander puts his hand between us and pulls the crotch of my panties aside. He draws circles on my clitoris with his fingertips, making me bend over even more and bite his lips with impatience.

"Please," I whisper breathlessly, unable to hold back any longer. He removes my hand from his cock and in one motion enters me, filling me to the last inch.

Emotions throw me over the edge and forces me to energetically bounce on Alexander, not worrying at all that passers-by might see or hear us. My palm slides across the foggy window, and the top of my head hits the ceiling of the car. Another sob, another slam of my hips against his trouser-clad legs, another slap of my clitoris against his crotch, and I explode with a wild cry. I rest my forehead against his and go limp as Alexander comes to the end.

A few minutes pass before I come to my senses and start laughing.

"It turns out that in movies they show the truth when the heroes have the most intense sex after an argument."

Alexander laughs and removes the stuck hair from my face, tucking it behind my ears.

"No poetry can describe your beauty," he says tenderly, looking at my face. This is the first compliment Alexander has given me after sex. Usually he doesn't like to talk, he just hugs me silently or immediately goes into the shower.

I smile and kiss him on the lips. Once again, he opens up to me from the other side. I don't know how many more facets he hides and how many he will show me. But I am ready to be endlessly a pioneer.

Chapter 25

Sophie

I think I can taste salt on my tongue even though the plane hasn't landed yet. Fifteen minutes have already passed since the announcement of landing, and all this time I have not left the window, not taking my eyes off the blue surface stretching below us. Alexander strokes my palm with his rough fingers, and this makes the moment seem even more unreal.

We spent quite a few hours on the flight, and all this time it seemed to me that I was sleeping, although I could not close my eyes for a second. Before this, I flew economy class and domestic flights only. Now I realize how great it is when you have the opportunity to purchase business class tickets. Sitting in solitude with your loved one, sharing this moment between just two. I promise myself that I will definitely achieve success, I will do everything in my power in my career, and I will organize my vacations to the highest standard available. And I will definitely arrange a similar return surprise for Alexander. He will most likely grumble that I spent money, but I don't care.

"Thank you," I whisper in his ear and kiss his earlobe when the landing gear touches the landing strip. Everything inside is trembling with overwhelming delight.

"Sophie," Alexander says tenderly, taking my chin with his fingers and giving me a light kiss on the lips. "We just landed, there's nothing to be grateful for yet."

From no one else's mouth does my name sound as delightful as from his. Every time I am ready to turn into a small puddle at his feet.

"You won't believe how much you've already done for me," I confess, feeling emotional. "Every day you open up new horizons for me. Just next time, please, give me the opportunity to take time off from work myself. I still feel uncomfortable about the situation with Christopher."

Alexander just laughs and shakes his head at my reproach. And I'm still not laughing. He personally called my boss, when I didn't yet know about the trip, and asked him to organize an unscheduled vacation for me, justifying himself by saying that he knew my boss and it was more convenient for him to plan our trip.

Barbados welcomes us with an ocean breeze and air too warm for my wool sweater. The bright sun reflects off the azure water and blinds my eyes, but this does not stop me from looking at the local colors while driving in a comfortable minivan to the west of the island.

As soon as Alexander gets cell service, his phone starts ringing non-stop. He calls his assistant and asks not to disturb him over trifles, only urgent and important calls, for everyone else he is unavailable for a week. I'm bursting with happiness that he cancels so many meetings and ignores work calls for our vacation together. Although I don't mind at all, understanding how important it is for him. But I'm still very pleased.

The hotel offers us cool drinks while we check in and listen to all the extravagances offered by the venue. Alexander immediately books us time at the spa and asks if I would like to sign up for morning yoga. But I refuse, planning to spend every morning in Alexander's arms, enjoying the sound of the waves and the cries of the seagulls.

The first half of the week passes as if we are in paradise. We leave our private villa only for breakfast, dinner, and walks along the sandy beach, watching sunrises and seeing off sunsets. Within a few days, I am so saturated with ocean salt and sunlight that my pale skin takes on a slightly bronze tint. Not as bronzed as Alexander's, but I no longer look like Snow White compared to him.

"I want to get a tattoo," I declare, running my fingers along the ink snake encircling his torso as we lie on a large sun lounger in the shade of a baldachin.

Alexander looks up from the tablet on which he is reading the latest news and turns to me, taking off his sunglasses. I expect to hear his moralizing that I shouldn't spoil my clear skin with ink drawings, but he surprises me once again.

"What would you like to get and where?" He asks interestedly, looking at my body, covered in a too revealing bikini, which he bought me on the second day of our vacation.

"Here or there," I show him with my finger locations at my forearms next to the bend of my elbow and at my left side ribs. "I know what I want but it is a secret."

Alexander's eyes sparkle and then he reaches for his phone. He actively types something in the messenger, and ten minutes later he returns to me, giving a ringing slap to my buttock.

"Get ready," he smiles. "You have a maximum of thirty minutes."

"What? Where?" My eyebrows rise in amazement, causing my glasses to slide down the bridge of my nose.

"To make your dream come true," Alexander winks at me and, throwing a towel over his shoulder, heads inside the house.

An hour later, a car with our hotel logo stops in the center of Bridgetown, opposite the tattoo parlor. It turns out that Alexander, with the help of our personal concierge, booked an appointment for me here.

"You're crazy," I laugh as we enter the tattoo parlor, filling the space with the ringing of metal bells on the door.

"Purely theoretically, you're the crazy one here. I'm just following your lead," Alexander teases me and I playfully shove him with my hip. This man will drive me crazy someday.

A tattoo artist comes out and introduces himself as Sebastian. His hair is braided in bleached dreadlocks, and his dark skin is covered with a variety of tattoos. He offers me a catalog with drawings for every taste, but I refuse, already knowing exactly what I want.

Alexander sits down on the sofa by the window and says that he will wait for me here, and to leave the tattoo I chose as a mystery. At this point I decide to do two at once. I will show one right away, and he will see the second at night, when he undresses me to the sound of the ocean waves and in the light of the moon.

In a separate booth, I take out my phone from my shorts pocket, which I keep turned off all this time. I don't want to involve the outside world in our fabulous trip, I don't want to think about my autumn city, the work awaiting me, gray everyday life and Christine who doesn't know where I am. Besides, I still haven't figured out how to justify my absence.

I find the saved pictures in the gallery and send them to Sebastian. We discuss size, placement, and color, and then we get straight to work.

It turns out that getting tattoos isn't that painful. It's only when he moves on to the linework on my ribs, that I understand what

Sebastian was telling me when he explained that each part of the body has its own degree of sensitivity.

I remain steadfast throughout the entire session. I manage not to cry from the first second of the needle touching my ribs, and then I get used to the unpleasant sensations. To distract myself, I look at the number of notifications. I notice that I have received many messages from Christine, but I don't read them, convincing myself that I will answer them as soon as I come up with an excuse.

"I'm ready," I say proudly, going out to Alexander. He gets up from the sofa and pays for the artist's work. I try not to think about how much more money he's spent on me. I feel uncomfortable, but in the end, he is a grown man and he's the one who decided to give me another surprise. I didn't ask him for it.

"Will you show me?" Alexander asks slyly as we get back into the car.

I show him the tattoo on my arm, which is hidden under a transparent film.

"What is this?" Alexander tries to understand, clasping my elbow and focusing his gaze on the drawing.

"What do you see?" I smile.

He runs his fingers over the ink thoughtfully.

"Atomic molecule?" He assumes, and I burst into laughter, expecting exactly such a reaction.

"These are two intertwined hearts, see? Here's one," I outline the contour of the first. "And here's the second one," I point to the other.

"Where is the second tattoo?" Alexander asks, and the corner of his lips rises when he meets my puzzled gaze. "Sebastian blew your cover when he told me the cost of both tattoos separately."

"What a tattletale," I'm angry at the artist for not keeping my secret.

"It seems like you're in deep trouble," Alexander laughs, pulling me by the shoulders and kissing the top of my head.

"Why?" I don't understand his strange reaction.

"You speak just like me, Sophie," Alexander grins. "So will you show me the second tattoo?"

The pleasant warmth from his words spreads throughout my body, making my heart race. My mom once told me a phrase that has stuck with me forever: "The lovers repeat each other's words."

Alexander is the first person with whom I do not deliberately imitate this fact.

"You'll see tonight," I smile slyly, intending to keep the mystery and intrigue until the sun has set and the moon fills the sky.

Chapter 26

Sophie

"Wow," I say in surprise when the waiter brings a giant metal plate with ice and a lot of seafood, some of which I see for the first time.

I hesitate to take one of the shellfish first because I have absolutely no idea how to eat it. I watch Alexander deftly pick up an oyster, squeeze lemon juice onto it and add sauce with a small spoon. I repeat the steps after him.

"God, how delicious this is," bursts out of me as I chew the fleshy component of the sea creature. It looks like snot but tastes incredible. Salty, but creamy at the same time. I've never eaten anything like this before. It's like tasting the sea.

For the next half hour, Alexander teaches me how to properly cut a lobster. He wields special scissors and tweezers as if he has been doing this every day since birth, but I am very bad at it. After another unsuccessful claw cut, he takes everything upon himself and simply puts the extracted pieces of meat on my plate, allowing me to observe his manipulations and savor the delicacies.

Alexander smiles, watching my reaction. I have already noticed that he likes to discover new sensations for me. And I like to be myself around him and enjoy every second spent together.

"It's so beautiful here," I smile, looking at the moonlit path of light reflecting from the water. My feet sink into the still-warm sand, and the light ocean breeze flutters the hem of my dress.

Strong tanned arms wrapped in a white linen shirt hug my shoulders. Alexander stands behind me, and I feel his breath on top of my head. I'm ready to enjoy this moment until the morning dawn.

"Thank you," I put my palms on his forearms and kiss the crook of his elbow, sitting comfortably in his embrace.

If someone had told me a couple of months ago that I would end up in heaven with my best friend's father, I would have laughed in their face. But right now, Alexander's arms seem to be the right place for me to be in my life.

"I'm glad you liked it," a hoarse voice drowns in my hair, spreading goosebumps throughout my body.

"It's so sad that we have to leave very soon," I sigh, remembering that sooner or later we will have to return to the cruel reality of life. Once again, a cold, inhospitable city with eternal hiding from friends and relatives.

"We will come back here again," Alexander once again fills me with hope for a future together, which I try to avoid. I just focus on enjoying the present, so as not to overthink the future and throw a tantrum again.

Reality unexpectedly invades my fairy tale, forcing me to think about the words that I have long wanted to say to Alexander. For some reason, now seems like the best time for me to share my thoughts with him.

"You know, two polarities collide in my head when it comes to you. On one hand, you're a caring, gentle, kind man; yet when Laura and Christine describe you as a man who abandoned your unborn daughter, always strict and serious..." I don't have time to complete the sentence because Alexander interrupts me.

"Let's not spoil such a wonderful moment with unpleasant conversation," he visibly tenses, and his voice sounds colder.

"I just want to know more about you," I make another attempt to get information out of him.

"Everything has its time, Sophie," he kisses the top of my head and releases me from his embrace, making me shrink from the abandoned warmth.

I have nothing to object to his desire not to discuss this further, and it's not my habit to pull information out of a person. If Alexander is not ready to discuss this topic, it means he is uncomfortable, or he does not want me to know the details of his past. I am sure that he had his reasons not to interfere in the upbringing of his daughter, although I can't imagine what could force a person to literally give up his flesh and blood.

Having spent enough time with him, I can conclude that most likely he did not initiate such a relationship with his ex-wife. Yes, he can be rude and hot-tempered, but he would never abandon his daughter just like that. But I can only guess what really happened.

Alexander takes me by the hand and leads me along the beach towards the copse of palm trees, leading me away from the water. As soon as we reach one of the trees, I find myself pressed by Alexander's powerful body against the rough trunk. Before I know it, his inquisitive hands are roaming under my skirt.

"What are you doing?" I giggle, trying to stop his attempts to lift the fabric above my buttocks.

"I want to see your tattoo," Alexander pants, covering my neck with hot kisses and pulling the strap of my dress off my shoulder, allowing the fabric to expose my chest.

He stops, looking at the ink adorning my ribs. Then he turns on the flashlight on his phone to make sure that his eyesight is not failing him.

"Snake?"

Yes, baby. Just like yours.

I just shrug and smile, satisfied with his reaction to my little surprise. Alexander hugs me tightly and puts his lips on mine, cupping my exposed breast with his palm and squeezing my nipple between his fingers. The slight tension between us after my ill-timed inquisition instantly evaporates.

"People can see us," I appeal to his mind, but I can hardly restrain myself from jumping on Alexander right here.

"Let them look, I don't care."

"Alexander," I moan, either begging for more, or begging him to stop.

"Give yourself to the moment, Sophie. Stop thinking."

I take his advice, letting desire cloud my head. Alexander picks up my leg, pressing it to his thigh. I don't even have time to notice how he lowers his trousers and his hard penis, without foreplay, invades my heated flesh. I bite Alexander's collarbone, suppressing screams mixed with sobs.

My legs inexorably give way as we walk along the gravel path to our villa. Stars are still dancing before my eyes, and my lower abdomen is throbbing after the intensity of my orgasm. I am ashamed to look towards the hotel workers when they pass by us. It seems like they have seen everything. It's immediately clear from my flushed face and disheveled hair that I've just had sex.

The same cannot be said about Alexander: he walks with a confident gait, holding my hand and typing something on his phone for his assistant. This vacation has convinced me more that Alexander is a workaholic.

I see Christine in my dreams all night. I don't know what exactly my conscience is asking of me: to respond to the many unread messages or to feel guilty (which, by the way, is completely absent) for the fact that I am hiding my relationship with her father. Due to uninvited dreams, I wake up early in the morning while Alexander is still sleeping.

I make myself a cup of coffee and go out onto the terrace to admire the sunrise. The sun rises from the horizon, illuminating the beach with the first rays of a brand new day. A local resident bathes his horses in the ocean. This sight is breathtaking, and I grab my phone from the table to take a photo as a souvenir.

After a few minutes of thought, I make up my mind to connect to the wi-fi and finally respond to Christine's messages. In my head, I had already worked out a plausible excuse for my absence: boss gave me an official vacation, and I went to my parents to spend time together and disconnect from the outside world.

I open the messenger and freeze, re-reading the messages several times. My brain begins to work at full capacity, comparing the story in Christine's message with subsequent events. Anger rolls over me like an icy wave, and a chill from overwhelming emotions sweeps across my skin, making my whole-body tremble.

I jump up from my chair, placing the ceramic mug on the glass table with a thud. I cover the distance with quick steps and open the door to the bedroom. Alexander sleepily opens his eyes, awakened by the door hitting the wall.

"When did you buy the plane tickets for us?" I blurt out, clenching my fists.

"What? What are you talking about? What time is it?" He blinks and looks around for his phone.

"It's time to tell the whole truth, Alexander," I mutter through clenched teeth, trying with all my might to restrain the fire of rage spilling out of me. "When did you buy the tickets? Before you beat up Liam or after?!"

The last words fly out of me as a scream.

Alexander freezes, continuing to look me straight in the eyes. The cold that suddenly appeared between us is like an ice floe pressing me against the wall. I take small sips of air, reading the answer to my question in Alexander's pupils. All the fabulousness of our trip is broken into small fragments, just like my rose-colored glasses. The glass exploding inwardly, scratching my corneas with the inevitable truth.

Chapter 27

Alexander

As a child, my small family, consisting of my parents and me, relocated to the bustling capital. Unfortunately, my father's demanding job at the university left him with little time for me, as he dedicated his days from morning till evening to fulfill the expectations placed upon him. His hard work and determination had secured his position, a feat that was challenging to achieve coming from a humble village background.

In his youth, my father undertook arduous journeys covering hundreds of kilometers to the nearest city in pursuit of a quality education. He passionately defended scientific dissertations and utilized his last resources to attend conferences in the capital, all of which took place before my birth. Throughout this period, my mother steadfastly supported us, working long shifts at the restaurant, fueled by her unwavering belief in my father's eventual success.

The turning point arrived when Jeremiah Bailey, my father, returned home with exhilarating news: he had secured the coveted position of assistant professor in the department of physical and mathematical sciences, eventually ascending to the role of department head. Despite the achievement, our living situation remained modest, and my mother took on an additional job, as the salary of an assistant professor scarcely covered the monthly expenses for a family of three in the capital.

As we settled into a small apartment on the outskirts, I found myself navigating life's challenges independently. School provided formal education, but the streets, frequented by local punks, offered unconventional lessons. These individuals imparted wisdom, emphasizing the importance of strategic fighting techniques and the judicious use of gloves to avoid leaving incriminating evidence on one's knuckles.

However, my well-laid plans took an unexpected turn when I failed to account for the presence of a remarkably intelligent and perceptive girl by my side. Little did I know, her presence would alter the course of my carefully crafted endeavors.

My parents had always been my guiding example. As a university student, I embarked on a journey as a stand-up comedian in a local bar. Gradually, I built significant connections with influential individuals, contributing as a writer on various TV shows and crafting jokes for popular sitcoms in my free time. These experiences paved the way for the position I currently hold.

During one of the shoots, I encountered Laura.

At that time, she was a breathtakingly beautiful woman who had recently returned to the capital after winning the Miss Universe title. Every businessman and congressman seemed poised to vie for her attention, yet she inexplicably took notice of me — a budding screenwriter making a name for himself. Our romance unfolded unexpectedly and swiftly.

A year after our meeting, Christine entered our lives. It was then that I discovered Laura was simultaneously involved in a relationship with a prominent businessman. Her plan was for him to leave his wife for her, with me serving as a source of comfort for her ego. However, an unforeseen pregnancy disrupted her intentions, and the businessman departed without even determining the unborn baby's father.

Laura endured a challenging childbirth. I catered to her every need, even disrupting film shoots to ensure she received the necessary medicine and nourishment. Then, one day, she thoughtlessly sent me to the hospital to retrieve essential documents, unaware that these papers included a secretly conducted paternity test.

The revelation of this betrayal struck me with a force I hadn't anticipated. The dreams of a strong, harmonious family shattered in an instant. Despite confirming Christine as my daughter, I found forgiveness impossible in the face of Laura's deception.

The trust reduced to ashes could not tether me to such a woman.

Aware of the situation, Laura issued an ultimatum: either I remained with them or risked being denied access to my daughter.

She didn't consider the impact on a child growing up in a household where animosity prevailed between parents.

I couldn't bear the thought of Christine being raised amidst such hostility, believing that hatred was a normal emotion between those who should love each other. With Christine's well-being in mind, I made a decision that felt right at the time: providing financial support for my daughter while refraining from active involvement in her upbringing. Little did I anticipate the consequences this choice would have on Laura.

The acrid sting of cigarette smoke filled the confined space of the car, prompting me to open the window wider, welcoming the chilly autumn air. Outside, the capital had been shrouded in days of incessant rain, mirroring the despondency that enveloped me upon returning from what was supposed to be a paradise — now turned into a personal hell.

I rubbed the bridge of my nose with my fingers, closing my eyes in an attempt to banish thoughts of Sophie's last words uttered on the final day of our vacation.

"I want to leave now," she wheezes, standing in the doorway of the bedroom.

"Sophie, let's talk like adults," I attempt to calm her down, but my words seem to fuel her agitation even more.

"Talk to you?" She grins malevolently. *"You're only good at waving your fists, not at solving problems through conversation."*

A surge of rage, fueled by the hopelessness of the situation, washes over me like a tsunami, clouding my ability to think rationally. It mirrors the moment I caught her alone with her ex, who dared to encroach upon what belonged to me.

"What do you expect me to have done?" I'm losing my temper. *"Just stand on the sidelines and watch that jerk grope you?"*

"You could talk to me, Alexander!" Her scream reverberates through my eardrums.

"About what? About the fact that I couldn't erase your ex from your memories?"

Sophie falls silent, staring at me as if I've lost my mind. This only intensifies my anger, widening the emotional gap between us with every unspoken accusation.

"Are you completely idiot?" She exhales, shaking her head in disappointment. Her arms hang powerlessly along her body, and the first tears stream down her face.

I despise the sight of women's tears, a painful reminder of my childhood when my mother wept on lonely evenings, waiting for my father. And then from Laura, when she pleaded with me to stay, falling at my feet.

"Maybe I needed to talk to Liam sooner or later," Sophie wheezes, swallowing tears with pride. "Not to go back to him, but to reassure myself of how much I love you."

She heads to the closet, pulls out a suitcase, and begins packing her things. Everything blurs before my eyes.

I flick the cigarette filter out the window. "I love you," Sophie's voice resonates in my ears, interrupted by the melody of another call from my assistant.

I impatiently pound the steering wheel with my palms and end the call. I can already predict the nature of the message she'll deliver — a new complaint from Stevenson, whose presence has fueled a cascade of problems since the moment I arrived. This troublemaker revels in flaunting every minor issue, deftly exploiting my earlier threat to him at the party.

Exiting the car in the all-too-familiar courtyard, I slam the door loudly, leaving the phone behind. Raindrops pelt my face, unnoticed in my focused state. At any cost, I need to articulate words to Sophie that I've hesitated to say before.

Dialing the memorized code on the intercom, I ascend to the floor of the worn-out building. Swearing to myself that if Sophie forgives me, this very evening, I'll take her away and arrange for her to move in with me. I don't care about public opinion. I'm unwilling to let her slip away for an extended period again.

I knock on the door. Silence. Once again, but the result is the same. I decide to ring the bell, hoping she might be in the shower and hasn't heard my knocks. I try not to dwell on the fact that she still may not want to talk to me.

The door opens just as I prepare to go to the car to retrieve my phone and call her. A bald man in a shabby old T-shirt stands on the threshold.

"What do you want?" he asks in a smoky voice.

For the first time in my life, I'm at a loss, unsure of what to think. I peer inside over his shoulder, attempting to catch a glimpse of the apartment. Could I have the wrong door? But the interior looks the same as before, except Sophie's outerwear has been replaced by a worn men's windbreaker, and the breeze from the open window carries the stench of cheap cigarettes.

"Is Sophie at home?"

"Who?" He rubs his forehead with his palm, trying to understand. "Oh, you're probably talking about the previous tenant. She moved out a couple of days ago under my strict guidance," he chuckles disgustingly and ambiguously. My fists itch to connect with his face, but I restrain the impulse, remembering Sophie's advice about handling problems with words. "What? She left some debts? I checked everything when I bought it. Everything is clean."

Relief washes over me as I realize Sophie didn't change residences to evade me, but confusion sets in because now I have no idea where to find her.

"Do you know where she went?" I inquire, aware of the likely unhelpful response from the man standing before me.

"Nah, dude, no idea," he shrugs his hairy shoulders. I cringe at the disdainful nickname and pivot on my heels, heading towards the elevator.

There's nothing left for me to catch here. Once again, I'll have to wait for her at work, looking like a maniac.

"Hey," the new tenant shouts at my back. "Some girl was helping her pack her things. With black hair, so curvy. Maybe she was staying with her?"

I exhale in irritation when a stranger makes inappropriate remarks about my daughter. Clenching my fists, I force a crooked smile and thank him for his assistance.

The Bentley's engine purrs softly as I pull out of the driveway, steering the car toward a familiar neighborhood.

I light another cigarette, exhaling smoke out the slightly open window, concocting an excuse for my late evening arrival at my daughter's apartment. I dismiss the idea of waiting until tomorrow. On a physical level, I need to be close to Sophie and remind her of my existence.

For the second time that evening, I knock on the apartment where she is supposed to be. Opting not to use my key, I cautiously press the bell button, trying not to be too forceful.

The door opens, and Christine appears immediately.

"Daddy?" Her eyebrows shoot up in surprise. "What are you doing here?"

"I decided to check on my daughter. Is this prohibited by law?" I nod in the direction of the living room, where the light is on.

"No, come in," Christine hastily lets me inside. "I'm just not alone. Soph is here. I didn't warn you, but she'll be staying with me for a while until she finds a new apartment."

"You don't need to warn me. This is your apartment."

The relief of confirming Sophie's whereabouts for the first time in days gives me a faint feeling of relaxation, and I don't even notice how Christine blushes at my words.

"Come into the kitchen; we're just having dinner. Soph has prepared her signature lasagna," she pretends to be an exemplary housewife.

Sophie is sitting at the dining table with her legs tucked under her, twirling her glass of rosé by the stem when I walk into the room. Her eyes immediately meet mine, but I don't feel the same warmth as when she gazes at me with an indifferent look, only wariness.

Her declaration of love hangs in the air without my answer, despite the icy thickness between us. Only a blind person would not notice the sparks that fly when we are in the same room.

"Good evening, Sophie," I break the silence while Christine is busy at the stove, putting food on a plate.

"Good evening, Mr. Bailey," Sophie responds coldly and too formally.

It seems that this ice will be much more difficult to melt than I thought, but I do not intend to give up so easily. Not with the girl who turned from a non-committal affair into something more for me.

Chapter 28

Sophie

Anything that can go wrong, will go wrong.

After a multi-hour flight, during which I hadn't exchanged a word with Alexander, the note affixed to my apartment door felt like a cruel joke. Without any prior call or communication, the landlord had chosen to surprise me with "wonderful" news through a hastily written notice. It turned out that the owner had decided to sell the apartment without any prior notice, and fate would have it that a buyer emerged precisely during my trip. I now had a couple of days to pack all my belongings, retrieve the cat from my neighbor, and move to an uncertain destination.

Despite unsuccessful attempts to find a new apartment, I had to concede defeat and seek shelter from Christine for an indefinite period.

When Christine came to assist with packing, the first thing she noticed was my tan. The rain and overcast weather did nothing to support my excuse of spending the entire week with my parents. The web of lies began to accumulate new layers.

I fed Christine a fabricated tale, explaining that my mother had read articles in magazines suggesting that the fastest way to acquire vitamin D was through ultraviolet lamps. Hence, it was imperative to visit the tanning salon regularly, especially during the cloudy autumn days in our region.

I still feel a pang of shame. Furthermore, Christine was so enthused by this concocted idea that she convinced me to accompany her to a beauty salon near her home. Now, I am the proud owner of a tanning salon subscription and the dubious privilege to get melanoma.

The worst part of this entire situation is that Alexander chose to pay an unexpected visit to his daughter. While I anticipated this outcome, the timing took me by surprise. Just a couple of days after our return, I was ready to repent for my stubborn behavior. However, moving out of the apartment and hastily returning to work left me with no time for reflection.

Now, here we are, seated across from each other, and I am steadfastly conveying to Alexander how angry I am with him.

In our brief time together, I've come to realize that he is quick-tempered, inclined to yield to emotions rather than resolving issues through dialogue. However, I still struggle to comprehend how he could resort to physically assaulting someone without first understanding the full story.

While I was always the first to reconcile with Liam and pleaded with him to avoid further fights, with Alexander, I find myself wanting to be a petulant girl, upset because he didn't immediately seek forgiveness after our quarrel. I'm unsure whether this is a display of femininity next to a strong and confident man or just plain foolishness that might come back to haunt me.

Regardless, the fact remains: when I see Alexander this evening, any thoughts of repentance for my hysterical behavior vanish, replaced by a stubborn defense of my position. According to my mother, waving fists is characteristic of bad boys, and it's better not to mess with them.

But then again, don't good girls love bad boys?

Christine scurries back and forth in the kitchen, showcasing her domestic prowess. She reheats the food, offers wine, and diligently wipes the countertop with a rag, a chore she's never bothered with in my presence.

When Christine finally settles and joins us at the table, the palpable tension conveyed through Alexander's intense gaze eases a little.

"Christine," he begins suddenly, his voice hoarse and sending goosebumps down my spine. I can never get used to the influence he has on me. "What would you say if I had a girlfriend?"

I choke on my wine, coughing and trying not to show my shock. But Christine is equally surprised by the question, so she doesn't notice my amazed gaze directed at Alexander.

"Um... Well..." She stammers, involuntarily starting to wipe the table with a napkin. "You didn't ask me anything about Lola."

"Lola is not the issue," Alexander quickly redirects the conversation away from his past relationships, avoiding any discussion. "She was just a frivolous hobby. What if I had a serious relationship with the woman I love?"

It feels like my eyes are about to crawl beyond my forehead at his reciprocal and veiled confession. Alexander looks straight at me. Seizing the moment of Christine's confusion, I begin to actively shake my head, urging Alexander to regain composure and not broach this topic now. I'm not ready to reveal the nature of our relationship just like that, not at this moment and certainly not in this manner.

My mind races back to the words I uttered at the hotel in Barbados. "I love you"—those words escaped me as casually as if I were talking about buying a jar of pickles. It was so natural and ordinary that I feared the gravity of my confession and how those words might alter the dynamics of our relationship.

Was I prepared for my spontaneous outpouring of feelings? Absolutely not. Perhaps that's why I felt such anger directed at both Alexander and myself.

Christine exhales sharply and looks at her father with a serious expression. "Honestly, I still hope that you will make peace with mom," Christine suddenly says, and my heart attempts to break free from my ribs.

The hope in her voice makes me swallow hard and look down. I had no idea how deeply the discord in her family affected Christine. After these words, it feels like I may never be able to meet her eyes without a sense of shame.

Alexander reads my reaction instantly, and I feel the touch of his foot under the table. I tuck my legs under me and take a big sip of wine. Instead of a pleasant berry flavor, it tastes sour and tart, making me wince.

"Christine, your mother and I have already settled everything a long time ago, and it cannot be changed," Alexander says sternly, directing his last words either to me or to his daughter.

"But she still loves you," Christine nearly jumps in her chair.

Alexander puts down his fork and closes his eyes for a moment, exhaling heavily. "I know it's hard for you to accept, but I don't love her. She did everything for this."

"Yes, you are right!" Christine jumps to her feet, causing her chair to crash to the floor. I wince, hoping this conversation turns out to be a nightmare. "It's hard for me to accept because neither of you tells me the truth! What happened between you two that you hate her so much?!"

"Christine," Alexander growls, rising from the table. "If your mother deems it necessary to tell you what she did, then she will do it. I don't have to make excuses for my actions to you."

"You don't have to?! You abandoned me and mom, left me to grow up without a father!" She squeals, and at that moment, I want to laugh hysterically, understanding how hot-tempered she is and how she always starts up half a turn. I'm sure that if her father weren't standing in front of her, she would have attacked her interlocutor with her fists long ago.

"Ask your mother why you grew up without a father," Alexander mutters, straightening his suit jacket and shirt cuffs.

Realizing that the conversation has reached a dead end, Christine clenches her fists tightly and tries to breathe deeply, but she doesn't succeed. I want to fall through the floor rather than be present at the Bailey family argument, especially since it started with a conversation about me.

"I think it's best for you to leave," Christine breathes out.

Alexander only briefly agrees and glances at me quickly before leaving the kitchen. I purse my lips, not knowing what to do in this situation. I want to rush after Alexander and talk to him, but I can't afford to do this in front of Christine.

He takes the phone from the table and quietly nods at it. I turn my gaze to Christine and, making sure that she is not looking in our direction, nod in response.

"See you later," Alexander says goodbye meaningfully and leaves, slamming the front door.

**

"Sorry for ruining the evening," Christine apologizes, climbing onto the couch with me as we prepare for bed.

"It's okay, anything can happen," I reassure her, but my heart aches from the secret that hangs over us like an invisible cloud.

"I don't really understand why he came," she grumbles, getting comfortable and clicking the TV remote control.

"He probably just wanted to sincerely talk to you and ask your opinion about a new relationship," I play the role of a peacemaker, trying to seem indifferent, although these words come to me with great difficulty.

Christine looks at me from under her furrowed brows. "I thought you were supposed to protect me as your best friend, not my father," she snorts, grinning. "And what kind of relationship can we be talking about? He's probably dating some whore again. I know that he can't have a serious relationship with anyone other than my mom. Although he won't admit it because of his pride, he still loves her."

I bite my cheeks until it hurts from the inside, not knowing how to respond to this remark. I am again torn into two parts. On the one hand, I personally know Alexander and his relationship with his ex-wife. On the other, his reluctance to discuss their separation and Christine's confidence in her parents' feelings.

"Okay, I'll go to bed," she gets up from the sofa, throwing the remote control in my direction. "Tomorrow morning, we going to Liam, remember?"

"I remember," I lie. Because of all the events, I completely forgot that we had planned to visit Liam in the hospital. "Good night."

"Yeah, you too."

When Christine leaves the living room and closes the door to her bedroom, I rush to the phone I left on the coffee table. My heart skips a beat when I see a notification about a new message from Alexander.

I'll pick you up at work tomorrow.
We need to talk.

Chapter 29

Sophie

I find it hard to breathe as the nurse stops in front of Liam's room. I'm unsure of what to expect. A bruised and plaster-covered ex? Or will he greet me with caustic comments from the doorstep about my unclear relationship with my best friend's father?

Why did I even agree to Christine's offer to visit Liam together? It seems like an extremely reckless decision. He might seize this opportunity to take revenge on me, and Alexander would undoubtedly reprimand me for this.

The memory of Alexander reverberates like a warm wave throughout my body. Though we haven't officially reconciled, his declaration of love through dialogue with his daughter gives me hope that a normal relationship (as far as possible in the current situation) is still possible between us, and that he hears my words. Fears of being considered a hysterical fool and cast out of his life have faded into the background.

"Liam, hi!" Christine exclaims as she bursts into the hospital room with a bag of fruits and snacks. "How are you?"

Liam flinches at the sight of me but immediately smiles tightly, redirecting his gaze to Christine. He looks completely different from the photos our classmates sent me. The bruises have already become barely noticeable, and the abrasions are covered with a dark crust.

"Hey. Much better now," Liam says sheepishly, sitting up in the hospital bed.

"I thought they'd already let you go," Christine jabbers. "How did you even manage to do that?"

"I got into a fight with *morons* outdoors," he winces. "The doctors should have let me go a week ago, but because of the concussion, my mother persuaded them to keep me for another week to make sure that everything was fine with my skull."

His heavy gaze pins me to the floor, and I guiltily shift from foot to foot. He knows exactly who beat him and why, but I don't know how to apologize to him. Nothing in this world justifies the violence he suffered.

After spending another fifteen minutes in the room, the tense silence in which Christine's ringing voice fills, I begin to glance at my watch. In half an hour, work starts, and I urgently need to leave. I can't even imagine how to leave without saying a word.

"Oh, Soph, is it time for you *to go*?" The observant Christine saves me by looking at her phone. "I'll go and get the car from the parking lot, and you two will coo," she winks and leaves the room, having previously pinched my hand suggestively.

I want to roll my eyes, but I restrain my inappropriate impulse and move a little closer to Liam.

"You better stay where you are," he puts out his palm in warning, making me freeze. "I don't want to lie in bed again with nausea and a swollen face for several days."

"I'm sorry," I whisper in confusion. "He shouldn't have... I'm so sorry..."

"How long have you been fucked with your *best friend's dad*?" Liam interrupts me dismissively. "Is he the reason you rejected me?"

I blink my eyes, not understanding where to put my hands and unsure of how to respond to such questions. I want to tell him to back off, but the gnawing feeling of guilt doesn't allow it.

"I think that my personal life is none of your business," I politely put him in his place. "What Alexander did to you was wrong, but I didn't ask him to do it, and I didn't want it to happen."

Liam grins nastily and folds his arms over his chest, looking at me with a contemptuous look.

"How did I not notice before how rotten you really are? You know, I don't want to have anything to do with you anymore. Don't ever come near me, and don't let me see you, otherwise, I'll write a police report against your... *fucker*."

I flush, feeling a painful burning in my chest. Once again, I hold back the impulse not to tell him everything I think about him.

"Goodbye, Liam," I proudly turn on my heels and leave the room, taking a breath. As soon as the door closes behind me, tears roll into my eyes.

"*He's not worthy,*" the voice of common-sense knocks in my ears.

"Well, have you made up?" Christine asks as she pulls out onto the road.

"You could say that."

"So, we'll have a reunion party soon?" She squeals joyfully, tapping her fingers on the steering wheel to the beat of the music.

"More like a wake for a relationship buried forever," I chuckle, remembering Liam's last words.

"What?" Christine is indignant. "How is this possible? I was really hoping that this incident would bring you closer, and you would come to your senses. You were a good couple."

"Christine, are you serious?" Irritation begins to fill every cell of my body, causing me to begin to shake with large tremors. "Return to the man who betrayed me? You yourself cursed him with all might!"

"Listen, well, anything can happen in life. A person stumbled, understood everything, and came back," she shrugs.

I massage my temples with my fingers, trying to dull the headache our conversation has caused.

"Be honest, were you the one who invited Liam to the housewarming party?" I make an assumption that has tormented me since that very evening.

Christine pretends that she is too focused on the road and does not hear my question. But when I repeat it louder, she bites her lip, and everything becomes clear to me. Such a trick was to be expected.

"Why? Just *why*? So that we can get back together? I thought you were on my side," I dig my nails into the soft skin of my palms to bring myself to my senses. "You saw how I suffered and how long it took me to recover. He broke my heart, and not just forgot to reply to the message, after all."

Christine huffs in annoyance and rolls her eyes.

"I wanted the best. I saw that you were already feeling better. I thought that you had cooled down and would take him back. He's still in love with you. He told me."

Great, my best friend is talking to my ex behind my back. What setup should we expect next? I resist the urge to get out of the car at the nearest traffic light and breathe deeply.

"Christine, let's agree once and for all, nothing connects me and Liam anymore, and there's no need to try to reunite us. Period."

"Okay, okay, whatever you say. I won't do it again, all wishes have been taken into account," she mutters.

***

Being busy with deadlines at work distracts me from angry thoughts about Liam and the frightening realization that Alexander did everything right. He is much more far-sighted than me and understands people better.

Sometimes, dealing with people like Liam, you can't put them in their place even in a fight. They will always stick to their opinion and make others guilty of all their sins.

I hand over the last drawings to Christopher and leave the office just at the moment when Alexander's car slows down on the side of the road. I jump into the front seat and close the door behind me.

"Hello," I greet with restraint, and then, not caring about everything and giving in to impulse, I lean over the armrest and kiss him on the lips.

Alexander cups my face with his hands and kisses me passionately. The butterflies in my stomach finally wake up after a long lull and actively flap their wings, making me smile and forget all the fears and uncertainties about the sincerity of his feelings.

We break away from each other only when we begin to suffocate, and my heart begs for mercy, beating at a frenzied rhythm.

"Sorry for losing my temper," I apologize, wiping my lipstick off his chin.

"I thought it was I who should ask for forgiveness for my eccentric character," Alexander grins.

"We *deserve* each other," I admit the disappointing fact of our relationship. We are indeed similar in some ways, for example, in jumping to conclusions.

Alexander brings me to his home and orders delivery of Japanese food. It still feels strange to be in this apartment, knowing that no one else will disturb us, and we don't have to hide in the bathrooms for privacy.

After my story that Christine once came into the apartment while we were having sex, Alexander changed the locks.

"Why didn't you tell me that you were evicted?" He asks as we sit on the carpet next to the coffee table and start dinner.

This simple question baffles me. My first instinct when I saw the notification was to call Alexander in tears and ask him for help. I stubbornly pushed this thought to the back of my mind, understanding how it would look from his side. A little girl has a quarrel with a man, and then she comes running to beg for money.

"I was afraid that you would perceive me as Lola," I admit quietly. "I didn't want you to think that I was selling myself to you."

Alexander puts down his chopsticks and makes me look him in the eyes, lifting my face with his fingers by the chin.

"When will you begin to understand that my concern for you is not paying for your body with money, and that my previous relationships are in no way similar to ours?"

I swallow convulsively, hypnotized by his serious gaze, and only one thought is spinning in my head.

"Say it again," I ask Alexander almost inaudibly, afraid to ruin the intimate moment.

"What exactly?"

"What you said at Christine's place."

I hold my breath when the corners of Alexander's lips twitch slightly and his large palms hug my cheekbones.

"I," he stumbles mid-sentence, and my heart plummets. "Love you."

I can't hide my happy smile, which stretches across half my face. With a wild squeal, I pounce on Alexander, embracing him in my arms, causing us to fall to the floor.

This evening we begin a new stage in our relationship, and I lock all the worst thoughts about his exes into the black box of my mind. They won't dare to sow doubts in my head anymore because I know that Alexander loves only me.

Chapter 30

Alexander

"I still believe you should talk to Christine and explain what transpired between you and Laura," Sophie asserts confidently, her bare feet on the cool marble tiles as she effortlessly flips a pancake in the frying pan. Meanwhile, my attention is divided between her culinary skills and the way my T-shirt rides up, accentuating the curves of her ass. In this moment, it's challenging to harbor any resentment towards her well-intentioned advice.

"You don't know the full story," I respond, taking a sip of coffee, my gaze fixated on the sun-kissed tendrils of hair escaping from Sophie's casual bun.

"Because you won't share it with me," she grumbles, turning towards me.

I'm tempted to sweep her into my arms, carry her to bed, and silence her with a cascade of kisses. The last thing I want is to delve into the intricacies of my past. After all, the past is meant to be forgotten and left undisturbed.

"Everything has its time, Sophie. I've already explained this to you," I state.

She rolls her eyes, returning her attention to the stove.

"Well, I still think you should move in with me," I bring up our previous nocturnal discussion, a topic she skillfully evaded by burrowing under my blanket.

"How exactly do you propose I do that? What should I tell Christine? I already fabricated a story about spending the weekend with my parents so I could be with you. Besides, there's the issue of my cat. I doubt you want him scattering litter all over the bathroom and leaving fur on your clothes," Sophie mumbles under her breath.

At times, it appears she's adept at finding a myriad of reasons to prioritize the convenience of others over herself.

"Your cat and I have already become fast friends, and I don't mind animals in the house. We can designate a separate area for him and invest in some sticky rollers if you're concerned about fur. As for Christine, just tell her you found a new apartment," I suggest.

"But she'll ask where I'm moving and want to throw a housewarming party," Sophie sighs. "No, that's a bad idea."

"That's why you should come to me next time you need help," my reproachful tone rings clear.

If only she hadn't taken offense, everything could be different. We might already be living together, and I'd be serving the cat breakfast while sipping on my morning coffee. But what's done is done. We'll tackle problems as they come, and I'll handle Christine's unnecessary questions.

The rest of the day is spent on the living room couch, wrapped up in each other in front of the TV. Sophie chooses a show produced by my channel, where several girls vie for the affection of one man, each date playing out like a scripted drama. I recall resolving a scandal once when the main character slept with multiple participants in one episode. It struck a chord with the viewers.

I genuinely detest this project, though I reluctantly acknowledge its lucrative returns.

Midway through another dramatic dialogue on the screen, Sophie's phone disrupts the tranquility with a loud melody. She quickly jumps off the couch, leaving the comfort of my arms, and retrieves her cell phone from the kitchen island.

"Hello, Christine," she greets deliberately loudly, implying that I should keep my voice down.

I turn around, observing Sophie's facial expressions transition rapidly from cheerful to serious. A foreboding sensation settles in my stomach. Despite our quarrel, if something has happened to Christine, I'll be the first to rush to her side.

I nod at Sophie, my concern evident. "What happened?" I inquire, but she raises a finger to her lips, signaling for silence. Several excruciating minutes pass in complete quietude before she finally begins to speak.

"Okay, dear, I understand you. I'll come now. Stay there," Sophie says with a tremor in her voice, swallowing visibly after concluding the conversation. She avoids meeting my eyes, shifting restlessly in the center of the room, likely contemplating how to approach the impending conversation.

"Alexander," she starts, her voice carrying a gravity and determination that leaves me breathless. "I won't lie to you about what happened, but only if you promise not to come with me and wait for a message from me."

Involuntarily, my fists clench, and my eyebrows shoot up. Is Sophie really giving me ultimatums, especially when it concerns my daughter?

"Sophie, you have to understand that if something happened to Christine, I won't be able to just sit idly by," I respond, attempting to maintain a calm tone, though my voice takes on a metallic edge.

"I know, but this matter is highly personal for Christine. She will completely shut down if I accompany you. I'm only asking you not to jump to hasty conclusions," Sophie explains, approaching me. Placing her hands on my shoulders, she gently but firmly guides me back to the sofa, positioning herself between my legs. Her fingers rhythmically stroke my hair, a hypnotic gesture meant to soothe my anxiety.

"Christine fell in love with a guy," she begins in a hushed tone, pausing before delivering her next words. "They spent the night together, and he just took advantage of her and left. She's feeling incredibly lonely right now and wants to confide in her best friend, not her dad."

I release a heavy exhale, attempting to process the weight of her revelation. Judging by Sophie's careful choice of words, the story remains incomplete. The thought of someone taking advantage of my daughter, who is just stepping into adulthood, is hard to bear. I've only just begun to shield and care for her. The protective instincts of a father scream at full volume within me, akin to blaring ambulance sirens.

Is this what women feel when their maternal instinct awakens? If so, I now understand the fervent protectiveness many mothers exhibit toward their children.

Without a doubt, I know exactly who this bastard is. It was evident to anyone paying attention that Christine had her eye on Jeff. She extracted information about him from me on numerous evenings. I never liked this asshole. Tolerating his company was a challenge, given that he was a competent professional and the only reason I interacted with him.

"I'm going with you," I declare, seizing Sophie's hands and pulling them away from my head.

"Alexander, what do you hope to achieve?" she attempts to reason with me. "Are you planning to barge into a hotel room with me, where your daughter is crying over the asshole who took her virginity and dumped her?"

She falls silent abruptly, realizing she may have revealed too much.

A red veil clouds my vision. A weighty stone presses against my chest, making it difficult to breathe. I'll kill the bastard. I will strangle him with my bare hands.

"Alexander!" Sophie shouts, and I feel a burning sensation on my face. I hadn't even registered her slap; my emotions had completely overtaken me.

"Please, don't, for my sake," she begs, cupping my cheeks with her palms and trying to kiss me. I break free from her grip. No, that will not work.

"Don't you dare tell me what to do now?" I say through clenched teeth, making my nodules begin to shake. "She's an innocent little girl. That asshole fucked her like a whore in a hotel room."

Sophie recoils from me, her eyes wide in shock.

"Can you hear yourself?" Her voice breaks into a scream, which begins to fill my ears. "Like a whore? So, that's who you think I am?"

"How does it concern you?" I'm sincerely perplexed how she managed to turn the arrows on herself. I wince at the disgusting ringing in my eardrums.

"So, you can fuck me in a hotel room like a whore?" She puffs, and I begin to understand what she means. "Don't you think this is a double standard?"

"You're an entirely different matter," I say, raising my hands in a conciliatory gesture. Reflexively, I squeeze the bridge of my nose with my fingers, attempting to quell the storm of emotions within me.

Why did she even equate these situations? With Sophie, everything was consensual and by mutual agreement. Despite being the same age, Sophie is much smarter and wiser than Christine, who remains excessively naive with her head in the clouds.

Sophie closes her eyes, exhales slowly, and clasps her hands behind her back before heading into the hallway. I follow her, contemplating the current situation. Perhaps she has a point. Christine needs the support of a best friend now. Sophie can provide that, but what role can I play? Should I unleash my anger, wreak havoc, and terrify my daughter even more by destroying everything in sight?

"I won't continue this discussion now and will just go to Christine," Sophie warns. "Promise me that you'll give us some time alone."

"You're right," I readily admit the obvious. "She needs you more at this moment. Just let me know if she's okay."

Sophie looks at me in amazement, freezing with a shoehorn in her hands. She carefully studies me from head to toe, ensuring I'm in a stable state, then nods in agreement.

I take the shoehorn from her hands and place it on the banquette. Wrapping Sophie in my arms, I tenderly kiss the back of her head. I don't want her to leave on a tense note.

"You are the smartest woman I have ever met in my life," I whisper, inhaling the berry scent of her hair. I feel Sophie squeezing me tighter, and having calmed down, she steps out of the circle of my arms.

"I'll text you when I get to her," she kisses me on the cheek, the same cheek she hit a couple of minutes ago, and leaves the apartment, closing the door behind her.

I stand in the middle of the corridor, staring at the closed door. The red veil of rage has long dissipated, leaving behind a ringing emptiness. I used to express my emotions physically, but now they are simply quelled by one small and fragile girl.

I don't know how to live like normal people. And, apparently, I will never learn...

Chapter 31

Sophie

It takes half an hour to reach Christine. During this time, I have the chance to thoroughly analyze what unfolded in Alexander's apartment.

Despite his temper, he listened to my words. Realistically, I don't hold high hopes that I can reform a forty-year-old man accustomed to living life on his terms. However, the glimmer of compromise in our relationship is heartening.

He makes an effort for me, and that effort is unmistakable and truly invaluable. Mom always emphasized that both partners must work on a relationship. If one person is shouldering the entire burden, it's not a relationship but a form of masochism.

Surprisingly, Alexander and I share a partnership built on mutual respect.

Beyond the grandiosity I initially perceived in him, Alexander turns out to be an entirely reasonable and intelligent man. Sure, he has his quirks, but who doesn't?

As a taxi pulls up to our destination, I realize with either a humorous or absurd twist of fate that it's the same hotel where Alexander and I spent our first night together. The city, it seems, is either remarkably interconnected or merely small.

Christine greets me at the threshold of the room, her eyes marked by tears. She trembles slightly from the emotions she's undergone, and the hem of a giant hotel robe entangles between her bare feet.

"How are you?" I ask her softly, gently hugging her shoulders as we both settle into a large chair in the corner of the room.

"I'm such an idiot, Soph," Christine sobs, fumbling with the terry belt with shaky hands.

"You're not an idiot," I reassure her, running my fingers through her damp hair post-shower. "You just fell in love and lost your head; it happens to the best of us."

"Don't try to calm me down. I'm worse than an idiot. I didn't tell you everything on the phone, but…" She takes a shuddering breath. "I knew for sure that he would be nearby. I booked a room in advance. I also asked a friend for an invitation to a party where Jeff was."

She pauses her story to blow her nose into a tissue and wipe her wet eyes.

"What happened next?" I gently encourage her to continue.

"He ignored me all the time. He was constantly with his friends and didn't pay attention to me. I danced on the dance floor, even sprayed the crowd with expensive champagne. Nothing worked. And then…" She swallows, looking away. "I just approached and offered him a one-night stand. I thought it would unfold like yours, and then he would fall in love with me. We came here. He, of course, got scared when he found out I was a virgin, but he continued. We did this in several rounds. I never thought that was possible. Only in porn or something else. In the morning, he just left, saying, 'Thank you for the night, it was fun. Goodbye, and I don't want to see you again.'"

"Asshole," I blurt out in anger, hugging Christine tighter after the last words. Though she bears some responsibility, I understand she may not realize it, and I'll address it with her later.

"Why did you lie to me about not being a virgin?"

"I was ashamed… You are so mature and experienced. You were already in a serious relationship, you slept with a stranger. But everyone ran away from me after a couple of dates."

Christine is certainly misguided. But I remain silent. This isn't the moment for her to hear moralizing from her best friend. Right now, she needs support, not judgment. Otherwise, I could just bring Alexander in, and he'd start lecturing her.

"Everyone has their own story, Christine. Just because this happened to me doesn't mean you should follow the same path.

Besides, nothing worked out with a stranger. So, I'm not that lucky," I shrug.

I want to sink through the floor. Why did I bring up the lie about the stranger again? I intended for Christine to move past this story as quickly as possible. Sometimes, my fervent desire to support someone compels me to blurt out utter nonsense.

"Seriously?" Sniffling loudly, Christine wipes her nose with the back of her hand and looks at me with pleading eyes.

"Yes," I nod. "It didn't work out with Mr. A."

I console myself with the notion that sometimes a lie can be more comforting than the truth, especially when you invent a bedtime story to soothe your best friend. Our parents used to tell us such tales when we were children to quickly calm us down before bedtime. So why should the situation be different now?

"Shall we then mourn our broken hearts?" Christine smiles through her tears and reaches for the uncorked bottle of wine on the bedside table.

I have no inclination to drink alcohol, but I must play my role to the end. It is my own fault.

"Let's do this. I'll just go to the toilet first, while you prepare the wine," I wink at her and quickly walk into the bathroom, locking the door behind me.

I retrieve my phone from the back pocket of my jeans and promptly send Alexander the promised message before he does something impulsive.

Christine is fine. I'll stay with her today, perhaps all night. Do not wait.

Chapter 32

Alexander

If anyone assumed that I'd simply sit back and wait for Sophie to call after the incident with Christine, they're in for a surprise. Far from calming down and lounging on the sofa, I took immediate action.

Despite my awareness of Jeff's character and his knack for taking advantage of infatuated girls, I never thought he'd stoop so low with Christine. There was too much at stake to risk a dalliance with the daughter of a business partner. Unfortunately, my misplaced trust in him shattered. This asshole cared little about the consequences of his actions, indifferent to whose heart he toyed with.

Fueled by rage, I navigate through Saturday traffic towards my office, where, according to Natalie's intel, Jeff shamelessly showed up for work after what he did to my daughter the previous night.

The anger inside me is palpable, my lungs releasing cigarette smoke in erratic bursts. Another butt finds its way out of the half-open Bentley window as I reach for a fresh cigarette, but even the solace of nicotine fails to ease my turmoil.

The apartment, once warm and cozy with the scent of berries, plunged into an unsettling darkness the moment Sophie slammed the front door. It felt as if a gust of wind had blown through, leaving behind a suffocating void.

It becomes apparent that Sophie's constant presence is my anchor to a semblance of peace. Without her, I find myself drowning in a sea of uncontrollable emotions, trapped in an endless quagmire.

For me, Sophie is akin to Gatsby's green light— a beacon guiding me through obstacles, including my own temper.

I can't help but chuckle at the irony. Who would have thought that, one day, my broken heart would erect so many protective barriers that gradually unveiled themselves over time?

The other challenge looming over me is Christine. No matter how many times I replay the moment I confessed to my daughter about Sophie being my girlfriend, I can't wrap my head around it. Christine is unlikely to forgive either me or Sophie for this revelation, and I can't afford to lose both of them now.

It's a perplexing dilemma. If I divulge everything to Christine, it could shatter the fragile relationship we've built. On the other hand, if I conceal my relationship with Sophie for too long, I risk losing a girl I genuinely care about.

I run my fingers through my eyebrows, holding a cigarette between them. Well, I'll deal with these problems as they come. For once in my life, I want to let go of control and simply savor the present, allowing the waves of life to carry me ashore.

Turning the steering wheel, I pull into the parking lot. I take a deep breath, then exhale.

"Problems can be solved with words," Sophie's persistent voice echoes in my head.

Exiting the car, I set the alarm and slip the keys into my leather jacket pocket. The brisk autumn wind only fuels my determination, rather than cooling my heated body. As I walk towards the entrance, I finish my cigarette, discarding it in the trash.

Jeff greets me with a deadpan expression behind his computer screen as I enter his office threshold.

"Hi, what do I owe you?" he slurs in a drunken voice.

It's evident that the sleepless night has taken its toll on someone. I clench my fists, recalling the exact reason I rushed to the office on a Saturday afternoon.

"To many now, Jeff," I mutter through clenched teeth. "What the hell are you allowing yourself to do?"

"What are you talking about?" the pervert blinks in confusion.

I lose my temper. "Why the hell did you fuck my daughter tonight?"

I approach his desk, delivering a forceful blow that sends the metal pencil holder clattering to the side.

"So, that's what you're talking about," Jeff's overwhelming indifference adds fuel to the blazing fire of my rage.

"What am I talking about?" I mimic him. "Care to explain before I throw you out of your desk?"

Jeff leans back in his chair, rubbing his tired face with his palms. My knuckles itch, eager to make contact with his skin.

"Listen, Alexander, it was mutual consent. She was all over me the entire evening. If I hadn't agreed, she would've made a scene right there in the club. Also, be thankful that this happened…"

I can't bear to listen to the excuses pouring out of his mouth. Across the table, I seize Jeff by the collar of his shirt and pull him towards me, causing his laptop to crash to the floor.

"I'll strip you of all your projects, you bastard. I don't care how valuable you are to the channel. If I catch you around again, I'll make you watch my leg meeting your ass from the inside!"

I shove Jeff, his face now covered in red spots, away from me, and he slumps back into his chair. Disgusted, I wipe my hands on my jeans and chuckle with satisfaction. Sophie is right; resolving issues with words is more interesting and entertaining than resorting to physical violence. A punch may knock out an opponent instantly, but here, you can play and make him squirm.

"But, Alexander…" Jeff attempts to say something but falls silent when our eyes lock. He realizes I hold more power and can carry out my threats as effortlessly as he used my daughter.

"Less talk, more action, Jeff!" I clap my hands, mimicking the gesture one would use with a disobedient dog, causing the enemy to wince in pain. "Gather your things and get out. I'll have security ensure you leave."

Returning to the car with a sense of accomplishment, my fists unscathed and my conscience intact, I realize I've kept my promise to Sophie and followed her advice. While I may have deviated slightly from the original plan, that seems like a minor detail.

Checking the phone, I left in the car's salon; I notice a new incoming message from Sophie. Her name in the notification prompts the corners of my lips to lift. "What are you doing to me, girl?"

Chapter 33

Alexander

The phone begins to trill, its notifications chiming in unexpectedly, at the moment our baseball team scores a point against a formidable opponent. While I wouldn't label myself a sports enthusiast, I can occasionally indulge in watching a ball traverse the entire field when there's nothing better to do.

I retrieve my phone from the sofa, swiping my finger across the screen. As anticipated, there are messages from Sophie. The first one features a photo of her standing in the bathroom, playfully sticking out her tongue and showcasing her cleavage. The subsequent image highlights her provocatively protruding ass.

I can't help but grin. She's a little tease.

Sophie enjoys teasing me with her photos, and my phone already boasts a collection: legs clad in stockings peeking out from under her work skirt; a mirror selfie with the pajama strap coyly pulled down; and one taken in my car while she waits for me after a shopping trip.

This is Sophie — a well-mannered and modest girl who, in my presence, transforms into a whirlwind of emotions and provocations. I'm uncertain if I'm the catalyst for this change or if it's merely the influence of a male presence in her life. I have no interest in how she behaved with her ex; I prefer to believe that her cheekiness is reserved exclusively for me.

I respond to her with a fire emoji, prompting another message from Sophie.

> I'm drunk, and I want you.

I furrow my brows.

> Are you and Christine still at the hotel? Have you had a lot to drink?

I rise from the sofa, pacing along its length, contemplating how to discreetly extract a tipsy Sophie from my daughter's company.

It's unsettling that, at this moment, my primary concern is Sophie rather than my own daughter, who is inebriated, emotional, and nursing a broken heart. I can't help but feel like a shitty father.

> Yes. A couple of bottles of champagne. Christine is in a daze.

Her message is accompanied by a laughing emoji, but it fails to amuse me. For reasons that are all too apparent, I'm uneasy when women indulge in excessive drinking, especially in the case of Christine. Immediate thoughts cross my mind about the potential transmission of alcoholism through parental genes.

> I'll pick you up now.

The action plan crystallizes independently as the car navigates the dark city streets, its headlights gleaming on the wet asphalt.

I can't help but question my morality if the thought of Sophie being alongside my daughter, secretly sending me photos, arouses me. And the certainty that we'll spend the night together after bringing Christine home only adds to the internal conflict.

***

I find myself carrying my drunken daughter out of the hotel in my arms. In her alcohol-induced delirium, she mumbles something about Jeff, clinging tighter around my neck. In this moment, I wish I could turn back a few hours and unleash my fists to obliterate the face of that asshole.

Sophie confidently strides beside me, casually swinging Christine's small travel bag in her hands. If it weren't for her radiant, satisfied smile, one would never guess she had taken a sip of alcohol. Normally, she offers a more reserved smile next to me.

We drive to Christine's house in complete silence, interrupted only by occasional playful glances and winks from Sophie. I want to laugh, but I refrain from doing so, not wanting to disturb my peacefully snoring daughter in the back seat.

"Thank you for helping," Sophie whispers as we both tuck Christine into bed.

She shuffles around, fidgeting from foot to foot, looking up at me through lowered, fluffy eyelashes.

"Are you bidding me farewell?" I narrow my eyes, running my thumb along her cheekbone, entwining my fingers in her loose hair.

If it weren't for the current circumstances, I might have taken her down right there on the floor, eager to savor her taste, especially after those provocative photos.

"Any other suggestions?"

I adore her. With all my heart. Just the way she is. She may exude modesty, but in the next moment, she gazes at me like a panther, licking her lips, conjuring up risqué images in her mind.

"Yes," I grunt and sling Sophie over my shoulder, carrying her across the apartment threshold.

She laughs heartily as I settle her in the front seat of the car, securing her seatbelt with her arms pressed to her body. It's just a precaution, ensuring she doesn't make a run for it.

"Does this count as kidnapping?" Sophie quips as the car starts moving.

"If convincing you to come home is kidnapping, then so be it."

Her laughter quickly fades. My attempts to persuade her to move in with me face resistance, and her reaction baffles me. While my daughter can be trying at times, there are ways to handle her, or we could concoct a story about Sophie's relocation.

I'll tackle that issue later. Right now, more pressing matters await.

Back at my apartment, it feels as if nothing has happened. In Sophie's presence, the space becomes cozy and warm. She effortlessly transforms it into a home, radiating warmth like the sun.

"How did your talk with Jeff go?" she suddenly inquires, kicking off her sneakers and settling on the sofa.

I glance at her as I hang our jackets in the closet.

"How did you know I was talking to him?"

Sophie sighs and shakes her head, my favorite smile returning to her face.

"Don't underestimate me," she laughs. "I know you can't stay calm in these situations. I just hope you spared at least a small patch of skin on his face without a scrape or bruise."

Little does she know how close I came to leaving that fool with no unblemished area on his body.

"I promised you I wouldn't lay a finger on him. So, I kept my word," I say, sitting down beside her and gently stroking her denim-covered knee. "I kicked him out of his workplace, warning that I'd strip him of all projects if he ever pulled such a stunt again."

"Why am I not surprised?" She embraces me tightly, her berry scent enveloping me. "I'm proud you resisted the urge to break his nose."

Our peculiar conversation starts to feel like the ramblings of a madman. It's akin to a session with a psychotherapist.

"I don't want to talk about this anymore," I cut her off with a kiss.

Pushing Sophie back onto the sofa, I lean over her, settling between her legs. She wraps them around my waist, lifting herself up to capture my lips. I gladly reciprocate, sealing our mouths in a passionate kiss.

Chapter 34

Sophie

After reaching a compromise, Alexander secured me an apartment in a nearby building. Clearly beyond the budget of an intern, the place is an architectural marvel. The exterior charm seamlessly extends to the interior — a spacious and inviting two-room space designed in the Art Nouveau style. It boasts an Italian kitchen, concealed interior doors, contemporary plumbing, a Japanese toilet, and high-end household appliances. It's more than just an apartment; it's the dream creation of an architect and interior designer. And I absolutely love it.

Entering the place, I hesitated even to let a cat in. Yet, for the feline resident, whom Alexander personally provided with a bed, a scratching post, a tower house, a cutting-edge automatic tray, and bowls. It seemed like a bit of an overindulgence. We had agreed that my cat and I would primarily reside with Alexander, making this apartment a potential costly storage space for my belongings.

When sharing my new address with Christine, who was ecstatic upon hearing the news, I attributed the affordable rent to my employer's generosity. She's savvy when it comes to real estate prices, so I find myself crafting another layer of deception.

A housewarming party is on the horizon, scheduled for a specific date. The mere thought of giving a tour of an apartment I've visited at most five times fills me with dread.

"Are you ready?" Alexander emerges from the bedroom, neatly tucking a snow-white T-shirt into his trousers.

"Yes, just a second," I insert a small gold hoop into my ears and spin around, showcasing my simple yet stylish ensemble — jeans, a long-sleeved shirt, and a sweater casually thrown over my shoulders.

"Beautiful as ever," he winks.

I respond with a joyful smile, feeling the nervous tension subside and allowing me to breathe calmly.

***

"Do you think they'll like me?" I ask Alexander as we step out of the parked car, heading towards a quaint country restaurant.

Judging by the serene atmosphere, it seems that only a handful of people frequent this place. It gives off the vibe of a private, exclusive club, reminiscent of the wine mansion where we had our first date. Despite my excitement about meeting Alexander's friends and deepening our connection, the reality of our clandestine relationship hits me once again, like a sudden fall onto wet asphalt. However genuine our interactions may feel, they remain a secret.

Alexander treats me as if we're in a typical, normal relationship between a man and a woman. Yet, his reluctance to transition me from the shadows to the spotlight begins to weigh on me. The justifications I've constructed in my mind for him lose their efficacy, and I resist pressuring him. My role in his life doesn't grant me much authority, leaving me with the sole option of finding compromises. I have no desire to relive the situation we faced on the island.

"Of course, they'll like you," Alexander reassures me, pulling me towards him and planting a tender kiss on the top of my head. "You're amazing, and they'll see it right away."

How does he consistently divert my thoughts from these challenging concerns?

I yearn to immerse myself fully in every moment with Alexander, to live without the nagging doubts and the shivers of uncertainty. There will be time to grapple with those feelings in solitude.

A warm and welcoming hostess, adorned in a vibrant kimono, leads us to a snug private booth. The entire restaurant exudes Japanese aesthetics, reminiscent of scenes from "Memoirs of a Geisha," with walls designed as delicate paper partitions.

Four individuals occupy a low table — a pair of couples whose enduring connections are evident. The girls engage in lively conversation, exchanging jokes about their boyfriends, while the men delve into work matters. Unaware of our entrance, their banter continues until one of them spots us.

"Alex!" A blond man rises as we enter. "I thought we wouldn't see each other again this year."

"Only in your dreams, Pierce," Alexander chuckles, exchanging a handshake. He then proudly ushers me forward, introducing me to his friends. "Sophie, meet my best friends from university — Pierce and John. And these," he gestures toward the women at the table, "are Julia and Sarah, their lovely companions."

The two blondes offer friendly greetings, casting intrigued glances my way. The brunette, introduced as John, shakes my hand warmly.

"We're thrilled to finally meet Alexander's girlfriend, whom he kept hidden from us for so long," Pierce winks, inviting us to join the table.

Breaking the silence, a familiar melody announces an incoming call, emanating from someone's phone. Alexander raises his finger, retrieving his mobile from his trouser pocket. A furrow forms on his brow. Intrigued, I steal a quick glance at the screen and freeze, recognizing the name I had hoped to see as the latest caller.

Chapter 35

Sophie

"Yes," Alexander replies firmly into the phone, abruptly leaving the booth. My gaze involuntarily follows him until the door closes in front of my nose.

Taking a deep breath filled with the delightful aromas of Japanese cuisine, I turn my attention to the company gathered at the table. An awkward smile plays on my lips as I notice their heads turning in my direction. Like owls, their eyes seem to flutter in unison.

Under the watchful eyes of my newfound acquaintances, I cautiously approach the table, uncertainty evident in my gait as I take an empty seat.

"Sophie, please, have a seat," Pierce graciously fluffs the pillow for me.

I settle next to him, crossing my legs in a lotus position, and offer a modest smile while quietly expressing my gratitude. I can't shake off the feeling of awkwardness, as though Alexander left to discuss matters with his wife, and I, in turn, am perceived as his mistress, with everyone casting judgmental glances my way. Yet, in reality, no one seems to care. Julia and Sarah continue chatting about their girly things, while Pierce and John focus on studying the menu.

"We're delighted that Alexander finally introduced you to our group," Julia turns to me, her good-natured smile lighting up her face.

She's truly captivating: the blonde up close reveals hints of dyed hair, with slightly darker roots accentuating her fair skin, and her blue eyes resemble those of a doll, framed by thick eyelashes. She wears minimal makeup, and it enhances her natural beauty.

"I'm also very glad to meet you all," I respond, smiling and glancing people around.

They're dressed simply, devoid of flashy logos or cheap embellishments, yet it's evident that their clothing is both expensive and of high quality. Their demeanor exudes refinement. I'm beginning to feel a sense of respect for the individuals seated before me. It occurs to me that we could potentially form lasting friendships.

"You know, this is more or less how we pictured you," Sarah observes, her eyes fixed on me.

As I bring a glass of water to my lips, my nervous hands cause it to tremble slightly. Swiftly taking a sip, I carefully return it to its spot, avoiding any potential spills.

"Did Alexander mention me?" I inquire, dabbing my lips with a napkin.

"No," Julia shakes her head. "But during our recent gatherings, he was unusually considerate, frequently responding to messages even when he normally switches off his phone. He hurried home before everyone else. So, naturally, we assumed he had someone special."

A pleasant warmth spreads through my chest, and I instinctively glance toward the door, picturing Alexander on the other side, phone pressed to his ear, tiredly rubbing the bridge of his nose with his fingers. Julia's words and warm welcome dissipate the lingering irritation from Laura's call.

The key is not to overthink it.

After all, Alexander's ex-wife and Christine's mother has every right to contact the father of her child. Perhaps it pertains to aspects of parenting. Alexander has always been remarkably honest with me, and I'm confident he'll openly share the reason for her call.

"Ladies," John interrupts, "enough gossiping; let's place an order already. I can't wait any longer. I'm ready to devour an entire elephant."

Sarah sweetly giggles, wrapping her arm around John's elbow and giving him a quick peck on the cheek.

"How about we order those delicious shrimp chips to nibble on while we wait for the appetizer?" she suggests, soothingly stroking his forearm.

"You're my clever girl," he kisses the top of her head and signals the waiter by pressing the button on the table.

This affectionate couple sends my blood sugar levels soaring. I can't help but smile. It's refreshing when people express their feelings so openly, without embarrassment or concern about onlookers. It's something I can only dream of.

"Sophie, what are you thinking of ordering?" Pierce asks, nodding toward the menu, which I'm clutching as if it might slip away. Usually, I meticulously study the menu online and have a rough idea of what I'll order. But right now, I feel completely indecisive.

"I don't know; I've never been here," I admit with a shrug. "Any recommendations, please."

"Oh, go for their introductory set," Julia suggests. "It includes five popular dishes from various categories. I think you'll enjoy it."

"Did I miss something?" Alexander finally returns, taking a seat beside me and covering my knee with his warm palm.

I gaze into his eyes, attempting to discern what transpired during his lengthy conversation with Laura. However, his look, as always, remains calm and confident. With such endurance, I'd recommend him for a career in politics.

"Only that moment when I nearly devoured everyone," John snorts, persistently pressing the button to call the waiter. "Is it broken or what?.."

Thanks to the guys' banter, filled with memories of their student years and shared experiences in a stand-up bar, I find myself relaxing. It feels as though we've known each other for years.

My laughter bubbles up as Pierce, John, and Alexander reminisce about their university days, recounting how ladies constantly pursued them, and they had to fend off the attention. With all three being undeniably handsome, I don't question a single word they say.

We finally roll out of the restaurant after everyone has savored a generous slice of Japanese castella honey sponge cake.

Julia, Sarah, and I exchange phone numbers, prompting our men to wait in their cars, signaling us impatiently with high beams. We exchange kisses on both cheeks and pledge to meet again as just the girls. Climbing into our respective cars, we exit the restaurant parking lot one after another.

"It seems like you've made friends," Alexander remarks, smiling at me.

"They're very nice and funny," I confirm, saving Julia's number in my phone. "We've planned to meet again this week."

"Give me a heads up so I can clear my schedule," he requests, changing lanes and overtaking Pierce. The guys exchange playful middle fingers, revealing their youthful sides, despite all being over forty. I cover my lips with my palm, concealing my amused smile.

"We'll go with just the girls," I tease, sticking my tongue out at him.

Alexander falls into a thoughtful silence, his brow furrowed as he focuses on the road. A sudden wave of panic grips my chest, sending chills through my skin and prompting me to wrap my arms around myself. I can't pinpoint the cause of this anxiety, but I intuitively sense a shift in Alexander's thoughts.

"Why did Laura call you?" I decide to broach the topic, perhaps not at the most opportune moment. I fear that Alexander might once again defer the conversation, but to my surprise, he starts to speak.

"She sought an audience. Once again, she's airing her grievances about my financial support for our daughter," he chuckles. "Seems someone is simply envious that her allowance now pales in comparison to the gifts for her own daughter."

I smile at my own naivety. I had guessed the reason behind her call, yet I tried to deceive myself. I resolve to trust my intuition more often.

"What was your response?" I glance at Alexander, who is attentively navigating the road.

"We agreed to meet," he shrugs, overtaking another truck.

I wring my fingers in indecision, attempting to frame the next question carefully to avoid triggering a negative reaction from Alexander.

"Just ask it," he exhales, finding my hand and placing it on the armrest, entwining our fingers. His reassuring gesture and the fact that he understood me without words embolden me.

"So, what happened between you two?" I whisper almost inaudibly, not wanting to disrupt this precious moment of our heart-to-heart conversation. "Is it the right time now?"

"Yes, Sophie, it is," Alexander sighs heavily, squeezing my hand in reassurance.

Chapter 36

Alexander

Sophie gazed at me with understanding in her eyes, her voice softening. "If you don't want to share or if it's too difficult for you, I'll respect that," she said quietly as soon as we arrived home.

It struck me as both ironic and endearing. When I had been reluctant to talk earlier, she had taken offense, but now, when I was ready, she welcomed my silence. The intricacies of feminine logic never failed to amaze me.

Taking a seat at the kitchen island, I poured myself a glass of water, trying to shake off the tension that lingered from Laura's call. Sophie, sensing my unease, darted around the kitchen, searching through drawers for something to occupy herself.

"Maybe some tea?" she suggested, holding up a package of chamomile tea that seemed to have found its way into my kitchen without my notice. Without waiting for my response, she nodded to herself. "Yes, exactly. It will be more comfortable this way."

Observing her movements, I waited for her to settle beside me. As she sat down, she curled her legs underneath her and cradled a large cup in her hands. It was a nightly ritual, a moment of quiet warmth before bedtime, her fingers seeking refuge from the perpetual chill.

I found myself marveling at these small details about her. How had a girl I had initially picked up in a hotel bar for what I thought would be a fleeting encounter managed to embed herself so deeply in my life? I had pegged her as either an experienced lover seeking no-strings-attached intimacy or a call girl aiming to relieve me of a month's salary by the end of the night.

Yet here I was, sitting across from her, contemplating the prospect of sharing my most traumatic relationship experience. When had she become more than just a passing figure in my life?

I had never shared this with anyone, not even my parents. They believed that Laura and I simply had a strained relationship, blaming themselves for what they perceived as a result of my flawed upbringing. To them, I was just a son who left his girlfriend and newborn child, supposedly driven by a fear of commitment.

"Ready," Sophie announced, the clattering of heavy cups on the marble tabletop pulling me back from my train of thought. I took a sip of chamomile tea, using the moment to compose my scattered emotions. I felt at a loss, unsure of where to begin. Conversations of this nature were uncharted territory for me.

Tough negotiations at work? No problem. Dismissing an employee without flinching? A walk in the park. Letting go of long-time staff members was never easy, but there were always justifiable reasons for their dismissal. So why was I now fumbling like a virgin on a first date?

"The most crucial thing you should know about me is that I never forgive betrayal. And there's a valid reason for this: my ex-wife cheated on me." I paused, memories swirling as I chose my words carefully. "Laura was involved with two men simultaneously when she became pregnant with Christine. I only discovered this after she gave birth, stumbling upon the results of a paternity test."

"Christine isn't yours..." Sophie began to suggest, but I interrupted her question with a dismissive wave of my hand.

"No, she is my daughter. Otherwise, I wouldn't be trying to build a relationship with her now."

"But why would Laura do that?" Sophie asked, a naive question from a woman still in the bloom of her youth.

"Everything was simple and prosaic. She had to choose between me, a carefree young man she met on a comedy movie set, and a wealthy, married businessman. I was more of a boy for fun at that time. Laura had hoped that her main option would leave his family for her. However, my swift sperm outran his decision-making. The news of an impending birth frightened the businessman so much that he fled to another country with his family.

A wry grin crosses my face as I recall Laura's feigned joy when she told me about her pregnancy, concealing the despair in her eyes and the shattering of dreams beneath her feet. The former Miss Universe has now become a complete alcoholic, abandoned even by her faithful daughter, let alone any hopes for a brighter future.

"What was your reaction?" Sophie gazes into my eyes with genuine sympathy.

I despise the sympathy directed at me. Why did I even think it was worth sharing the story of Laura with Sophie? Was it her hysteria on the phone that drove me here today, or the strange sense of connection I felt when Sophie seamlessly integrated herself into my circle of friends?

"What do you think? I told her I couldn't forgive her and live together. I offered financial support and the role of a 'weekend father.' But that wasn't enough for her. Laura pleaded to stay, and when she realized I was resolute, she resorted to threats of cutting off communication with our daughter. In the end, she followed through. However, I could never abandon my daughter so easily; I sent alimony and gifts despite being forbidden to approach her, even within a few meters."

Another sip of the calming herbal infusion and another dose of compassion from Sophie. I feel the urge to hurl the mug against the wall, relishing the splash of liquid and fragments, but I restrain myself.

Unexpected irritation tightens its grip, squeezing me in a vice. I feel akin to a little child who has scraped his knee, now crying and frustrated with his own clumsiness.

"I'm so sorry," Sophie whispers, rising from her chair to envelop me in her warm embrace.

However, instead of experiencing the anticipated warmth and tenderness, there is only coldness and denial within my soul. I hug her mechanically, out of habit, but my thoughts are in disarray. It's as if someone flipped a switch.

Today, we've crossed a certain point of no return. Meeting my friends, her meticulously planned encounter with their girlfriends, and the invitation to the drama of my life — all of it signifies a shift. It feels like Sophie is growing into me with every atom, insidiously slipping under my skin and becoming an integral part of me. I allowed it to happen, and now it's frightening. For the first time, I acknowledge that something has the power to scare me.

It was much simpler when I viewed it as my own madness, an excuse for the chaos in my life, without contemplating where our game might lead. Now, as relationships cease to be a sealed secret and assume certain boundaries and obligations, the once carefree and fun dynamic loses its luster.

The weight of responsibility anchors me to the ground, making it feel impossible to move. Just a few days ago, I was willing to defy judgment in front of my daughter, indifferent to what others might think of me. But now, there's a different reality to contend with.

There's a nagging thought that perhaps I toyed with this forbidden secret between us, and we've ventured too far...

Chapter 37

Sophie

"Holy moly, your office has splurged big time!" Christine exclaims, nonchalantly kicking her shoes into the corner of the hallway.

With a resigned sigh, I bend down to carefully relocate my shoes to their designated spot. "Oh, what a beauty!" Christine admires, running her fingers over the glossy surface of a state-of-the-art refrigerator with a transparent door.

In a rush, I grab a kitchen towel and hurriedly scrub away the greasy stains left by her hands. Tossing the rag onto the countertop, I gulp down a glass of water and put it back with a thud.

"Soph, why are you so on edge?" She bats her eyelashes, observing my anxious actions.

I wish I had an answer. Lately, my mood has been erratic, and my patience nonexistent. Every little thing seems to get under my skin. Just the day before yesterday at the grocery store, I intentionally nudged a woman who was blocking the aisle. I'm still haunted by the shame of that moment.

It all began after my conversation with Alexander. I had eagerly anticipated him opening up about his past, hoping it would bring us closer. Yet, instead of bridging the gap, something peculiar occurred.

On the surface, everything appears unchanged. Alexander remains gentle, courteous, and caring. However, an odd premonition, akin to a sixth sense, niggles at the back of my mind. I can't pinpoint its origin or fully comprehend its meaning.

"Pay no mind to it," I dismiss, waving off any concern. "Just PMS."

"Well, whatever you say," Christine shrugs. "Just don't pull a freak-out when the guests arrive, or you might scare them away."

I look at her in surprise. Guests? What is she talking about?

"Christine," I call her with a hint of warning, "what guests are you referring to? We agreed that we would celebrate the housewarming just between us."

"Soph," she says dreamily. "You and I are two lonely ladies now. I'm without my Jeff, and you're without the mysterious stranger you never introduced me to," a hint of reproach lingers in her words. "Did you honestly think I'd let both of us wallow in sadness?"

My hand itches to give Christine a reality check and knock her out of the clouds. Will she ever emerge from the viscous swamp of her naivety?

I clench my fists and count to ten. The more I interact with Christine, the more I consider ending our friendship before it's too late. Yet, my conscience holds me back each time; after all, Christine has been there for me in difficult times. There's also the fear of being left completely alone if I ever need support.

Selfish? Perhaps.

But doesn't "a human need a human"? I have no one closer than Alexander and Christine. Stella from work is just a colleague, and I can't divulge everything to my parents.

"Okay," I exhale, "a couple of people at most. Not more!"

Christine claps her hands joyfully.

"Only two people have been invited," she winks at me with a sly smile, and suddenly, I'm not so sure about this idea. A sense of impending regret washes over me.

The intercom rings just as Christine and I manage to sip the cool champagne, miraculously not forgetting it in the freezer, preventing an explosion of sparkling spray in the refrigerator.

"Here they come," she squeaks, rushing towards the front door. "Sit still and don't move! It's a surprise!"

Nervously tapping my nails on the tabletop, I run through all our mutual acquaintances in my mind. I can't fathom who Christine might have invited as a surprise. Unless... well, no, Liam would be a terrible housewarming gift, and she surely understands this after our recent conversation in the car. But then again, this is Christine.

"Ta-da!" She announces, appearing in the kitchen doorway with two guys I don't know. "Soph, meet Jack and Sean. My friends from the club. They organize awesome parties there."

I scrutinize the uninvited guests and realize it's not just a trick of the champagne playing with my perception; Jack and Sean are indeed twins. Two dark-haired brunettes with playful curls on their heads, bright blue eyes, and straight noses resembling those of Greek gods. They even dress alike in dark sweatshirts and black jeans, with only different socks and prints on their sweaters giving them away.

"Pleasure to meet you, Sophie," one of the brothers winks at me, planting a gallant kiss on my hand. Such a gentleman. He exudes a Colin Firth charm straight out of Pride and Prejudice.

"Mutually, but you can call me Soph," I refrain from offering my full name. It's a term of endearment reserved for Alexander alone, and only from his lips does it sound most beautiful.

"Cool house, Sophie," John remarks, surveying the surroundings.

"Thank you," I mutter words of gratitude solely due to my upbringing.

Casting an irritated glance toward Christine, I understand all too well why she summoned them. I can predict that, after a couple of glasses of sparkling wine, she'll be engrossed in capturing photos and videos with them, posting the content on her social networks.

For what purpose? In the hope that Jeff might chance upon her page, peruse the photos, and suddenly remember her name? I highly doubt it, especially after Alexander dealt with him decisively.

I'm frustrated with myself for being spineless and irritated with Christine for daring to think that strangers could be invited into my home. She's indifferent to who crosses the threshold of her apartment, driven by the desire to flaunt. For me, my apartment is my sanctuary, my personal space — where I unwind and find solace.

Moreover, Alexander is the one who rents it. I'm uncertain if he'd approve of such an impromptu party. Thankfully, we agreed beforehand that I would spend this evening with Christine, and he wouldn't visit.

As expected, after a few glasses, Christine records a selfie video, dancing with John and unabashedly rubbing herself against him.

At what point did my apartment morph into a nightclub?

I sigh wearily, observing Christine's drunken state while nibbling on yet another snack. Mentally, I vow to kick everyone out, including Christine, as soon as it hits 11 PM.

"Soph, come here, let's take a picture!" Christine shouts over the music, beckoning me with her palm. Sean, who had been breathing in my ear for the past while, abruptly stands and rushes up from his seat. He grabs my hand, attempting to pull me into the middle of the living room.

"Come on, Soph, dance for me," Sean encourages, and I pull my hand out of his grasp, repulsed.

Rolling my eyes, I reluctantly allow them to take a few group photos before retreating to the sofa, where my perpetually hungry cat has taken advantage of my absence to pounce on the snacks.

"Ugh, Oliver, you'll ruin your stomach," I scold the greedy cat, pulling him away from the chips and settling him on my lap.

"Beautiful little animal," Sean smiles and joins me on the sofa again.

"Thank you," I reply, forcing a restrained smile. *Go. Fucking. Away. From. Me.*

"Listen, what are you doing tonight? I would like to..." Sean doesn't get the chance to finish his probably inappropriate sentence because my phone starts ringing.

I snatch the phone like a life preserver. Whoever is calling, know that I love you, saintly savior!

I answer without even looking at the screen, keeping my eyes on Sean as I lean towards the balcony with Oliver in my arms. I put the phone to my ear.

"Hello?"

"What the hell is going on, Sophie?" Alexander's voice growls into the phone, its coldness sending shivers down my spine.

I fly out onto the balcony, swiftly locking the door behind me.

"Alexander? What happened?" I ask with concern, my heart starting to dance, tapping its own rhythm against my ribs.

"What happened? I think I should be the one asking you."

I frown, confused about what he's talking about. My disturbed cat tries to comfort me by rubbing against my feet on the chilly balcony floor.

"Alexander, I don't understand..." I mutter in confusion, glancing back towards the living room. Christine is dancing with the guys, who, without hesitation, are now getting too handsy with her. I need to put an end to this before it leads to disastrous consequences.

"Why the hell are there strange men in your apartment?" His voice booms through the speakers. "I thought we figured out how I felt about this."

Chills grip my arms and legs. How did he know? Does he follow Christine's social media pages? Surely, she has already posted photos.

"Alexander, Christine invited them. I didn't know..." I mumble excuses.

"Everyone must leave your place in fifteen minutes, otherwise I'll come myself, and I won't care what anyone thinks."

Short beeps are heard in the speaker. I stare at the phone in my hands.

Crap.

Alexander opened up to me, shared his situation with his ex, and after a short time, I did the same... It doesn't matter that I didn't invite the guys. I can imagine what it looks like from Aleksander's point of view — it's like I'm trampling on his trust with bare feet.

As always, the cause of such absurdities is my best friend, who is now happily waving to me from the living room, unaware that she has once again done something foolish.

Chapter 38

Alexander

The point of no return looms as I step across the threshold of the restaurant. The outcome of this conversation, a delicate dance of emotions and uncertainties, hangs in the air, casting a shadow on the unknown path that stretches before us.

Seated at a table near the window, Laura, a mere silhouette of her former self, nervously toys with a napkin, her gaze fixated on a cup of tea. Surprisingly absent is the familiar gleam of an intoxicating beverage. The toll of alcoholism has drained the vibrancy from Laura, leaving her hair resembling straw, dark circles accentuating tired eyes, and her skin sagging in places it shouldn't. Botox and fillers, once attempted remedies, now only accentuate the stark transformation — rendering Laura a canvas fit for a role in a "Frankenstein" film or a "before and after" magazine spread.

"Alex," she exclaims, her voice evoking memories from a bygone era, causing a reflexive wince as though I've bitten into a sour lemon. It has been ages since she uttered that nickname, a reminder of a lifetime that seems to have passed since she last called me by it.

"Laura," I acknowledge with a brief nod, silently urging her to resume her original position. She complies, sinking back into the chair, the napkin returning to her lap. Even alcohol could not erase her manners, ingratiating tone, and ability to irritate.

"You've become so serious," she observes, as if she doesn't follow me in gossip columns and doesn't check pages on social networks through fake accounts.

Ignoring her remark, I signal the waiter for an Americano, a mere pretext to linger. My intention is clear — as soon as I finish my drink, I'll leave immediately.

"What do you want to talk about, Laura?" I inquire, adjusting my shirt cuff and turning a silver cufflink with a deliberate gesture that doesn't escape Laura's predatory gaze.

What a regrettable oversight it was in my youth not to catch the similar glances she cast at other men, utterly unabashed in my presence. Perhaps then, I might have discerned sooner who she truly is and how she regards me.

"About you spoiling Christine too much," Laura remarks as I express gratitude to the waiter for the coffee.

"Perhaps if you hadn't kept my daughter from me for twenty years, only accepting alimony and gifts, then I would have distributed my generosity over several years, and not tried to give it away all at once," I chuckle, lifting the invigorating drink to my lips.

The hot coffee scalds my tongue and palate, but I'm oblivious, relishing Laura's reaction to my words. It appears as though she might erupt with anger, yet she refrains, understanding that displaying emotions plays against her.

"Listen," she begins with restraint. "I'm not trying to dissuade you from this. Christine is gentle; she knows no limits," Laura clears her throat, and my eyes narrow suspiciously, sensing a hidden agenda in her words. "Maybe, as in her childhood, I will hide half of the gifts and give them away when the time comes."

Unexpectedly, a fit of laughter seizes me. I can't help but marvel at the rapidly changing expression on my audacious ex's face. Laura has shed all remnants of conscience.

Even during Christine's teenage years, Laura appropriated half of the gifts I sent to my daughter for herself. One could still attribute it to maternal concern, and I often questioned the wisdom of gifting expensive jewelry to a teenage girl. Yet, what Laura is attempting now surpasses all conceivable and inconceivable bounds of propriety.

"You know, Laura, I believe that Christine is already old enough to play in belated Santa. Admittedly, I might have been a bit excessive with gifts lately. That's a matter I'll discuss with Christine. However, your shamelessness is entirely out of place here."

My ex-wife's complexion rapidly shifts to a reddish hue, and her skin becomes blotchy, resembling a ripe fly agaric mushroom.

"Don't forget that I still pay you child support, even though our daughter is now an adult. Or has your alcoholism escalated to the point where you can't afford a bottle anymore?"

"How dare you?" Laura hisses, crumpling the napkin in her fist. "I devoted the best years of my life to your daughter. I could have graced red carpets and magazine covers! I might have even won an Oscar!" She squeals, flinging the long-suffering snow-white rag onto the table.

"No one forced you," I lower my voice. "If you don't recall, I was more than willing to raise my daughter. It was you who, for your own gain, chose to use her as your shield."

"What do you understand about motherhood?" Laura points her finger at me. "You're an insensitive asshole. You haven't even started a new family during this time."

"I didn't start one because you crushed all my faith in a strong family and the existence of a faithful, loving woman," I think but refrain from saying aloud. There's too much honor for this spiteful person with whom I once managed to fall in love.

"The conversation is over, Laura," I declare, rising from the table, abandoning the half-drunk coffee. I toss a banknote; with the change, she can buy a few more bottles of vodka or whatever she chooses to drink.

There are individuals in life who have the power to evoke the most negative emotions within you. Astonishingly, some of them were once considered family.

How did we end up on opposing sides of the barricades? Could I have endured the ignorance of her infidelities had I not stumbled upon the paternity test? Would I have found the strength to forgive her when she pleaded for me not to leave?

No, the answer is a resounding no.

In those days, I was young and resolute. I envisioned the perfect family, and settling for anything less was inconceivable then — and remains so now. That's why I keep everyone at a distance. Everyone except...

The tranquility in the car is shattered by the sound of an incoming message. I've been sitting in the restaurant parking lot for about five minutes, lost in thought as I stare blankly at the windshield.

The message is from Christine.

It's odd; she should be with Sophie today. I unlock my phone, hoping against hope that nothing untoward has occurred, yet again.

A photo appears on the screen, showing my daughter and her best friend embracing two unfamiliar guys.

"Celebrating Sophie's housewarming. You should have seen the apartment her employer rented for her! Fingers crossed it's for her skills, not just personal qualities. If you know what I mean," accompanied by a laughing emoji.

Furrows cut deep into my forehead, the skin seemingly on the brink of bursting under the pressure of wrinkles.

What the hell is going on? Sophie, what the fuck are you doing?

I slam my palms on the steering wheel in frustration. We had a heart-to-heart talk. This is precisely why I hesitated for so long. The moment you open up to someone, they plunge a knife into your back.

Through the car window, I catch the wicked grin of Laura, stationed on the restaurant porch, her gaze fixed on me, unwavering.

Bitch. Do you really think I'm losing it over you? You won't get that satisfaction.

I dial Sophie's number immediately, spewing incomprehensible threats fueled by emotion. In the background, the speaker echoes with music and cheerful laughter, intensifying my irritation.

Tires squeal as I speed out of the parking lot, leaving Laura's silhouette behind in the rearview mirror. Encounters with her never lead to anything good.

Unfortunately, on the journey home, wet snow begins to melt under the wheels, creating a disgusting slush that hampers visibility. Nevertheless, I press the gas pedal to its limit, overtaking trucks. I want to get home quickly, pour myself a glass of whiskey to soothe my nerves, and collapse on the sofa, mindlessly flicking through channels in search of something mindless and amusing.

The thought of going to Sophie's doesn't even cross my mind. There's simply no inclination, even if it means evicting unwanted guests from her apartment. I don't want to delve into the details of what happened there or who made it onto the guest list.

A peculiar apathy once again envelops my heart, encasing it in a thorny vice.

The front door clicks shut just as I finish my first glass of amber liquid, standing beside the kitchen island in my lounge pants. I don't turn around because I know exactly who has arrived.

The sound of a jacket hitting the floor, the rhythmic slapping of bare feet on the parquet floor, heavy breathing, and then a wet body crashes into my back, wrapping cold arms around my bare torso.

"I'm sorry," Sophie whispers, her cool lips planting a kiss just below my shoulder blade.

Chapter 39

Sophie

I stroke Alexander's heaving chest, my fingers entwined with the dark, curly hairs adorning his bronze skin — a reminder of our blissful vacation and the joyous moments beneath the warm sun and ocean breeze.

For the past fifteen minutes, we lie ensconced in the quiet embrace of the bedroom, seeking solace after my sudden arrival. His perpetually warm body cocooning my chilled limbs, the ends of my hair, still damp, delicately graze my bare shoulders, eliciting a shiver of goosebumps. The wet snow catches up with me on my way to Alexander's, a relentless companion. I had hurriedly ushered Christine and the oblivious twin brothers out the door before reaching him.

Surprisingly, Christine had accepted my request to leave with unexpected calmness. Ever since I supported her during the situation with Jeff, a thaw had commenced in our relationship. Gone were the reminders about Liam, the unsolicited advice, and the dismissive treatment. Except, of course, for those occasional impulsive decisions, like today. But that was quintessentially Christine — something she couldn't easily shed.

I showed up at Alexander's doorstep, mascara smudged, clothes clinging to my drenched body, I couldn't fathom why he didn't recoil from my bedraggled appearance. Instead, he engulfed me in passionate kisses, sweeping me off my feet and onto the bed. Words became an afterthought.

With a contented squint, I reminisce about how he tenderly peeled away the clinging clothes, his palms gliding over the wet skin, and his tongue skillfully licking away the melted droplets. It was a warming ritual beyond imagination. I felt an urge to purr, akin to a cat sated with milk and valerian.

Alexander exhales, the air escaping his lungs in a soft whistle. His warm breath, faintly carrying the aroma of whiskey, brushes against the top of my head. Surprisingly, even the lingering taste of alcohol doesn't taint his kisses, as it once did with Liam.

"I love you," I confess, surrendering to my emotions. My heart races, but my admission receives no immediate response. Instead, there's a gentle stroke of his thumb along my forearm, a touch from his rough palm.

Despite our closeness, he remains emotionally distant, and a flicker of fear tugs at me. Yet, it's not enough to raise the alarm. I understand that the unspoken incident with uninvited guests hangs between us. I'll address it, but not now. For the moment, I want to revel in the burning fire of his skin. Strangely, it's at this very moment that I feel the happiest in the world. I had dreaded his reaction after the call, conjuring up the worst scenarios in my mind. Our unexpectedly tender connection becomes a delightful surprise.

No, it wasn't just sex. That's too crude a term for what transpired in this room. Alexander and I made love for the first time. Yes, precisely, we made love. For the first time in all our shared moments, I view our intimacy as something spiritual — a union of souls.

How did this happen? Not during that argument when we inspected fogged-up car windows, not beneath weightless silk sheets with the accompaniment of noisy waves outside the windows, but right now. Why did it take us so long to reach this point? In my mind, the alarm bell doesn't ring "yes, stronger, like this," but "God, I love you."

I kiss Alexander's collarbone and create a trail of kisses leading to his dry lips. They don't resist, yet they don't respond with too much eagerness.

"Sophie, I need to take a shower," Alexander says hoarsely, prompting him to leave the bed, and forcing me to move away.

I sink into the soft pillow, my eyes trailing the contours of the naked male body until it disappears behind the bathroom door. Pressing cool fingers against my heated forehead, I lament the passing of a moment I wish could stretch into eternity. I would barter my soul to the devil just to linger beside him, savoring every second as our skin melds together.

Regret courses through me for not agreeing to live with him. Perhaps, in doing so, this quarrel wouldn't have erupted, shattering his trust in me. Maybe Alexander would have opened up much earlier than he did. But dwelling on what could have been won't change our current reality. It feels as if he once spoke those exact words to me.

Opting not to wait for Alexander's return from the bathroom, I find his shirt in the closet and slip it on. Buttoning it up and rolling up the sleeves on my way to the kitchen. I inhale the lingering scent of his favorite cologne.

The cool marble slabs underfoot contrast with the warmth building within me as I arrange an impromptu dinner from the contents of the refrigerator on the kitchen island. Placing a glass of whiskey at the sink and returning the bottle to the minibar, I can't help but note the unusual choice of drink for Alexander, who seldom indulges in anything stronger than wine at home. I push aside thoughts about the reasons behind his preference.

"It looks delicious," Alexander chuckles, snagging a piece of cheese with two fingers and tossing it into his mouth. Water trails from his wet hair, creating wet paths on his bare torso and saturating the elastic of his home pants — an enticing sight I could admire endlessly.

"I intended to cook something better, but the fridge had limited options," I admit with a shrug, placing the hot glass teapot on a cork stand. "We should go to the store for groceries."

"We should," he responds somewhat distantly, his focus on the sandwiches made from nearly dried bread and relatively fresh ham.

I reflect on the last time I visited Alexander's house — about a week ago, I reckon. Our schedules seldom align; either I'm toiling away late at work on a new project, collapsing into bed exhausted upon returning home, or he's grappling with after-hours challenges, resolving issues with problematic actors.

Typically, I manage the contents of Alexander's refrigerator, compiling a list of necessities. We either venture to the store together or, in his absence, I make a quick stop on my way home from work. Did he really not buy anything during my absence? Although, it looks a lot like him. He probably ate food from delivery.

As I pour tea into cups and break off a piece of my favorite oatmeal cookie with chocolate chips, I catch Alexander's attentive gaze fixed upon my actions. An awkward smile plays on my lips, caked with cookie crumbs. A light icy crust begins to cover every inch of my skin, because the usually warm gaze now seems distant and more like the gaze of a scientist observing an experimental subject.

Clearing my throat, I realize I can no longer postpone the impending conversation. "If only you knew what it cost me to kick your annoying daughter out of the apartment," I start, attempting to infuse my voice with an unobtrusive and slightly humorous tone.

"Christine can be quite persistent when she wants to be," Alexander remarks, taking a sip of tea.

Exhaling, I set the cup down and move around the island to sit beside him. I rest my palm on his shoulder, but his expression remains impassive.

"Listen, I understand how it looked when you saw the photo," I clear my throat, striving for confidence, "but I genuinely didn't know who Christine would bring. We agreed to celebrate together, but she deemed it too dull. You're aware that once she sets her mind on something, it's unchangeable."

"Sophie," Alexander interrupts my explanation, "I realized during our phone call that you're not to blame for this situation."

"Then why are you acting like this?" I withdraw my hand from his shoulder, reaching for my cup to conceal my nervousness.

"How?" he asks, perplexed, raising a questioning black eyebrow.

Only the warmth of the cup cradled in my hands prevents me from throwing my arms around emotionally.

"Detached," I muster the strength to utter a single word in a composed voice.

"You imagined it," Alexander remains steadfast, rising from the bar chair.

I observe him as he takes his mug to the sink and finally turns to face me. Clenched fists hide in his trouser pockets, and he closes his eyes, exhaling heavily.

"Sophie, you really just imagined it. I freaked out today when I saw some guys groping you, and you know how it affects me and how long it takes me to recover."

I know. I know him down to every detail: exactly how he likes to drink coffee, what cuisine he prefers, how many times a week he goes to the gym, what positions he likes in sex, what shampoo he has been using consistently for years, what brands of clothing he wears and much more. Isn't this a sign of how much he trusts me?

Springing from my chair so quickly that it crashes to the floor, I care little for the noise. I envelop Alexander in a tight hug, feeling the almost audible crunch of his ribs. His arms gently embrace me, fingers running through my hair.

How much have we weathered together? How many trials and tests of strength has our relationship endured for me to doubt it so easily! We've uplifted each other, yet here I am, like a blind kitten colliding with walls I've built in my head.

Despite my efforts to convince myself that everything is fine, the lingering unease persists. I hope it's just overthinking. It's time to let go of these doubts and surrender to the waves of happiness crashing on the shores of my life.

Chapter 40

Alexander

Lately, my life feels like a performance in the theater of the absurd. Like the last idiot, I find myself hiding from my girlfriend, crafting ridiculous excuses. I've even managed to untangle all conceivable and inconceivable issues with Stevenson, not to mention the paperwork, which I used to delegate to my assistants.

Starting a relationship and then struggling to find an exit — it's complete folly. Such behavior might be expected from a twenty-year-old, not a man in his forties.

I'm embarrassed to meet Sophie's gaze. I'm ashamed to admit to myself that I overestimated my resolve, thinking I could withstand the complexities of our forbidden relationship. Initially, it was exhilarating, with a touch of poignancy, living on the edge. My blood boiled from secret meetings and furtive glances. But what now?

Now, as the relationship grows too serious, I've thrown in the towel. I risked everything only to retreat. Very clever and mature, Alexander. Bravo!

I sigh, reclining in my office chair. I believed I had already faced the most challenging moments in my personal life, only to discover that the most intriguing experiences were waiting for me. After parting ways with Laura, I was one hundred percent certain I'd never allow myself to be entangled in a serious relationship again.

I always intended to settle for a mutually beneficial arrangement: I assist another beautiful aspiring actress in breaking into the industry, and in return, she offers me her company. I provide what they desire, and in return, I receive physical satisfaction.

However, things took an unexpected turn when, in the midst of a bustling hotel bar, I encountered her — sitting alone, sipping a cocktail. The call girl turned out to be an innocent doe who moaned beneath my touch, surprised by her own feelings, as if she had never been with an experienced man before.

It seems I'm in the midst of a midlife crisis. I found myself entangled in a committed relationship with a young woman, a decision that risked jeopardizing the improving relationship with my daughter.

The devil had his hooks in me.

Already in the bar, I realized that with her it would not be like with other girls for one night stand. Now we act like a couple who have been married for several years. Discussions revolved around urgent gastronomic shopping, home essentials, and plans for our next vacation.

The dissonance was palpable. Unlike Lola, who remained quietly at home, dutifully attending castings without asking unnecessary questions, Sophie took an active role in caring for the apartment and creating a cozy atmosphere.

"Mr. Bailey, the university director is calling. Would you like to take it?" My assistant's head appears in the doorway.

"Yes, Natalie, thank you," I nod, and she disappears as if by magic.

I pick up the landline phone and stir the now-cooled coffee with a small spoon.

"Good evening," I greet my important interlocutor.

"Good, Mr. Bailey, this is Jason Donovan," the brusque voice echoes through the speaker. "Sean has already briefed me on your needs. I believe we can handle this without any issues. The main condition is that the enrollment occurs no later than the next academic year. Otherwise, I won't be able to help you."

"Thank you, Mr. Donovan," I express my gratitude, jotting down notes on a small piece of paper. "You've been a tremendous help. I'll transfer the money this week. Have your bank details changed?"

"Well, Mr. Bailey, my son-in-law's friends are my friends; I'm always happy to help," the voice on the phone chuckles hoarsely. "My secretary will send everything you need, including bank details, tomorrow. Call if you have any questions. Good evening."

One problem down. It's quite reassuring when your best friend's wife is the daughter of the director of the architectural university where your daughter studies. All issues, even with enrollment, are resolved in an instant.

I hum with satisfaction, gazing at the completed tasks on my schedule. The real estate agent has been informed, the money for the apartment has been transferred, and the university matters are well under control. Tomorrow, I'll wrap up the remaining tasks. Now, it's time to head home.

Driving, I find it hard to focus on the road, my mind consumed by a constant stream of thoughts. They say, "If you love, let person go." But how do you release someone who loves you back without causing pain?

You might wonder, why let go if everything is mutual? Unfortunately, I have an answer to that question. Despite the mutual feelings, I can't envision a future with Sophie. My selfishness has kept her with me for too long, but we can't conceal our relationship forever. Hence, I face a choice: take our relationship to the next level or call it quits.

I choose the latter.

Neither Sophie nor I are prepared for a serious commitment. She's too young, and I've endured too much to allow her closer. Our forbidden secret has stretched on for too long. It's time to end this charade and spare Sophie from further pain.

I can't offer her more than I do now. During our dispute over fucking Liam, it felt like I was being replaced, prompting me to confess my love and fight for her. Yet, looking back, I realize my actions were irrational.

I'm not cut out for family life, and it's time to acknowledge it. I can't recall the last time I lived with someone for more than a year. Keeping Sophie as my "actress" would be too cruel. That's precisely what I attempted when persuading her to move in with me. However, Sophie doesn't require anything in return. Her feelings are genuine, and she hopes for reciprocation.

How blind I was, oblivious to the underlying motivations behind my actions. Fortunately, Sophie's persistence led me to the decision to rent her an apartment instead of moving in together. My baby, as it turns out, was more farsighted and intelligent than I gave her credit for.

Riding the elevator to my floor, a realization settles in — I must put an end to this captivating yet drawn-out tale. It was intriguing, enjoyable, undeniably passionate, but it's time to return to reality and confront the truth.

Sophie and I share little in common. She envisions a future with a family and children, while all I can offer is introductions to my closest friends and the perpetuation of our clandestine relationship.

Inserting the key into the lock, I mentally commit to calling Sophie tomorrow, arranging a meeting on neutral ground to explain myself.

However, as soon as I swing open the door, fate once again throws me a curveball — enticing aromas waft from the kitchen, causing my stomach to knot and saliva to pool at the corner of my lips. Sophie's clear voice harmonizes with the song emanating from the sound system.

Damn it! Why is fate punishing me like this?

Chapter 41

Alexander

The alluring aroma of something delicious wafts from the kitchen, accompanied by the rhythmic percussion of a spatula against the side of a frying pan and the bass of a song that beckons one to dance and sing.

Sophie, with her thighs barely covered, dances in front of the stove.

She is the first who has cooked in my kitchen. It brings me back to that morning when she made me breakfast, likely wearing the same shirt she has on now. I try to recall if Laura ever greeted me from work like that when we lived together.

No. Initially, Laura hesitated to share living space, claiming her apartment was closer to work. Later, I realized her refusals were likely due to another man. Then, during her pregnancy, Laura suffered from morning sickness, complaining that the smell of food triggered nausea.

The rest of my past relationships featured women who simply disliked cooking. They found it easier to order food and pass it off as their own creations.

Sophie belts out the lyrics to a 2000s hit. I banish thoughts of my past and carefully remove my outerwear.

Engrossed in her cooking, she doesn't notice as I push back a bar chair and take a seat at the kitchen island. I observe her actions, rubbing the bridge of my nose.

I had intended to talk to her at the earliest opportunity, so why is my heart dancing wildly under my ribs and my brain sounding an alarm? Fate has presented the perfect moment, yet I hesitate, thinking the conversation can wait. Why?

Is it guilt? Sophie has gone out of her way after a hard day to surprise me with a delicious dinner. Nothing ever goes as planned with her — from the very beginning, from our initial meeting.

Lost in thought, I seem to be thinking too loudly. She turns in my direction, as if someone calling her name.

"Oh," her startled falsetto voice echoes through the apartment, "Alexander," she places her free hand on her heart. "How long have you been sitting here?"

Her lips stretch into a satisfied smile, her eyes glowing with warmth as she turns her whole body towards me, revealing red lace lingerie through her half-buttoned shirt — my shirt. Something painfully tickles in my chest.

"I just came in," not a single muscle betrays my internal tension.

"You're on time; dinner is almost ready," she announces. Spaghetti boils on the stove in a shiny silver pot, and meat simmers in a frying pan.

I nod briefly, rubbing my hands together, signaling to Sophie that I need to go to the bathroom for hygiene procedures.

"Fuck," I exhale convulsively, leaning my fists on the countertop on both sides of the rectangular sink. The music from the living room becomes quieter, no longer interrupting the flow of thoughts in my head.

I didn't think it would be so difficult.

I lift the handle of the water switch, turning it all the way to the right. I scoop up the icy liquid into my hands and wash my face to calm myself down and gather my strength.

"Come on, Alexander, you can do it," my inner voice repeats.

"I can't," I answer him, spitting the water.

How can I say goodbye to Sophie, who is carefully preparing dinner for me, standing in underwear and my shirt, in my kitchen? What's on her mind right now? Does she believe she's showing attention, lovingly stirring the minced meat in the sauce simmering on the stove, to a man tired after work?

A wave of emotion washes me down the drain with the cold water when Sophie switches the audio system to my favorite evening jazz playlist. I angrily hit the tap, cutting off the flow of water. I lower my head, avoiding the reflection in the mirror. Right now, I don't want to see myself.

Realizing that I have been in the bathroom for too long to wash hands, my brain finds a compromise with my conscience: let today be our farewell evening.

It would have been simpler if we hadn't seen each other until tomorrow. Much easier, especially considering our hectic work schedules over the past week. But, as I've come to acknowledge, things seldom unfold according to my plans with Sophie. She breaks them into pieces like an icebreaker.

"Spaghetti Bolognese for dinner today," she announces, placing a beautifully crafted plate of pasta in front of me as I return to my seat.

The aroma is as delightful as the presentation. Sophie has outdone herself, turning a simple dish into a culinary masterpiece. The effort she's put in makes me feel even more ashamed.

"Are we celebrating something?" I inquire, noticing the bottle of red wine in her hands.

"No," Sophie shrugs, handing me the corkscrew. "I just wanted to treat you after a challenging day. I know how busy you've been at work lately."

"Shut up, shut up, shut up!" My inner voice screams after her words. It's unusually talkative today.

I pour the wine into glasses, the gurgling sound attempting to drown out my tumultuous conscience.

"You're not on vacation either; you shouldn't," I take the first sip, its astringency burning my throat.

Even my favorite drink fails to brighten up this guilt-laden evening. It serves as another reminder that I am undeserving of Sophie's care and love.

"It's not difficult for me," she smiles. "Besides, the project is progressing well. The client left satisfied after the presentation."

Throughout the evening, I attempt to stay quiet, allowing Sophie to lead the conversation. Her animated tales about a recent work meeting bring a touch of brightness to our dinner.

Her excitement over the project's success fills me with an unwarranted sense of optimism. She'll be alright, I tell myself. Yes, it might hurt at first, but she'll get through it. She will go into work that brings her joy and forget about me.

"Did you enjoy it?" Sophie whispers in my ear, her arms enveloping my neck as she places the empty dishes in the sink.

Her fingers cool my bare skin beneath the collar of my shirt, and her heaving breasts press against my forearm, stirring desire within me. Sophie has a way of infusing even the most callous person with her emotions.

"Everything was delicious," I sincerely admit, my fingers gripping the marble tabletop. Yet, I realize I'm losing; resistance to her allure is futile, especially after the more than usual amount of wine I consumed tonight.

"What about this?" Her soft lips find mine, leaving a burning trail of a kiss with the taste of viscous dry wine.

I groan, acknowledging my helplessness. Sophie's outfit already hinted at her desire for a passionate continuation of the evening.

"What did you expect, Alexander? Did you think she would leave like this after dinner?" My vociferous conscience remarks sarcastically.

My fingers ache with the desire to feel the soft skin beneath them. I yearn to dive into the pools of her passionate eyes, trace the contours with my palms, taste the sweetness of every inch of her body, absorb her scent and emotions. One last time...

With a growl, I push myself off the island with my hands, rising to my feet and grabbing Sophie's wrists. I catch her surprised look, and before my inner voice protests again, I hoist her delicate body over my shoulder.

Farewell dinner, farewell sex, tinged with the bitterness of an impending breakup.

Chapter 42

Sophie

For the first time in my life, I am glad to be separated from my beloved man for a week. After a prolonged hiatus, Alexander has become insatiable, like an untamed animal. Despite a lingering emotional detachment between us, I attribute it to work-related stress, as I see no other apparent reasons for this shift. Alexander tends to keep his troubles to himself, revealing them only when resolutions are already in place. Consequently, I patiently await his willingness to share his concerns, ready to offer support in any way possible.

Encouraged by my success with a client today, I decided to surprise Alexander with a new lace lingerie set, intending to welcome him in style after his challenging day.

Taking a risk, I also arranged a surprise dinner, uncertain whether he would return home or spend the night at the office. Today, luck appears to be on my side — the dinner not only succeeds but is also appreciated by its passionate continuation.

"Turn over," Alexander hoarsely requests, leaning over me and scrutinizing every inch of my body, igniting a hot fire on the surface of my skin.

I obediently comply with his wishes. Tonight is exclusively for him, and everything will unfold as he desires. While Alexander usually pays close attention to my needs in bed, tonight, I want to focus solely on pleasing him. It seems Alexander senses this shift and willingly embraces the rules of the game.

His hands glide smoothly down my back, caressing the straps of my scarlet lace bra that gleams brightly in the moonlight. Following his hands, his lips leave fiery trails, scratching my skin with prickly stubble. He goes down to the elastic band of my panties and pries it up with his teeth. He slowly pulls them off, helping himself with fingers.

An involuntary groan escapes my throat, and I arch my lower back, offering assistance to Alexander. A sharp slap burns my ass, and then his hot palms grip my waist, lifting me up and compelling me to kneel.

The distinct sound of a zipper being undone echoes through my senses louder than it should. It momentarily makes me recoil from the overwhelming desire, but my actions don't go unnoticed. Alexander halts me, placing his hand on my back. I hold my breath as it gradually ascends, squeezing my neck before entwining my hair around his fist.

I bite my lip, relishing the delightful pain at the roots. My arched chest rises with frequent sighs. I shiver as the cool cotton of Alexander's shirt meets my bare skin, allowing the warmth of his body to permeate through me.

"Whatever happens, know that you are the best thing that happened in my life," his breath, tinged with the taste of wine, caresses my neck and earlobe in a ragged stream. "You're the best."

My brain struggles to process the weight of the spoken words as, in the same moment, Alexander bursts into my body with a powerful push, making me forget about everything in the world.

Lying on the bed, my body feels limp, entangled in the sheets. I attempt to catch my breath, but it seems like an elusive task. It's as if my soul has detached from my body and now hovers above the bed, observing me entwined with Alexander, both of us damp from our most passionate sex.

If enduring prolonged periods of separation is the price for such heated nights, then I am willing to endure the agonies of being apart.

Amid the constant roar in my ears, I listen to Alexander's heavy breathing and accelerated heartbeat. His hand rests on my lower back, fingers gently stroking the slowly cooling, sticky skin.

With every fiber of my soul and body, I yearn to merge into him without a trace. To unite us and become an inseparable entity forever, as it occurs during the moments of our sex.

Occasionally, I sense him from a distance. For the past week, a strange anxiety has haunted me, dissipating only when our lips meet. Could it be that we missed each other so intensely that it manifested on a physical level? Does this deep affection signify the kind of love depicted in fairy tales?

From childhood, we are taught that we will encounter a prince who will rescue us from imprisonment. After Liam, I dismissed such notions as nonsense and fiction, but now...

Alexander genuinely liberated my soul from the shackles of suspicion and mistrust. With him, I feel freer: I no longer care about others' opinions, I've stopped taking everything to heart, and men no longer appear as complete traitors.

How did it come to be that he didn't evoke doubts in me? Perhaps it was due to our unconventional meeting circumstances. Or maybe, deep down, I knew that Alexander wasn't like everyone else. Having weathered many trials, I realize he is my man. He and I share similarities and differences simultaneously. We both experienced betrayal from loved ones, yet we each coped with it in our unique ways. When we met, we helped each other confront our demons.

I snuggle closer to Alexander, planting a kiss on his collarbone. Lost in my thoughts, I don't notice his chest rising steadily. Asleep. My Alexander has drifted off. I smile foolishly at my discovery.

"Good night," I whisper into the darkness and adjust the blanket over his torso.

Entering the bathroom, I securely close the door before turning on the light. I take a quick shower to freshen up and regain my composure. After our intense sex, my mind is a whirlwind, and my body bears the marks of kisses and caresses.

As I towel myself dry, the trill of a phone emanates from the bedroom. I hasten to exit the bathroom, eager to intercept the unexpected call. Who would ring me at such a late hour? My imagination immediately conjures up various scenarios, ranging from a heart attack to a dreadful accident involving my parents.

I swiftly wrap a towel around myself, but before I open the door, I catch Alexander's voice. It's his phone. I'm not sure what compels me to eavesdrop instead of simply leaving the room, but now I'm standing with my ear against the door, listening intently.

"Is everything okay?" I hear Alexander's muffled voice, followed by an unsettling silence.

Foreboding signal begins to sound in my mind.

"I understand. I'll be right there," his once-sleepy voice transforms into a cold seriousness. There's a commotion and the rustling of bedcovers.

Deciding that continuing to lurk outside the door serves no purpose (if it ever did), I tighten the towel and step out of my hiding place. The bedroom is now bathed in light, and Alexander is hastily pulling on his jeans beside the closet.

"What happened?" I watch his brisk movements with growing concern.

Alexander turns to me but remains silent, gesturing for me to follow him into the hallway. A familiar stern expression freezes on his face: his eyebrows slightly furrowed, lips compressed into a thin line, and his eyes radiating coldness.

Chills race across my still-warm post-shower skin, and focus on the back of my head. What could have prompted him to leave his bed at nearly four in the morning? Even at work, he never allowed such disruptions, firmly telling his assistant that any issue could wait until morning and his arrival at the office.

"Christine called," Alexander announces, pulling a leather jacket over his muscular shoulders, clad in a sweater. "Laura isn't feeling well. She's with her now, waiting for an ambulance."

"What happened to her?" I shuffle anxiously on the cool hallway tiles, the chill biting at my bare feet.

"I don't know," Alexander bends down to pull on his sneakers. "Christine is in a panic. She couldn't put a word together."

"Should I come with you? I just need five seconds to get dressed," I ramble, succumbing to panic and desperately trying to recall where in the closet I left my jeans after changing.

Alexander shoots me a sidelong glance that pins me in place. Silly me, I hadn't even considered how it might appear if we arrived together.

"I'll be back soon. Go back to bed," Alexander snaps, grabbing his car keys from the table.

I nod briefly in acknowledgment.

"Text me when you find out what happened," I call after him as the door slams shut, cutting us off from each other.

Chapter 43

Sophie

About an hour later, I find myself in the kitchen, nursing a cup of scalding hot coffee. The idea of sleep eludes me; it's as if life has been cleaved into "before" and "after," and our passionate encounter with Alexander feels like it happened many weeks ago.

A wince escapes me as I bring the cup to my lips, the aroma of the burnt brew assaulting my senses. I set it aside and glance at the stove, now marred by remnants of spilled coffee. In Alexander's house, there's no fancy coffee machine, and he never got around to teaching me the art of brewing in a cezve. I hope he won't be too upset when he returns, accusing me of attempting to ruin the expensive induction surface.

With a sigh, I rise from the bar chair, opting to grab a can of energy drink from the refrigerator. Alexander seems to keep a stock of them for rushed mornings. I choose my favorite, the blueberry-flavored one, a personal touch since he used to stick to the classic unsweetened version.

The can opens with a hiss, filling the kitchen with the scent of berries. Unsure of the exact dose of caffeine I need when my nerves are already frayed, I decide against falling asleep. Sooner or later, fatigue will catch up with me after the night's passionate encounter and brief sleep. However, I want to greet Alexander with energy and readiness to support him, regardless of the news he brings.

Sipping the fragrant energy drink, I wander around the living room until I find myself standing at the threshold of a small home library. The room houses a pool table and a plush sofa, complete with a game console. Occasionally, Pierce and John join Alexander here to unwind after work. However, such gatherings are so infrequent that the gaming paraphernalia has accumulated a layer of dust.

I've only been in this room a couple of times, never really contemplating the books Alexander favors or the games he enjoys with his friends. The console boasts classic games like FIFA, Mafia, Mortal Kombat, DOOM, and GTA. Surprisingly, the bookshelves prove to be more intriguing. They hold a diverse collection, ranging from esotericism to romance and historical novels. I never would have guessed that Alexander indulged in such varied reading.

As I glance at the book spines, my eyes suddenly catch a frame lying face down. In a somewhat clandestine manner, I look around, almost expecting someone's presence, even though I'm alone in the apartment.

With care, I flip over the frame, shrouded in several layers of dust, and discover a rather intriguing photograph. It captures a younger Alexander and Laura, the latter holding a small bundle of fabric. A closer look reveals a maternity hospital sign in the background, suggesting it's a photo from Christine and Laura's discharge.

The youthful version of Alexander in the picture radiates happiness, sporting a wide smile that forms familiar wrinkles at the corners of his eyes. One of his arms lovingly encircles Laura's shoulders. However, Laura appears to be the opposite; her lips show no hint of a smile, her hair pulled tightly into a ponytail, and the bundle in her hands seems almost about to slip away, as if she's reluctant to hold it. While exhaustion after childbirth could explain her demeanor, knowing the intricacies of their relationship, it appears more troubling than ordinary weariness.

I carefully return the frame to its place, tracing a clean silhouette in the layer of dust. It feels as though I've opened a door into a person's soul, a door I shouldn't have even touched. Why does Alexander keep the photo this way? As far as I know, he moved to this apartment long after parting ways with Laura.

Attempting to unravel a mystery that eludes my understanding and feeling a sense of freedom in the solitary apartment, I grab a can of energy drink from the table next to the console and make my way to the home office.

The room greets me with impenetrable darkness. It takes me a moment to find the switch before the office is bathed in the bright light emanating from the ceiling chandelier.

I find nothing out of the ordinary. This room seems even more desolate than the library, as if it has never been touched. The fact that there's nothing in the desk drawers only reinforces my perception. According to typical expectations, there should be a photograph of loved ones on the desk, but even that is absent.

Exiting the office, disappointment engulfs me. Alexander's soul appears shrouded in darkness. I sensed this from the beginning, at our initial encounter when, perched at the bar, he brushed aside questions, even seemingly benign ones like "what do you do for a living?" If memory serves, he replied that it wasn't interesting, and I assumed he probably worked in IT.

I place the now-empty can of energy drink on the kitchen island's countertop and sink into a chair, reaching for the abandoned phone.

Opting to kill time, I decide to scroll through my social media feed, only to be met with an unexpected surprise in the very first photo: Christine has just updated her feed with a picture of a cheerful Laura, Alexander, and herself in the kitchen, sipping coffee. The caption reads, "early breakfast is a great time for a family reunion."

I can't believe my eyes and scrutinize the photo for any detail that might indicate its age, but I find none. Alexander is donned in the same clothes he wore when he left the apartment just a couple of hours ago.

A shiver runs down my spine, leaving my head filled with a painful void. I'm at a loss for what to think. I can't fathom that Alexander, still warm from our recent intimacy, hurried to reconcile with his ex, deceiving me with a false claim that she needed urgent assistance.

He would never do that. Not with me sitting here, waiting anxiously, and investing my energy in preparing a surprise dinner for him, succumbing to the pleasure of his caresses...

The longer I stare at the photo, the quicker my body fills with rage from head to toe.

I tear the towel from my hair, the same one Alexander gave me when I moved to this new apartment, and it flings onto the countertop, knocking down the energy drink can. The clatter of aluminum hitting the floor serves as a call to action.

I dash to the stove, grabbing the cumbersome cezve with the stubborn coffee remnants sticking to it. Fueled by anger, I strike the dirty hob. Lost in the red haze before my eyes, I fail to notice the crack forming on it. With erratic movements, I rampage through the first floor of the apartment, sweeping away everything in my path and unleashing a torrent of curses aimed at Alexander.

Chapter 44

Sophie

I hear the door open while packing my things into a bag in the midst of the trashed bedroom. I jump up, accidentally kicking an empty bottle of red wine with my bare foot, and rush like a hurricane into the hall, the phone clenched tightly in my palm. Like the ultimate masochist, I took a screenshot of the photo not to lose strong evidence, and now I'm going to present it to the accused.

"What happened here?" Alexander surveys the kitchen-living room without even removing his outerwear. Glass crackles under the soles of his sneakers.

I'm slightly shaky from the alcohol I've drunk, but I'm doing my best to stand my ground and meet Alexander's gaze, focusing on his deceitful face.

"You," I point a finger in his direction with my free hand, causing Alexander to frown and look me up and down. "Where have you been?"

"You know perfectly well where I was. Don't you find this question stupid?" He lifts one leg, shaking off a branch of a bush — the flowerpot with which I managed to drag from the terrace and smash right in the middle of the apartment. "It's better to finally answer the question and tell me what happened here."

"Oh, no, my dear," I grin hysterically, unable to contain the full wave of sarcasm. "You're the one who should tell me what happened!"

Alexander takes a step towards me, but I take two steps back. I bite my lip because I belatedly feel a fragment of something unknown digging into my foot. But that's the last thing that worries me right now.

"Sophie, are you drunk?" He asks insinuatingly, as if he were talking to a mentally ill person.

Everything inside me begins to boil when the bewilderment on his face gives way to a strange sympathy. Fury, inflamed by alcohol, controls me and forces me to pick up the first thing that comes to hand from the floor. This turns out to be a vinyl record from Alexander's jazz collection. I launch it into the air towards him, but he deftly dodges my throw.

"Are you crazy?!" Alexander growls, looking at the pieces of his favorite vinyl.

"You're the one who's crazy!" I scream at the top of my lungs, thrusting the screenshot in his direction with a trembling hand.

Emotions on his face change again, but I don't have time to catch which ones, because in an instant Alexander puts on his cold mask. Now he looks like an unshakable rock.

"Do you have anything to say in your defense?" I ask him without lowering my voice, shaking the phone in the air.

Alexander's fists clench, and he exhales imperceptibly. But he forgot that I know him as well as myself, and even in a drunken stupor, I can notice any little thing connected with him.

"I'm not going to make excuses for you," he mutters. "We'll talk when you come to your senses."

In two steps, he covers the distance between us and throws my staggering body over his shoulder. All my insides rise to my throat, the phone falls to the floor, and I begin to pound my fists on his back.

"Let me go, you bastard! You are a lying asshole! I trusted you! I believed you!" Tears begin to flow down my face.

The hysteria turns to helplessness, and I allow him to lay me down on the bed in the guest room. The only place where my vengeful hand did not reach.

"You'll get some sleep, and then we'll talk. And don't even dare leave this room until you sober up."

Alexander furiously wraps my limp body in a blanket, pressing my arms to my body, and then turns off the light and leaves, closing the door to the room.

Tears continue to roll from my eyes, and at some point, I begin to choke on them. I suppress my heart-rending screams into the pillow. A drunken brain does not allow me to think and connect thoughts into a coherent chain. I try to cling to at least one, but I can't, and after half an hour of hysteria, I fall into a healing sleep.

I wake up to chills enveloping my skin, hot from a hangover. I shudder, grabbing the edges of the blanket, and suddenly realize that my body is no longer bound by the thick fabric. I rise up on my elbows, rubbing my eyes and looking around the unfamiliar room. The apartment is unusually quiet. Fighting a headache, I lower my feet onto the cool parquet floor and immediately groan: a sharp pain pierces my foot.

Examining the cause of the discomfort, I see that someone bandaged my leg while I was sleeping. Memories descend on me like a tub of icy water. Alexander, Laura, Christine, a photo of them together, a caption about their reunion, and then the red veil of my anger and a destroyed apartment. Crap.

I rub my face with my palms until it turns red and, gathering my strength, I get out of bed. Surprisingly, I don't feel sick, just a headache, like I was hit with a stone.

I hesitantly open the door, freezing for a split second, and trudge to the first floor, which is already flooded by the setting sun. How long did I sleep?

Alexander sits at the kitchen island with his back to me and drinks coffee from a paper cup, looking at something on his phone. Mine is on the edge of the countertop. How strange it is that it was thanks to Alexander's gift that I learned about his lies and betrayal. Fate is a strange thing that clearly has a wicked sense of humor.

"Good... evening," I hesitate, not daring to take a step closer. How should I behave after everything I've done? I want to fall through the ground.

"Good evening," Alexander greets without turning around. Previously, he would have added my name at the end, but not now...

I am surprised to notice that the chaos I caused at night has disappeared without a trace. All that was left was a burnt stove with a crack in the middle and a broken vinyl player on the stand under the TV. I was smart enough not to touch the expensive TV...

"I'm sorry for causing... a mess here. I feel ashamed..."

"Sophie," Alexander interrupts the groans of my conscience in a stern voice, "we need to talk."

His icy voice sends chills down my spine. When he turns his stern and focused gaze, it makes my legs go weak. He gestures for me to sit next to him, and I obediently obey his request.

"Yes, of course," I nod, intertwining my fingers in a lock on my knees. I'm preparing to listen to moral lectures about damaging other people's property, but his next words plunge me into silent shock.

"We have no future," Alexander begins to hammer nails into the lid of my coffin. I can hear a hammer on metal and wood in my head. "You are only twenty, and I am already in my fifties. We are too different. I decided that we need to break up."

I look at him with a puzzled look. Did he make the decision for both of us? Previously, he was not bothered by the age difference. So why is he bothering with this now? Did he understand the difference between a mature woman and a teenager after a conversation with his ex-wife?

"Is it all because of her? Do you still love her?" I ask in a drooping voice because I understand that there is no turning back. If Alexander has decided, then he will not back down.

"Don't interrupt me and listen calmly," he puts the paper cup on the countertop. "You can continue your studies and go to the master's program, as you wanted. I've resolved the issue with this. You just need to submit an application before the next academic year. The apartment is paid for the entire duration of your studies. And don't give up your internship. I'm sure you have everything to make it work out."

I flutter my eyelashes, trying to process the information he gave me. Master's degree? Apartment? What is he talking about?

"Are you paying me off?" I wheeze, looking dumbfounded into the eyes of a man whom I seem to be seeing for the first time.

"I'm not paying off, but I want you to have the decent future that you deserve," Alexander says a little softer, pursing his lips.

Everything inside me is turning over. That's how he decided. Throw money at me and hope that this will be enough for me after all the declarations of love that turned out to be empty words. He treats me just like he treats his actresses. Only he forgot that our relationship is completely different.

But since you want to play this game, Alexander, then I will play along with you and come out of it with my winnings.

I gather all my remaining pride into a fist and lift my chin, rising from the chair. No hysterics and no drama, Sophie. Don't show him how painfully he hurt you, take your consolation prize. You can cry at home. Alone with your resentment.

"Well," I pick up my phone from the tabletop. "Thank you for... caring, Alexander."

I turn around and go into the hall, limping due to my sore foot. When I see a packed suitcase with my clothes and a bag of cat supplies for Oliver at the door, tears come to my eyes. He took care for a quick break-up... What a strategist you are, Alexander...

I pull on my boots and down jacket, swallowing the lump in my throat and quietly wiping away the first wet streaks on my cheeks. I take my bags and unlock the door under a gaze that I can feel even with my back.

"Sophie," Alexander suddenly calls, but I don't turn around. I don't allow myself to do this, so as not to be tormented by flashbacks every time I close my eyes.

"Goodbye, Alexander," I give my voice a cheerful tint, but it's not easy for me. "Thank you for everything and… I hope you two will be happy together."

Chapter 45

Sophie

This morning, the remnants of my shattered world haunt my every waking moment. Unfulfilled hopes crumble like ashes around me as I open my eyes. I believed HIM, in every uttered word. After convincing myself that trust was a luxury I could no longer afford, I let him in. And now, what's left?

For two days, I've been cocooned in the darkness of my apartment. The only reason that makes me get out of bed is the cat that purrs heart-rendingly at the bowl five minutes before breakfast and dinner. I hardly eat, I rely on small snacks and water, because my tears have completely dried me out.

While listening to the "breakup playlist," I screamed and stuffed all the clothes into the washing machine that smelled of Alexander's tart cologne. Then I cried angrily into the pillow, tearing out my vocal cords.

Today marks the end of my privilege to hide under the covers. Monday demands that I gather the shattered pieces of myself, put on a brave face, and return to work. I refuse to surrender to the despair. I'll carve a path to success in my career, leaving Alexander to rue the day he let me go. I will be successful, beautiful, and happy, irrespective of any man. That's a promise I make to myself.

Concealing the dark circles under my eyes with makeup and donning a sleek black dress, I stride into the office. Stella awaits at my desk, her fiery red hair bouncing with every step. The familiar routine brings a semblance of peace to my battered soul.

"Williams, there you are," Stella beckons urgently, motioning for me to hurry.

Quickening my pace with clicks of my heels, I decide to walk like a businesswoman — confident, poised, and determined. It's a step towards healing.

"Stella, what's going on?" I throw my coat on the chair and my bag on the table.

"Christopher needs you. Urgent edits for the Black Pearl project. He wants you in there ASAP, without even glancing at the documents. So, move!" she says, throwing a stack of papers on my desk.

Without a proper briefing? This must be serious. Christopher detests unpreparedness.

"What kind of last-minute changes are we talking about?" I ask in a hushed tone as I follow Stella toward the boss's office.

"Customers, you know how they are — always tweaking things. After working here as long as I have, you'll get used to it," she replies, opening the door.

I mentally scoff at another one of Stella's classic phrases, the "if you work as long as me" line. She has a penchant for dispensing advice, whether it's needed or not. Initially, she came across as easy-going, but the more I work with her, the more I see her underlying insecurity.

Stella knocks three times before opening Christopher's office door, ushering me in and leaving me alone with him.

"Good morning, Mr. Harrison," I greet, taking a seat at the lengthy conference table.

His office is more of a meeting room, dominated by a large conference table, a choice that seems to suit Christopher's needs. I can appreciate the practicality of it; small tables wouldn't accommodate the drawings and numerous papers with technical specifications.

"Good morning, Sophie," he replies, glancing up from his computer, appraising my outfit. It seems I might have overdone it, though I am well within the office dress code.

"Stella mentioned the client's requested changes to the order," I attempt to initiate a work-related conversation.

Christopher responds with a slight smile — a rare gesture that signifies his satisfaction with an employee. I wonder if he attributes this update to Stella or if he acknowledges my efforts.

"Have you had coffee yet?" he asks unexpectedly.

Christopher usually skips small talk, so this deviation catches me off guard. I'm unable to answer immediately, as my morning routine was rushed and I couldn't spare a moment for breakfast.

"Um, no, not yet," I admit, laying out the papers on the table and scanning them, though my eyes don't grasp a single line.

"Me neither," he mutters, pressing a button on his landline phone. "Two cappuccinos with regular milk, please." He looks up at me. "Sophie, you drink regular milk, right?"

He looks up at me, questioning my coffee preferences. I'm taken aback that he's concerned about the details.

"I usually drink it with oat milk, but regular milk is fine too," I respond.

"Make two with oat milk," he instructs into the phone. "I'll give it a try. Never had coffee with plant milk before."

I feel a sudden weight of pressure. What if he doesn't like it? Has Christopher ever let an employee go over something so trivial?

Awkwardly fidgeting with the documents, I tuck my legs under the seat, realizing I haven't responded to his comment about coffee. Before I can come up with a suitable answer, Christopher interrupts the awkward silence.

"So, the customer sent new edits last night," he says, putting on his glasses and retrieving his copy of the documents. "But it's okay. We just need to update some details on the façade."

I exhale a sigh of relief, either because the conversation has shifted towards work or the realization that I won't be consumed by this project day and night again.

"Could you fill me in on the client's requests?" I blurt out before thinking, my eyes meeting Christopher's with a hint of apprehension. "Sorry, I haven't had a chance to review the edits yet."

To my surprise, Christopher bursts into laughter. I've never noticed this side of him — a pleasant, velvety laugh that he seldom shares in the presence of colleagues.

"Sophie, relax. We're almost at the finish line; there won't be any major changes. The client just wanted to tweak some design elements. Nothing critical," he reassures me.

His words trigger an unwarranted panic within me. Sophie, regain composure, present yourself as a professional in your field.

"Okay, Mr. Harrison, I understand," I inject confidence into my voice. "What do you need from me?"

Christopher's secretary, a cute brunette with long silky hair, enters the office. Rumors about her relationship with Christopher have been circulating since the beginning of her tenure, sparking debates among colleagues.

"Your coffee, Mr. Harrison," she says, placing cups in front of both of us. "Need sugar?"

"No, thank you," we respond simultaneously, earning a slight approving smile from Christopher.

With a brief nod, the secretary exits the office. We proceed to discuss crucial details and enjoy two cups of cappuccino with oat milk (which, incidentally, Christopher seems to prefer now, vowing to avoid regular milk). I return to my workstation and immerse myself in the day's tasks — making design changes to the necessary documents and providing comments on corrected 3D building layouts in line with the new instructions.

The busyness of the day is so consuming that thoughts of Alexander and his betrayal barely cross my mind. Only when I step onto the office porch do memories of him flood back. He used to meet me from work, halting right in front of the entrance, his kisses sealing our reunions before leading me either to his place or mine.

I exhale a visible breath, creating a puff of steam in the frosty air. Closing my eyes, I attempt to erase warm and cozy moments with Alexander from my thoughts. Yet, it proves impossible. Even reviving the breakup scene in my memory. It is simply erased either by thoughts of our joint vacation and sex under palm trees and the night sky, or by numerous trips through the city center at night, when he held the steering wheel with one hand and stroked my knee with the other. I can almost hear his favorite jazz music, sending a shiver down my spine.

"Sophie, are you waiting for someone?" Christopher's voice reaches my ears.

"What?" I open my eyes and find myself face to face with him. "Oh, sorry. No, just lost in thought," I take a step back to allow him to pass.

He nods silently and starts descending the steps, but then he halts abruptly and turns back in my direction.

"Can I give you a ride?"

His proposition leaves my head feeling empty, as if tumbleweeds are rushing through it. Give me a ride? Me?

"No need, thank you," I reply with a polite smile.

"Well, okay," is it just me, or do I detect notes of disappointment in his voice? "Bye then. Talk to you tomorrow."

"See you tomorrow."

Christopher steps down onto the asphalt, walking around the porch toward the parking lot. However, he stops downstairs, opposite me, and raises his head, meeting my gaze.

"By the way, you did a good job today," he adds casually. "I didn't have to correct any mistakes. Keep it up. Wait until tomorrow for the final sketches, and you can send everything to the customer for approval."

"Who? Me?" Surprised, I even point a finger at myself, glancing around to make sure no one else is nearby.

"Yes, you."

"But, Mr. Harrison, you usually handle the final drafts yourself."

"Usually, yes. But this project is just as much yours as mine. For a newbie, you did an excellent job, Sophie, and I think you can be trusted with more responsibility. Next time, you will negotiate with the client. Good evening," he salutes me with a wave and leaves me alone.

Keep it up, Sophie! Well done!

Chapter 46

Sophie

The remaining week unfolds in endless meetings to finalize the construction contract, alongside Christopher and a lawyer from our architectural bureau. I wake up, go to work, navigate the city in the boss's car (half the time stuck in traffic, of course), return from work, and collapse into oblivion.

During our wanderings between offices and discussions of contract points, our small team develops inside jokes, and the awkwardness of the first day disappears forever. Now I'm "Miss What-Where-When?" as I constantly clarify various aspects of work processes. Unfortunately, architectural school doesn't teach how to conduct negotiations and work with contracts. Christopher comes to my rescue, patiently explaining in detail how to engage with clients and what to pay attention to.

Closeness with the management and a warming in our professional relationships happen unexpectedly but smoothly. This could be the description of my boss. Christopher is a spontaneous person but presents his ideas beautifully and unobtrusively. We've already managed to go to lunch at a new interactive Japanese restaurant (quite entertaining: we were forbidden to use our hands, received massages, and were fed with spoons) under the pretext that the boss couldn't make it to the opening due to work, and "when, if not now?"

"Sophie, you need to live in the moment," Christopher enthusiastically declares, taking the wheel of his car. "If reincarnation exists, which I strongly doubt, then this is the only, unique life you're living. Do it with pleasure. Am I right, Mr. Brosnan?" he asks, looking at him in the rearview mirror.

"Absolutely right, Mr. Harrison," the lawyer nods, reading comments on the contract. Sometimes I feel like he never lets go of the papers and works every free second.

"Daniel and I go on our pub route every Saturday, trying out new alcoholic beverages and meeting charming ladies."

My surprised gaze flickers between the boss and the lawyer. I would have never thought that these two are such close friends. At work, they maintain maximum neutrality and professionalism, giving no hint that they get drunk and pick up girls together on weekends.

"And why are you looking at us like that, Sophie?" Daniel chuckles, taking a break from the documents. "We're two eligible men in the prime of our lives. I'm deep into divorce, and Christopher is practically a virgin."

Mr. Harrison throws the parking ticket back, aiming for his colleague's face, and both burst into a low laugh. Unbelievable. I'm in a car with two men whose faces are framed by beards streaked with gray, and they are cracking friendly jokes in my presence. I don't know how to react. Etiquette and embarrassment prevent me from joining their conversation, and I blush as quickly as a mercury thermometer changes its readings in sudden temperature changes.

"Sophie," Daniel calls me from the back seat, "wouldn't you like to join us this Saturday?"

While I stare blankly ahead, Christopher shoots a squinted look at Daniel. Finding nothing better, I decide to maintain the tone of a casual conversation and turn everything into a joke.

"Mr. Harrison, did Mr. Brosnan just invite me to pick up girls in bars with you?"

"You can just call me Christopher," he requests without a hint of irony. "I'm afraid that with such a charming lady in the company, we'll probably be shielded from one-night stands. But I'm absolutely fine with that."

Those words make me look at him from a completely different angle. A handsome, well-groomed, self-assured man in a three-piece tweed suit has just given me an undisguised compliment. Who am I in his eyes? A valuable employee, a young beautiful woman, or perhaps both? In the enchantment of Alexander, I didn't even consider other men around me as potential partners or objects of desire.

Listening to myself, it feels like there's a Sahara desert inside. I want to agree to their offer just to avoid spending the weekend alone, but at the same time, I fear that our friendly gatherings will alter Christopher's attitude, and he'll stop being objective with me at work.

"Okay," I plunge in headfirst. It can't get worse than it is now, and distracting myself from the scratching cats in my soul is beneficial. "I'll be your guardian, Mr. Brosnan and Mr. Harri—" I catch a reproachful male glance and hide a smile. "Christopher."

"Sophie, just call me Daniel. It would be strange if you addressed your boss by his name and your colleague formally."

"Okay, Daniel," I respond, no longer feeling embarrassed, and reward them with a smile.

I hope my agreement won't affect the relationships in the team. As if reading my thoughts, Christopher turns to me, pausing at a red traffic light.

"Sophie," he says sternly, "as a newcomer to our bachelor group, I want to clarify just one rule: no matter what happens outside the office — at work, we remain professionals."

"Of course, Mr. Harr... Christopher," I overcome myself. "I understand perfectly."

Thoughts of Alexander are overlaid by constant concerns about whether I've done everything I was assigned. It's about to seem like my soul has healed. But upon returning home this Friday, I'm hit by a new wave.

Due to prolonged negotiations and the solemn signing of the contract, I return home almost at midnight. Even at the door, I hear the desperate cries of my cat, whom I left hungry. I've never turned the keys in the lock so quickly in my life.

I burst into the apartment, knocking everything in my path, and kneel beside the bewildered cat.

"Forgive me, my bun, my hungry one, my good one," I squeeze Oliver in my arms, causing him to scream even louder and scratch my hands.

Swallowing tears and cursing myself and Alexander for teaching me not to worry about the cat's dinner, I pour a double portion of the pet's favorite food into the bowl. When we were in a relationship, Alexander took on this role when I was late or held up at work.

Memories are the only paradise from which no one can expel us. And I allow myself to immerse in it.

Through the mist in my eyes, I watch as Oliver voraciously devours his dinner. I sit on the floor by the leg of the bar table and hug myself. I can't deny it anymore: no matter how much I pretended and busied myself with work, I still miss Alexander.

Between us, there was much more than a short-lived relationship, and I know it for sure. Although he annulled it all with just one action. And now I can't forget him and probably never will. He left an indelible mark on my character and my body. Alexander set the bar so high that he instilled in me the fear of not finding a better life and sex partner.

Without further deliberation, I reach into my coat pocket for my phone and open the taxi-hailing app, specifying the all-too-familiar address.

"Sorry, baby, I have to leave again," I stroke the cat, who doesn't notice me and goes to sleep on the couch.

Chapter 47

Sophie

I stop at the apartment door and slap myself on the cheeks with frozen palms. I rushed out of the house, even forgetting my bag, and now there's no makeup or mirror to tidy up. Not that I need it. The person inside the apartment will understand my state without words, and there's no need to hide my poor appearance.

With a sigh, I press the doorbell button and listen for the rustling behind the door. Thank the gods, she's home and, I hope, alone. I wouldn't want any extra eyes.

I barely have time to step back when the door swings open so abruptly it almost grazes the tip of my nose. Christine scans me with a squinted look from head to toe, focusing on my reddened and swollen face. We've been through a lot together, but I've never seen her like this.

"Hello," she greets coldly, showing no intention of letting me in.

Stiffening at such a reaction, I spasmodically try to understand what I did wrong. Maybe I woke her up? But Christine is standing in front of me in a sweater and jeans, as if she recently returned home. I doubt she sleeps in this attire.

"Uh, hi," I awkwardly smile, attempting to ease the tension between us. It feels like electric sparks of tension are flying, and I don't understand their origin.

I fervently believed that after the situation with Jeff, our relationship somewhat improved. Although lately, we haven't exchanged messages, but I attributed it to Christine's busy schedule in university, and I had other things on my mind. Emotionally, I wasn't ready to meet her, as she reminded me of Alexander. But tonight, I just didn't know who else to turn to, who else to complain to, and alone with my feelings, I can't endure any longer. My nerves simply can't take it, and I want to confide in my best friend over a glass of wine, sitting in the kitchen, as we used to do.

"Sorry for coming so late and without warning," I try to break the silence between us. "I need to talk to someone. Can I?"

Christine glances at me again and finally steps aside, allowing me inside.

"Thanks," I exhale in relief, crossing the threshold.

I'm not mad at Christine for that photo with my parents that led to my breakup with Alexander. She's just a daughter who wants her parents to be together again. Can you really be angry to someone for that?

"Tea?" Christine asks, walking to the kitchen. I quickly shed my outerwear and follow her.

"Yes, that would be nice, thank you," I sit at the table. "Can I help you?"

"No need, sit down," she clatters with dishes.

Accompanied by the boiling kettle, I wait for Christine to set the table. I twirl an oat cookie in my hands from a crystal bowl, mentally going through the words I want to say to her. I must not reveal Alexander, so I'll have to use the legend of the mysterious Mr. "A" from the hotel bar and our unclear relationship.

"So, are you going to sit there or finally tell me why your face is all flushed?" Christine pours herbal tea into cups. I smirk; she picked up the habit of drinking herbs in the evenings from me. Although right now, undoubtedly, something stronger would be preferable, but this will do.

"Well," I gather my strength to avoid saying too much. "Remember that man from the bar I told you about?"

"Of course, how can I forget," she chuckles, taking a seat across from me.

"I told you we were no longer together, but we kept in touch for a while. And now we've finally parted ways for good."

I observe Christine's reaction, but her face remains impassive. She looks me straight in the eyes with a glassy stare and calmly sips her tea. I contemplate what to say next, but I don't get the chance because she doesn't let me, hitting me right in the solar plexus with her words.

"So, did dad dump you?" she raises her eyebrows in feigned surprise. My heart pounds in my eardrums.

I straighten up, tensing like a string, and press my toes against the warm parquet floor. How did she find out? Did Alexander tell her? But why? It seems like the silent question: *"Did you know I was dating your father?"* is written all over my face because Christine smirks and places her cup back on the table.

"Did you think I was blind or completely stupid, and the letter 'A' in your phone didn't give it away?" she sarcastically remarks, continuing to batter me with her gaze and words. "Especially when you, like a complete idiot, waited for him in the freezing cold and hopped into his car."

Did she already know back then? Well, that settles it... We've spilled our secrets. I want to shyly cover my face with my hands, but I restrain myself. There's nowhere to hide; what's done is done. There's no point in denying what happened.

"Nothing worked out with Mr. 'A,'" she mimics, recalling my words from the distant past. "And why did you lie to your best friend's face? You know, it was amusing to watch your attempts to hide the truth."

"Christine, I didn't want this, really," I cover my eyes, intertwining my fingers under the table. Palms begin to sweat. "When we met, I didn't even know he was your father."

"Oh," she snorts, "save those excuses for someone else. You found out later and still acted like a complete jerk, running away from my birthday. I was worrying about you!"

I can't endure her judgmental gaze and rub my face with my palms.

"I was scared of losing you," I keep silent about the arrangement with Alexander. "Why didn't you tell me right away that you knew?"

"I just didn't care," she condescendingly remarks, shrugging her shoulders. "Mom had a plan to get dad back and you got in the way."

Well, it seems their plan worked. Now Alexander has returned to Laura. Everyone should be happy. Except for me.

"I didn't plan our relationship," I almost whisper in self-defense. "I just fell in love. Unexpectedly, even for myself Alexander reciprocated," Christine winces when I mention her father by name or talk about love. "We loved each other — that's for sure, and I would have told you about our relationship. Circumstances just didn't allow it."

"Do you think he loved you, and you're important to him?" Christine interrupts me indignantly. "He doesn't care about anyone but himself. Not even his own daughter! And what makes you better? Allowing him to fuck you?"

"You're wrong..."

"What?!" she waves her hands in frustration. "Oh, and why did he suddenly remember my existence after twenty years?"

"Your mother forbade him!" I blurt out without thinking, caught up in her tone on the verge of yelling.

Christine leans back in her chair. Emotions on her face change like a kaleidoscope but settle on something between surprise and irritation.

"You know nothing about my family," she hisses.

I want to say that she doesn't even have a clue about what really happened between Laura and Alexander, but I bite my tongue in time. I have already said too much.

"You know nothing about our relationship with Alexander to judge us so easily," I throw back at her. One-one. I didn't want this rivalry, but Christine's behavior forces me to speak to her in the same tone.

"I'm sure you should leave my house right now and never come back," irritation seeps through each of her words.

Without a word, I stand up and walk purposefully to the hallway. Christine doesn't even see me off, staying in the kitchen. There's absolutely no thought in my head, no anger or resentment towards her. Sooner or later, our paths were bound to diverge. We're just too different. To the point where our parting under these circumstances doesn't even cause an ache in my chest.

I sling my coat over my shoulder and jump into my shoes, not bothering to tie the laces. I'll do that in the taxi. I don't want to stay here for another minute. The door turns out to be unlocked when I press the handle and open it. But just at the threshold, another surprise awaits me.

"Sweetie, I was just looking for the keys," Liam raises his head, meeting my surprised gaze. "Oh, Soph, hi."

I look at my ex as if I've seen a person crawling out of a dumpster with moldy bread in their teeth and a banana peel on their head.

"Did you tell her?" I suddenly ask, a suspicion settling in me.

"Huh?" he stares at me in confusion. The bruises have already healed, too bad. "Oh, you mean about spreading your legs for her dad?" Liam shamelessly smirks. "I should thank you for that because Christine called me herself, asking if I knew about you and him. Funny that it was you who turned out to be our cupid, isn't it?"

I grimace and exit the apartment, purposely brushing against Liam's shoulder, making the bag in his hands fall to the floor.

"Hey, careful, bitch! Don't forget what I warned you about in the hospital!" this asshole yells at my back.

Laughing, I turn to him in the middle of the corridor.

"Don't come near you? And what's next? Will you tell her about me and Alexander?" I burst into sincere laughter. God, how could I have dated such an idiot?

Liam purses his lips, picks up the bag, and slams the door with a loud bang. I feel nothing but a wave of euphoria from the emotions after the conversation with Christine. Probably, this is how it should be when unnecessary people are sifted out of your life.

Chapter 48

Alexander

I've been sitting in the car for damn fifteen minutes, unable to get out and join my friends waiting for me in the bar across the street. Because I know the barrage of questions will start any moment now: "Where's Sophie?", "Why are you without Sophie today?", "Did Sophie get mad at us?", or "Did we say something wrong, and now you're hiding Sophie from us?".

Sophie. Sophie. Sophie. My hurricane that left chaos not only in the apartment but also in my head.

What should I say to their questions? That I messed things up with her, and now, like an idiot, I'm tormenting myself with my own decision, circling the city at night to the music she once played for me?

I hit my head against the headrest when memories of that day flood back.

Laura's apartment door is open when I arrive after a rushed call from Christine. I step inside and hear cheerful chatter mixed with laughter coming from the kitchen. Judging by the cleanliness of the floors and the mood of the girls inside, there's no sign of an emergency here. I want to spit in irritation right on the floor.

Deciding not to announce my presence, I silently move further into the apartment. Leaning against the door frame, I observe an astonishing scene: Laura and Christine are casually chatting about their girly stuff, both wearing smiles, each holding a cup of tea. Oddly, it's not a glass of spirits. It would look more natural in the hands of my ex-wife.

"Ahem," I clear my throat, signaling my presence.

Both comediennes jump as one. Laura immediately assumes the role of an incurably sick person, putting on a mask of suffering, while Christine leaps from the table and rushes towards me, raising her eyebrows in a makeshift expression of concern and comically trembling her lower lip, as if on the verge of tears. Actresses without an Oscar...

"Daddy, I'm so glad you came!" she squeals, wrapping her arms around my waist and pressing against my chest. "Mom felt so bad, I didn't know what to do."

I push Christine away, who seems to have forgotten that she's not five years old anymore, and grip her shoulders tightly, looking into her eyes.

"Is this really true, or are you staging another play?" I say deliberately sternly, although I already know the answer to this question.

"Daddy! How can you think that! Honestly! Mom is really, really sick," my daughter bats her eyelashes, trying to avoid my gaze.

I sigh wearily. How tired I am of this theater!

"Christine, please leave the room, and let me talk to your mom alone."

She quickly glances at Laura and, receiving a brief nod, exits the kitchen. Look at this well-coordinated team!

I take a seat at the table, clasping my hands together, and shoot my ex-wife a stern look. She continues to play her role of a dying swan, hugging herself and crumpling her pajamas as if trembling, lips quivering, eyes closed. It's so repulsive that it makes me nauseous.

"Laura, it seems you didn't understand anything from our previous conversation," she tries to interrupt me, but I raise my hand, asking her to shut up. "I'll repeat it once again: after what you did, everything between us is over. Back then, many years ago, you missed your only chance, though I doubt we would have lived happily. Eventually, we would have split anyway. Now I have my own life, and you have yours. We're connected only by our common daughter. I'm grateful to you for her, but that's my limit. Nothing has changed on my part: I don't love you, and I don't want to be with you."

A minute passes in silence, and I contemplate getting up and leaving when suddenly Laura smiles. However, the smile vanishes from her face a moment later, and she resumes her usual expression.

"If this is some kind of joke for you, I'd better leave," I attempt to stand up, but she stops me, grabbing my fingers.

"Alexander, nothing has changed on my part either: I'm ready to wait for you until you get tired of your Barbies. They will squeeze everything out of you sooner or later and leave, and I will stay with you forever," Laura says with a voice hoarse from smoking, looking into my eyes.

I frown, pulling my hand out of her firm grip.

"Do you even hear yourself? Where is your former pride? Where is that beauty pageant winner who toyed with naive guys and turned up her nose at them in favor of fat wallets? Or did she suddenly disappear when the man you never believed in managed to achieve his goals?" I spit out a long-held resentment.

"Alexander, when it comes to love, there's no room for pride," Laura purrs in a sweet voice.

Love? Is she talking to me about love? I snort, standing up from the table.

"You never loved me, and you probably don't even know what love is. It's time you admitted it to yourself," I declare.

"And do you know what love is?" Laura screeches, tearing off her mask and revealing her true face.

"Unlike you, I do know," I chuckle. "And you know, truly falling in love makes me realize that I've never felt anything like that for you."

The tea mug flies past me, shattering with splashes as it hits the parquet.

"Find a job, Laura," I enjoy the abrupt change in her expression. "You won't get a penny from me anymore. Christine is already grown up and lives separately, so I see no point in alimony."

"You set me up! You set everything up!" she screams at my back as I leave the kitchen and head away from this madness.

"Dad, are you leaving already?" Christine pops out of the bathroom, not understanding what's happening.

"Yes, and it's time for you to leave too. Go back to your place, and my advice to you — don't listen lies of your mother. Don't repeat my mistakes," I grab the doorknob, then turn to my daughter. "We'll meet next week, talk, and discuss everything. I'll call you."

Chapter 49

Alexander

"There he is! We thought you wouldn't show up," John stands up from the table and shakes my hand, patting my back with the other.

Nothing has changed in our favorite bar since our last hangout. It still smells of garlic croutons, which are in the top 5 most popular dishes on the menu, and it's still noisy and crowded.

"Sorry for being late, got caught up at work," I take off my coat and throw it over the back of an empty chair.

"Stevenson again?" Pierce smirks, tearing himself away from studying the bar menu.

"Yeah," I lie, scanning the room for a waiter. "Where's Julia and Sarah?"

"They decided to have a girls' night tonight. Wanted to invite your Sophie, but she refused," John says her name, and I sharply turn my gaze to him. They invited Sophie? Why didn't she go with them? Is she busy, or does she not want to see them because of me? No, Sophie is a sensible girl, and she really liked Julia and Sarah. So, she's busy. But with what? Or with whom? I don't even want to think about it.

"We thought you'd come with her," Pierce's voice interrupts my thoughts. "Does she have her own girls' night, or did you lock her at home?" he jokes, but I'm not in the mood for laughter.

I order a glass of red wine from the approaching waiter and wait for him to leave before announcing the latest news.

"We broke up," I say shortly, watching as John and Pierce's jaws slowly drop.

John recovers from shock first.

"What do you mean, broke up? Why?" he asks.

"Just like that," I shrug, folding a napkin into a paper airplane.

"Now I understand why you're so gloomy," Pierce chuckles.

"No, no, no, wait," John interrupts him. " 'Just like that' is not an answer. You never introduced your girls to us, but you introduced her, and you both were glowing with happiness last time. Even another call from Laura, after which you're usually down in the dumps, didn't seem to affect you. You were sitting there like a peacock with your tail up, patting her knee and smiling," he snorts. "Spill it."

I wait for the glass of red wine I ordered and drink half of it in one gulp, gathering the strength to tell my friends about my stupidity.

"It's bad," Pierce's eyebrows shoot up at the sight of my thirst.

"I'm an idiot," I rub my face with my palm.

"We know that. Tell us something new," John chimes in.

"I screwed up," I lean back against the chair. "First, I convinced both myself and her that because of our relationship, Christine would finally turn away from me for good. Then I got too involved in this game: eternal secrets, secret dates. It was so intense and on the edge that I got stuck in this swamp, and then I didn't even realize how I started to develop feelings for her."

"Wait a minute," John interrupts me. "I don't understand a damn thing. What does your daughter have to do with this? You even introduced her to Lola. What's wrong with Sophie?"

"She's Christine's best friend," I sigh.

"Are you out of your mind? How old is she?" Pierce chokes on his beer.

"As old as needs to be," I snap.

"Stop it!" John stops our argument. "Now, continue. I still don't get anything from your story."

They quiet down and look at me attentively.

"I fell in love like a teenager," I shyly cover my face with my hands, rubbing my skin until it turns red. "And then I got scared myself. Too much pressure: the perpetually troubled Christine, who, because of her character, would never be able to accept our relationship and most likely turn away from me for good, and I dragged Sophie along with me; her drive and love; our age difference and the swirling questions in my head 'what if she hasn't had enough fun yet? What if she treats me like Laura?' I got scared. I started preparing myself to break up with her."

"Idiot," Pierce snorts.

I silence him with a look, letting him know that I'm not finished yet.

"And then Christine called. She screamed into the phone that Laura was in bad shape, urgently needed help. I was with Sophie at that moment, we were having... a farewell sex, which she didn't even suspect. I planned to break up with her in the morning," I almost want to laugh at my own stupidity. "I rushed off, leaving Sophie at my place. I arrived to Laura's place, and this stupid bitch was fine. She was sitting there laughing at my daughter's jokes in the kitchen. They wanted to set up an ambush and set me up."

"Did they succeed?" John asks.

"They succeed to piss me off and make me make a final decision: to cut all ties with Laura forever."

"That's right, I've been telling you that for a long time," Pierce nods, munching on a garlic crouton.

"In the end, looking at all this mess, I realized one thing: Sophie is the best thing that ever happened to me, and breaking up with her would be the height of idiocy."

"So, what the hell?" John protests.

"Hold on," I interrupt him. "Listen to the end. I come home after Laura's stunt: the whole apartment is a mess, the terrace is wide open, dirt from the plant pot is everywhere, furniture overturned. I panicked, thought we got robbed, prayed that Sophie was safe. And then she comes out. Completely drunk. Shoves a photo in my face. Turns out Christine, an actress just like her mother, snapped a picture of us with Laura while we were talking in the kitchen and posted it online. Sophie thought I left her in the middle of the night after sex and rushed to make amends with my ex. It triggered me. It felt like I was back in the past when drunk Laura used to throw similar tantrums. Well, you can imagine the rest."

"Damn," Pierce whistles. "Now that's what I call soap opera. Never thought of turning your life into a series? You've got the resources; I think the project's profitability is guaranteed."

I ignore his jokes and finish the wine in my glass, taking a deep breath. It gets easier. Turns out, to understand the full idiocy of the situation and evaluate it from the outside, all I needed to do was share it with someone. I truly am a complete idiot. I called Sophie "little girl," but in the end, I turned out to be the little boy. I got scared of my feelings and the past, created drama out of nowhere... Very dignified for a forty-year-old man, you can't say otherwise. Bravo, Alexander!

God, what an idiot I am.

"I hope you realize everything perfectly well on your own, and I don't need to sit here and lecture you about what a jerk you are and that you shouldn't project your past onto the present," John asks, sipping whiskey from his glass with a businesslike demeanor.

"Hey, did she seriously drag one of those giant trees into the apartment?" Pierce persists.

John and I burst into laughter together. I catch myself thinking that for the first time in the past week, I'm genuinely laughing.

"You know what?" I stand up from the table under the questioning gazes of my friends. "I have to go."

I hastily put on my coat, driven by a firm confidence in my decision.

"Good plan, brother," John grins, saluting me with his drink. "Good luck. Don't mess things up again!"

Chapter 50

Sophie

Dressed to the nines, I stride irritably across the cobblestones, the heels of my ankle boots clicking. The bar Daniel and Christopher invited me to is located on the pedestrian street we used to love strolling down with Alexander. So, I keep getting thrown back into moments from the past.

There's no trace left of my former combativeness after the conversation with Christine and Liam. Now I feel like a fool who's overdressed and overdone with makeup. But there's no turning back: I'm almost there and backing out at the last moment (especially when I'm already half an hour late) would be quite ungraceful. Especially in front of my bosses.

Entering the bar, I scan the tables. What a mess. There's hardly room to swing a cat. All the seats are taken by men in expensive suits and painted beauties in designer clothes, sipping high-proof drinks and smoking hookahs. Good thing I ditched the comfortable jeans and flat-soled boots right away. I'd look extremely out of place here.

"Do you have a reservation?" a pleasant voice asks as the hostess materializes before me.

"I should be… meeting some friends," I hesitate, trying to spot my colleagues through the crowd and the haze of tobacco smoke. The dim lighting in the room doesn't help at all.

"Let me show you to your table. Under whose name is the reservation?" she asks, her finger with its long manicure tapping the tablet.

"Um... Most likely under Mr. Harrison. Christopher Harrison."

Girl looks up at me sharply, her dry smile turning friendly. Interesting reaction to my boss's name. I hope she wasn't one of those ladies who fell for the charm of these two single men at the height of their powers for just one night.

"So, you're with Christopher? Let's go then," she nods toward the back of the bar and leads me to the designated table.

"Sorry for the slightly inappropriate question, but why did you react like that to his name?" I ask, taking off my coat and voluminous scarf along the way.

"Mr. Harrison and his friend Mr. Brosnan are regular patrons here," she smiles. "Very pleasant and decent men, I recommend them," she adds with a wink.

I'm not sure who she mistook me for, but I feel uncomfortable. Maybe I overdid it with the short dress and high heels after all?

"Here we are, please," she points to the table in the corner of the room, situated between the panoramic window and the bar counter.

Daniel notices me first. Rising from the couch, he reaches out for my coat, handing it over to the hostess.

"Sophie, I'm so glad you could join us," the lawyer embraces me.

"Thanks for the invitation," I reply, taken aback by the emotional outburst of the always pensive and focused man. Apparently, this bar isn't their first stop for the evening.

"Sophie," Christopher nods and extends his hand. I place my palm in his, expecting a firm handshake, but my boss surprises me by kissing the back of my fingers. "Take a seat," he gestures to the spot next to him, neatly opposite Daniel.

I sit in the designated spot and focus on studying the menu intently, hiding behind my loose hair. The discomfort returns with renewed force. Maybe I shouldn't have accepted the invitation to Saturday drinks with these two. I feel like I won't be able to easily separate work from personal matters. It's hard to get the thought out of my head that Mr. Harrison is my boss.

"What will you be drinking?" Christopher inquires. "I recommend taking a look at their wine list. It's excellent."

I flinch. Anything but wine.

"I'll have a Negroni," I blurt out, the first thing my eyes land on in the cocktail list.

"Bold choice," Daniel comments, chuckling.

Only after the first sip do I understand why he reacted that way. The drink turns out to be very strong and bitter. I decide it's for the best. Just what I need to unwind.

Gritting my teeth, I down the first half. The cocktail I chose turns out to be completely out of my taste, but it starts to grow on me by the second. My tongue loosens, and a pleasant warmth envelops my body. Now I'm chatting away about movies, literature, and personal topics, keeping the conversation going as if I were a pro.

"Did you resolve that issue with Marie?" Christopher asks, taking a sip of his whiskey. I've already noticed that he prefers stronger, aged drinks.

"Thank God, yes," Daniel snorts. "Increased the alimony and let her live in peace."

"And who's Marie?" I chime in, slightly dazed by the amount of alcohol I've consumed.

"She's Daniel's ex-wife," Christopher replies.

"Ah, I see," I drawl, exhaling the fragrant smoke from the hookah. I've never liked them, but they always go down well when I'm drunk. Especially when Christopher taught me how to blow rings. Now I'm puffing away like a steam engine. And it looks beautiful; I've always admired the aesthetics of femme fatales with a cigarette held elegantly between their fingers.

"What about you, Sophie?" Daniel turns to me. "When was your last relationship?"

I cough at the unexpected question. This is definitely not the topic I want to discuss right now. Especially when I came to distract myself from failures in my personal life.

"I broke up with a guy a few months ago," I evade, deciding to keep quiet about my relationship with Alexander. Let them think that Liam was my last.

"How long were you together?" Daniel persists.

"Three years," I shrug, taking another drag.

Daniel lets out a surprised whistle, while Christopher silently observes our dialogue, furrowing his brow thoughtfully.

"Quite a while. Why did you break up?" he asks.

"He cheated on me," I reply, succinctly and without further elaboration. I hope this ends the unpleasant conversation.

"Danielle, don't embarrass Sophie," Christopher comes to my rescue, reclining on the couch and placing his hand on the backrest next to my shoulders, so close that I can feel the warmth emanating from his skin. "Let's ask something pleasant instead."

We sit for another half hour. Daniel and Christopher talk about something of their own, and I silently watch passersby through the window, not touching the remaining drink in my glass. I don't want to drink or smoke anymore. My mood gradually deteriorates, and the scenery outside the window dredges up warm memories of the two of us until it becomes almost painful.

My head starts to pound, whether from the alcohol I've consumed or the unfamiliar amount of nicotine in my system. I contemplate an urgent escape plan. I have neither the strength nor the desire to stay here any longer. The evening, which was supposed to distract me, instead throws me back into the past, which pulsates with pain in my temples and aching melancholy in my chest.

"I think I'll go," I smile uncertainly, interrupting the men's conversation.

"Sophie, is something wrong?" Christopher asks, concerned, this time placing his hand on my shoulder. But I want to be home so badly that I don't even notice the gesture. Why hasn't teleportation been invented yet?

"My head hurts, and I don't want to ruin the rest of your evening," I say, not needing to search for excuses, just speaking the truth.

"Of course," Daniel nods. "Headaches are no joke. We still need you in good health."

"I'll walk you," Christopher takes my coat from the hanger and helps me put it on.

I take a generous gulp of the freezing air when we step outside, but it doesn't get any better. My head continues to split apart.

"Tell me your address," Christopher asks, holding his phone.

"What?" I look puzzled at his profile.

"I'm calling a taxi," he smiles, displaying the open app.

"Oh, no, it's okay, I can manage," I reach for my bag to get my phone, but Christopher covers my trembling hand with his.

"Sophie, I'm walking you. I can't just let you go home in this condition. You're as pale as a sheet."

"What about Daniel? It wouldn't be right to leave him alone."

"Oh, don't worry about him. He's already found himself a charming companion. He won't be left in proud solitude, that's for sure," Christopher winks. "Shall we go?"

I ponder for a moment and then agree. I really don't feel well.

The journey home passes in complete silence. Christopher refrains from disturbing me further and occasionally throws concerned glances my way while I, leaning my forehead against the cool glass, breathe heavily.

"I'm sorry I ruined the evening," I apologize when we stand near my building.

I hope he won't insist on coming in to make sure I'm okay. But judging by the fact that Christopher didn't let the taxi go, asking it to wait for him, he doesn't intend to invite himself in for a cup of coffee. That's reassuring. I just want to be alone under a warm blanket as soon as possible.

"You didn't ruin anything at all," Christopher softly smiles. "You only made it more interesting."

An uncomfortable silence hangs between us.

"Hurry home and don't catch a cold," he says first.

Christopher brushes his cool fingers against my cheek, tucking the wind-blown hair behind my ear. I freeze, unsure how to react. There's chaos in my head and heart. I appreciate his concern, but at the same time, I want to see a completely different person opposite me.

"Goodnight," I whisper, swallowing a lump in my throat and lowering my gaze.

"Goodnight," Christopher bids farewell and kisses my cheek with warm lips.

Stunned, I watch him until he gets into the car, and it drives him away from my courtyard. I inhale sharply, because it seems to me that the blue Bentley parked nearby overtakes the taxi and pulls onto the road first.

I close my eyes and shake my head, and when I open them again, the silhouettes of both cars have vanished. I must have been so drunk that I'm now hallucinating.

Once home, I wrap myself in a voluminous blanket, like a cocoon. My breath catches in my throat, and my heart skips a beat as I close my eyes and imagine Alexander in Christopher's place. I can't do this anymore.

I reach for my phone under the pillow and open a familiar conversation.

I miss you.

I write quickly, so as not to change my mind, and press the "send" button. But the message doesn't reach the recipient, remaining on one side with a solitary checkmark beneath the letters.

I close my eyes again and allow myself to cry loudly.

Chapter 51

Alexander

The night passes like a in fog. I remember slamming the gas pedal to overtake that idiot's taxi and the desire to block the road and knock out every tooth of that bearded jerk. But I restrained myself. I gripped the steering wheel so tightly it felt like I might peel off the upholstery with my fingers, but I managed to overcome the burning desire to destroy everything in my path. Another call from my assistant, something about Stevenson showing off again, but I couldn't care less. I turn off my phone so no one else disturbs me and rush home. For the first time in years, I allow myself to get drunk and sleep to my heart's content.

I accept the paper cup of coffee and breakfast from my favorite café's courier. I have no energy to go to the office; my head is pounding as if a steamroller rolled over it. Hangovers and regrets — reasons why I've refrained from alcohol in large quantities, not counting the drunkenness of my ex-wife. That's done with. She won't manipulate me anymore, not even indirectly.

Standing over the kitchen sink, I pour the coffee into a proper cup and scoff at the cracked kitchen stove. It's a daily reminder of Sophie. My heart feels as this piece of household equipment right now. Intellectually, I understand that nothing special happened; he didn't even kiss her on the lips, let alone go home with her. But the fact that someone touched Sophie hurts to the core.

The only clear realization this morning is that I'm not ready to let Sophie go just like that. I still love her, and I doubt I'll ever stop. She's unlike any of my exes. Sophie is a hundred times smarter and more mature than all of them combined. And I'm just an idiot for allowing myself to succumb to weakness and break up with her, especially in such an ugly manner...

After breakfast, I turn on my phone and immediately receive several notifications. I don't have time to check them because Natalie is calling.

"Mr. Bailey, finally!" Natalie exhales in relief into the receiver. "Stevenson is literally trying to break into the office. He's stubborn as a mule."

"Natalie, you saw how I dealt with him. I trust you can handle it yourself. I'm unavailable to everyone today."

"But, Mr. Bai..." She interrupts in panic.

"Family reasons, Natalie," I emphasize the first word.

"Understood, sir," Natalie composes herself and hangs up. Smart girl, she knows that when I'm busy with family matters, it's better not to disturb me. She's been with me faithfully for over ten years.

Next, I call Christine and schedule a meeting with her later in the evening. It's time to resolve this unspoken issue with her mother. I realize it will hurt her, but she needs to know the truth, and Laura will never confess to what she's done.

Then I browse through the incoming messages, nothing interesting: a bunch from Pierce and John with questions like "how did it go?" and "did you mess up this time?" a reminder about the party this Wednesday, which my channel is covering, and another promotional email. And then I see it.

Stunned, I tighten my grip on the coffee cup. Sophie?

> I miss you.

That's it. Short and to the point. My heart skips a beat, and my head starts buzzing more actively. My girl misses me. So much so that she overcame her pride and wrote to me about her feelings. I look at the time the message was sent: almost immediately after returning home, after that kiss...

Like an idiot, I stare at the message for a few minutes and decide not to reply for now. First, I'll talk to Christine.

I nervously tap my fingers on the table, glancing at the clock. My daughter, as always, is in her element: half an hour late. Or maybe she just decided not to come out of spite, or Laura persuaded her not to. After another ten minutes of waiting, when I'm about to ask for the check and leave, Christine silently takes the opposite chair.

"Hi," I greet her, trying to conceal my irritation. It's absolutely unnecessary right now.

"You wanted to talk?" Christine gets straight to the point, then beckons the waiter and orders a glass of white wine. I grimace because I really don't want to see her slightly tipsy, but maybe it's for the best. It'll be easier to accept the truth that way.

"Do you want to eat first, or shall we start right away?" I backpedal.

"Let's get down to business. I ate at home," she says coldly.

Without further ado, I tell her everything. About how I met her mother, her betrayals, and the ultimatum banning me from seeing her. I don't even withhold my doubts from the past about whether I'm Christine's biological father.

By the end of my monologue, my daughter finishes her first glass of wine and immediately asks for a second. I don't blame her, fully understanding the emotions she must be experiencing right now. She lived with the belief that her mother was an angel in the flesh. Yes, flawed, but still her beloved mother, who raised and cared for her.

"So, she was right," murmurs Christine to herself as she gradually comes to her senses.

I scowl. Did Laura concoct something again, expecting me to tell our daughter the truth and make sure she wouldn't believe me? I wouldn't be surprised.

"Who?" I ask, more out of formality, already knowing the exact answer.

"Sophie," surprises me Christine. I frown even harder, so much so that my forehead begins to ache. What does Sophie have to do with this?

"What?"

"Oh, don't play dumb," she brushes it off. "I know you were dating."

I didn't get it. Did Sophie tell her everything? When? Why? Did she want to spite me? But that's not like her at all.

"How did you find out?"

"You two are lousy spies, you know," Christine smirks. "I first suspected from your meaningful looks and her mysterious 'Mr. A,' whom she slept with in a hotel at my suggestion. And then I was convinced when I saw her getting into your car after my housewarming. In case you forgot, the windows in my apartment overlook both sides."

Damn, I'm speechless... I can't find words to describe my state, and I have no idea how to react. Apologize or ask why the hell she advised her friend to sleep with the first person she met to forget her ex?

"Don't worry about it so much. You've already broken up," Christine says indifferently, shrugging.

"What if we get together again?" I'm testing the waters.

"I think Sophie will be happy. She came to me in tears the other day."

Her words leave a gaping wound in my heart. How bad was Sophie feeling that she risked going to Christine?

"Did she say anything about us?"

"No, she tried to pretend it wasn't you. But I told her I knew about you and kicked her out."

"Kicked her out? Christine, are you out of your mind?" There's a persistent desire to defend Sophie. It's not her fault that I messed things up for both of us. I'm pretty sure that at the time of our breakup, Sophie was already prepared to take our relationship to the next level and sacrifice her friendship with my daughter. For me...

"What was I supposed to do?" Christine protests. Her cheeks noticeably redden after telling about her mother. "Do you know how upsetting it is when your friend hides the fact that she's sleeping with your dad?"

"It was my wish," I take all the blame to somehow redeem Sophie in my daughter's eyes.

Christine scans me with her eyes, then takes a generous sip of wine, her attentive gaze never leaving me.

"Well, I'm inclined to believe that," she delivers her verdict.

"Listen," I exhale loudly, clenching my fist under the table, "everything I told you about your mother is true. And I understand how painful it is for you and how it will hurt when I say the next thing, but I ask you to understand, not to jump to conclusions, and not to give in to emotions, but to think everything over carefully. I love Sophie, like I've never loved anyone before. And I'll understand if you don't accept our relationship, but I want to ask forgiveness from Sophie, and if she forgives me, then we'll be together whether you like it or not."

Christine empties her second glass of wine in one gulp and abruptly rises from the table. I suspected she would do just that, so I'm not particularly surprised and am ready to listen to the torrent of abuse she's about to unleash on me.

"You know, yes, you're right. I'll never be able to accept your lies. Just like you'll never be able to accept and understand my relationship with Liam," Christine defiantly raises her chin and strides quickly towards the exit.

Damn. Liam... Well, I expected everything but this. She really hit me hard. The response hit the mark precisely.

In a fit of anger, I pound my fist on the table and crumple the napkin.

Breathe, Alexander, breathe.

Am I going to go and beat up that asshole who's so skillfully wormed his way into your life? No. I won't dirty my hands on him again.

Christine is a grown woman, and although she sometimes doesn't realize what she's doing, it's time for her to live her own life and learn from her own mistakes. I won't be able to protect her constantly, and she'll definitely decide about Laura herself. I have no doubt that if Christine is already on her way to her mother's house, the anger from our conversation won't be directed at me.

Resigned to my small defeat, I step outside, inhaling the crisp air and exhaling it back in a generous cloud of vapor. I head towards my car when my phone starts blaring with the familiar tune once again.

"Yes, Natalie," I answer much more amiably than in the morning.

"Mr. Bailey, I remember I promised not to distract you today, but I want to share some good news," the assistant sings joyfully. "I handled Stevenson myself today, just as you taught me. He and his manager haven't issued any ultimatums yet, and the filming day proceeded as scheduled."

"Excellent, Natalie, you're a star."

"And here's something else. I wanted to remind you about the AVD-Invest party celebrating the groundbreaking ceremony for the 'Black Pearl.' You must be there. Their CEO specifically requested your presence. Our filming crew is fully prepared for this Wednesday, and the host finally confirmed his attendance."

"Great, that's really..." I pause, frozen, holding onto the car handle. "Wait, did you say 'Black Pearl'?"

"Yes, that's the one. That long-awaited project. Remember, we were striving for exclusivity in covering it a few months back?"

"Yes, yes, I remember," gears in my head start spinning at lightning speed. "Natalie, do we have a guest list?"

"Of course, Mr. Bailey. It's already been sent to the TV-host for review."

"Could you check if the architectural firm handling their project is on the list?"

"One moment, I'll check," Natalie responds eagerly and starts clicking her computer mouse, the sounds of which reverberate in my eardrums like thunder. "Yes, they're on it. Invited are their CEO,

Mr. Dogerty, his deputy — lead architect Mr. Harrison, his assistant Miss Williams, their lead lawyer Mr. Brosnan..."

"Hold on, Natalie, that's enough, thank you," I end the conversation and plop down into the driver's seat with a joyful smile.

If this isn't fate, then I have no other explanations for why our paths are crossing again. I open the dialogue with Sophie and look at her last message. Don't worry, darling, we'll meet and discuss everything in person. Just wait a little while longer.

Chapter 52

Sophie

"Hello, my darling," my mom's voice chimes through the phone. "How are you? It's been so long since we've seen each other or talked. You've completely forgotten about your old folks."

Despite her stern tone, mom is laughing. How I've missed that familiar voice.

"Hello, mommy," I try to inject a cheerful tone into my voice, wiping away tears with cold fingers. "I'm fine. How's everything with dad?"

"Oh, you know, same old, same old. Home, work, home, work. Everything as usual," Mom chirps. "Come visit us soon. We're planning a barbecue for the holidays. And for Christmas, we'll have our traditional duck with apples and your favorite cake. Will you come?"

"I'm not sure yet, Mom. We just finished a project. Today we have a corporate event with the client to celebrate," I dab at my damp skin with napkins, watching my uncontrolled emotions in the mirror. "Can you imagine, they've entrusted me to lead the next one independently."

"My smart girl! I told you that your employer would definitely like you. You're beautiful and smart!" Mom exclaims.

"Mom, stop it," I smile against my will.

"What, stop telling the truth?" Mom chuckles. "As always, you underestimate yourself, my darling."

My head is full of turmoil after the long weekend our bosses organized before the celebration for completing the project. Christopher's kiss don't leave my mind, nor will Alexander's unanswered message.

So, it's hard for me to hear praise from Mom. I feel like a complete failure. There's a charming man caring for me, asking about my well-being after Saturday, offering to bring medicine when I decline a meeting due to a fabricated ailment, and yet I can't get my ex out of my head.

"Mom," I start hesitantly, "listen, you and Dad have a big age difference. Did you ever have problems because of that?"

Mom falls silent. Damn. I shouldn't have asked. Now she'll start imagining things she shouldn't. I hear rustling in the phone's speaker, followed by the sound of the door closing. Images flash before my eyes of Mom leaving the room, wrapping herself in a warm blanket, and going out onto the balcony to gossip with a friend.

"Dear, there are always ups and downs in relationships," Mom begins gently. "You know, there are no perfect couples who never argue. Ultimately, relationships involve two individuals with differences in character, especially when there's an age gap, and sometimes friction occurs, it's inevitable. Your father and I still argue to this day. But with time, it dulls, and the arguments don't seem as intense or as important as they did at the beginning. Now it's just playful banter. For example, yesterday we argued about musical preferences. You know how much Dad hates George Michael's tracks, and I simply adore them. Well, we argued, I endured another lecture on good music, laughed at our stubborn old man, kissed, and moved on. Why do you ask? Is something wrong?"

I remain silent, fully feeling the warmth of nostalgia for my teenage years when Mom drove me to school, and we sang her favorite songs, while Dad covered his ears if he was nearby. Tears well up once again, and I sob uncontrollably.

"Well, sweetheart, what's wrong?" Mom says gently.

"Promise not to judge?" I choke out into the phone.

"Sophie, when was the last time I judged you?" Mom protests. "Except maybe in your childhood when I changed your diaper, and you made such a mess that I had to soak you in the bath with several bars of baby soap."

I laugh through my tears. Mom always knows how to lighten my mood.

"I met a man," I begin tentatively, considering how to delicately present the situation to my mom.

"Ooh, do tell! I'm all ears," she responds eagerly.

"He's twenty years older than me," I continue with a sigh.

"Well, that's quite a gap, but love knows no age," my mom's voice carries no hint of judgment. It becomes a little easier to talk.

"He was married, and he has some unpleasant memories of his marriage. His wife cheated on him, then they had a daughter together, and she forbade him from seeing her unless he stayed in the marriage. But he couldn't because of the betrayal, so he just decided to provide financial support," I explain, my mom listening attentively without saying a word.

"Recently, we broke up because of his ex wife. Something happened to her, and he rushed to help her in the middle of the night, even though they hardly communicate. And then I saw a photo of them together in the kitchen, where she was perfectly fine, and they were all lovey-dovey. I freaked out, and when he came back, we broke up," I omit the whole truth because I don't want to tarnish Alexander's image in my mother's eyes.

"Alright, did you discuss this situation with him before breaking up?" she asks.

"Not really... Honestly, I wasn't in a state to discuss anything," I fiddle with the nail polish.

Mom falls silent for a few more seconds, contemplating the information I've given her.

"Firstly, Sophie, I've taught you since childhood not to jump to conclusions," my mom says deliberately stern. "Especially based on silly photographs. You don't know what really happened there to freak out. Secondly, if you're asking for my advice, then I'll tell you this: age difference is nonsense, and you can get rid of the ghosts from the past. Your dad didn't exactly meet me with a bouquet of flowers either. You wouldn't believe how many times his ex barged into our relationship. They, by the way, dated for several years before that and even planned a wedding, but broke up on the eve because she dumped him. We got married only after you were born. That's how afraid your dad was that I'd leave him at the altar. But we got through it."

"You never told me that," I mumble thoughtfully, trying to recall any mention of my dad's past, but nothing comes to mind.

"There was nothing to talk about. What's done is done. No need to dredge it up when everything's fine. But you didn't finish listening to my advice. So, listen carefully: if you love this man, just talk to him and calmly discuss what happened. I'm sure he's a reasonable person, and you'll come to an understanding. If not, then there's no point in suffering over jerks."

"Mom, you know I love you, right?"

"I love you too, my dear," she says softly, so softly it feels like she's hugging me right now. "Pull yourself together and don't lose heart. If he hurts you, just let us know, we'll send your dad to him. He'll show him what it's like to hurt Sophie Williams!"

After the conversation with mom, a sense of emptiness contrasts with a feeling of clarity. My mom's advice sounds reasonable, and I do feel like a fool for not immediately sorting things out with Alexander. But how do you talk to someone who doesn't even bother to reply to messages?

The urge to call Alexander and ask for a meeting vanishes instantly when I notice the time. I realize I have an hour and a half before leaving the house, and here I am still in pajamas with dirty hair.

I set a new record for getting ready. I hastily tie up my still damp hair, slip into a light tight-fitting silk dress, and apply quick makeup with a focus on red lips. When Christopher sends a message saying he's already downstairs, I grab my coat, slip on my boots, holding my heels in one hand and my purse in the other, and leap out of the apartment, promising the cat I'll be home soon.

"Good evening, Mr. Harrison," I greet my boss as I close the door behind me. Today, he came with a driver, so we settle into the back seat.

"Mr. Harrison again?" Christopher scoffs. "Good evening, Sophie."

I let his remark pass over me. The car moves off, and I, feeling the tension of silence, don't know where to put myself in the confined space. I realize we need to discuss his Saturday kiss and clarify everything so as not to give him false hopes.

"Mr. Har..." I pause. It would be strange to call him by his first name now. "Christopher, I would like to discuss what happened on Saturday."

He looks at me attentively, waiting for me to continue.

"That kiss... I don't know what it meant to you, but I'm not ready for any kind of relationship. I'm still dealing with a breakup and still love my ex-boyfriend. I don't want to send mixed signals or lead you on. That wouldn't be fair to you," I blurt out.

Christopher remains silent, his scanning gaze fixed on me. I brace myself for a barrage of questions or judgment, but he unexpectedly smiles.

"Sophie, I would be happy to have someone like you by my side. Smart, beautiful, and wise. But I'm not some jerk to force you into anything. I understood everything from your reaction."

"Thank you," I exhale in relief. It turns out Christopher is also a wise person.

"And don't worry, it won't affect our work relationship."
"Friends?" I ask the mature man, naively extending my pinkie.
Christopher laughs heartily, intertwining his finger with mine.
"Friends."

I step out of the car already in heels, and we briskly make our way to the restaurant doors. We leave our coats, and a waiter leads us into a huge Empire-style banquet hall, festively decorated for the Christmas. Everywhere are banners with the client's and our architectural bureau's logos. Half of the colleagues also came to celebrate the beginning of the joint project. Daniel is flirting with ladies, and Stella is sipping champagne, chatting with a group of strangers to me.

Christopher takes two glasses from the tray and hands one to me.

"Sophie, I need to talk to some people," he nods towards the men in perfect black suits. "Enjoy yourself, relax. If anything, you know where to find me. Anytime, don't hesitate," he brushes his hand over my forearm and leaves me in proud solitude.

I stand there, hesitating to even join my colleagues. Thoughts of Alexander once again engulf me at the wrong time. Should I have called him immediately? What if it's too late now?

I shake my head and take the first sip of champagne, which tickles my nose with bubbles. I need to relax and spend this evening in a cheerful mood. I'll worry about all the problems tomorrow. I try to detach myself, gripping the glass tightly. I make a promise to myself to drink half and then join Stella. There's no point in standing here like a statue. I turn around, trying to find my red-haired colleague, who has already fluttered away to a group of coworkers.

I bring the glass to my lips, intending to fulfill my plan, and freeze halfway. A pair of deep brown eyes meet mine.

"What is he doing here?" flashes through my mind as Alexander begins to move in my direction, his gaze unwavering.

Chapter 53

Sophie

I watch Alexander's every move, desperately hoping until the last moment that he's looking past me. But hope dies last. The man of my dreams is moving straight towards me.

No matter how prepared I felt for this conversation, when there are only a few seconds left before he reaches me, I want to shamefully tuck my tail and run in the other direction. A swarm of thoughts whirls in my head. What does he want from me? What will he say now? And what should I say? After all, I've already told him. Sent a message, but he didn't reply.

As always, Alexander looks immaculate: a luxurious dark blue suit with a double-breasted jacket, shoes polished to a shine, a watch on his wrist, and hair slicked back. My breath catches as the familiar scent of his cologne caresses my nostrils. My hands start to tremble, which doesn't go unnoticed amidst the waves of champagne.

Alexander stops just inches away from me. He's silent. He looks and he's silent. It's piercingly acute, as if he's peering into my soul and pulling out all the most intimate thoughts. And then he covers my hand, halting the storm in my champagne glass.

"I miss you too," his velvety voice penetrates my ears, enveloping them from the inside. Time seems to stand still, and the world narrows down to just the two of us.

One short sentence. One response to my message. But not through a phone, but in person. If it weren't for Alexander's hands, the drink would have spilled long ago, and the shards would have scattered across the corners.

"Why didn't you reply right away?" I don't recognize my own voice, as if I'm hearing it from the outside.

"It's a long story," his lips twitch. Before I can protest, he adds, "Which I'll gladly tell you, but in private."

"Do you think I need to hear it?" remnants of indignation and hurt make their way out, escaping with clumsy words and a lifted chin.

"WE need it," he emphasizes the first word. My heart skips a beat and starts racing.

"We. We. We," drums beat in my head.

"Are you sure?" I ask with doubt.

Alexander sighs heavily and removes his hand. I want to scream for him not to let me go. Everything inside me rebels against the cold I feel without his touch. How acute it is right now, when the faint chance of our reunion flickers on the horizon.

"Shall we talk?" he nods towards a small corridor with a nook and a door for the service staff.

"Do we have anything to talk about?" Oh God! Why can't I just say yes?! Stubborn as a mule.

"We do," Alexander cuts in and wraps his arm around my waist, setting the direction.

I step forward with wobbly legs and hand the glass to a passing waiter. I don't want to cloud my mind anymore. Now I need clarity of mind and a calm emotional background. Mom is right; we need to listen to each other, and most importantly, understand.

We step into the dark corridor, stopping a distance away from the door. I lean against the wall, facing him, waiting expectantly as I gaze into his black eyes.

"I really miss you, Sophie," Alexander begins. "I acted like a complete idiot when I left you and spewed nonsense. Age difference and all that talk are irrelevant. You're the most mature and intelligent woman I've ever met in my life."

My heart somersaults. We're silent, staring at each other. I digest what's been said. It turns out the reasons for our breakup were fabricated. Why?

"Are you with Laura?" I force the question out. I'm afraid to hear the answer.

"No, I wasn't, and I don't plan to be. We stopped talking completely that morning," Alexander admits, and it hits me like a lightning bolt. I stop understanding what's happening.

He ended things with Laura, but when he came home, he broke up with me. A lump forms in my throat, and my head feels fuzzy.

"Why?" I ask, my voice strained.

"I got scared," he tightens his lips into a thin line. It's evident that these words are difficult for him.

"Why?" I feel like an idiot asking such simple questions, but there's nothing else.

"Let's talk about it in a more pleasant setting," Alexander suggests, placing his hand on my forearm. Goosebumps run down my skin from the familiar touch. Emotions swell inside me, on the verge of bursting. Just a little more, and I'll shatter into a million pieces right under his feet.

I can't utter a word. Stupor engulfs my entire body. Pride and hurt battle with tenderness and love. The eternal struggle of heart and mind. Just say yes, Sophie, I beg. Snap out of it. Remember Mom's words.

"Will you allow me to take you out for breakfast tomorrow and explain everything? Will you listen for at least fifteen minutes?" Alexander asks again, seeing that I'm not reacting to his words. He places his other hand on my bare shoulder and gently strokes my skin with his thumb.

I nod silently.

"Thank you," he smiles with his usual warm smile. "Just know that I want to be with you and only you."

It feels like a stab to the heart. Why are you doing this to me?

"Will you allow me to be your companion tonight?" he asks another question.

Again, I nod silently.

"Then let's go," he wraps his arm around my waist, pulling me close, and leads us into the banquet hall, where everyone has already gathered near the stage.

The evening passes in complete stupor. I don't understand what's happening, and there's complete dissonance in my head. Alexander's hand rests on my back the entire time, stroking the exposed patches of skin, sending a million goosebumps down my spine. Even after all this time, my body responds to his touch just like before. It's as if we never parted.

The only thing unfamiliar is that we're in front of everyone. Alexander, without hesitation, introduces me to his numerous acquaintances and colleagues, sometimes kissing the top of my head and pulling me closer. I try to engage in conversation with everyone, or simply nod in a friendly manner at the right time. But my thoughts are in a completely different dimension.

What happens now? Are we back together?

Tomorrow, we'll discuss every question that concerns me, and today, I'll try to relax. Alexander admitted he misses me and that he got scared. I'm sure he has valid reasons for it. And he's not with Laura. That's the most important thing. He didn't leave me for her. He didn't betray me.

Finally, everything Alexander said sinks in. My lips involuntarily stretch into a smile. I stop listening to the CEO of the client company speaking from the stage. He seems to be thanking everyone involved and congratulating on the successful start of construction. I slide my hand under Alexander's unbuttoned jacket and embrace him around his waist. He's surprised but doesn't show it. He only momentarily moves his hand away from my back and places it on my shoulders.

This evening was initially supposed to be one of the key moments in my nascent career. Yet, it turned out to be the most important in my personal life as well. Fate is the villain, and she knows how to manipulate time and present interesting surprises.

After the formal speeches and a small buffet, the entertainment part of the evening is announced — champagne flows freely, and the music plays non-stop. One of the first performers on stage is none other than Mom's favorite singer. I poke Alexander in the side and chuckle. This is a sign sent from above.

"What's up?" Alexander asks tenderly. His breath tickles my hair.

"Do you want to dance?" I raise a playful gaze at him. A slow song just started playing. It seems like the perfect time to declare a truce. I've been acting all evening as if I were the offended Snow Queen. Mom wouldn't approve and would say, "Be smarter, Sophie."

"With pleasure," his eyes sparkle with my initiative.

I thought we'd dance somewhere on the sidelines of the hall, but Alexander intertwines our fingers and leads us to the center of the dance floor. He confidently enfolds me in his arms and starts dancing. His boldness rubs off on me. I press closer, closing my eyes with happiness. It's the first time we're openly displaying our feelings to those around us. I can't believe this is really happening.

Butterflies flutter in my stomach, tickling me from the inside. If I could squeal with delight right now, I definitely would. But I don't want to scare off this moment of tenderness.

As the music draws to a close, Alexander loosens his embrace and steps back slightly. Frowning, I lift my head, meeting his warm smile. And then something happens that I never expected. Alexander leans in and kisses me on the lips. Not deeply, but not hastily either, keeping the kiss within the limits of what's acceptable in a public place. My legs go weak, and my head completely stops functioning. His hands hold me tighter.

He did it in front of everyone. No more secrets or mysteries.

Alexander breaks our kiss. We stand there like two idiots, looking at each other and smiling, as if the world around us doesn't exist.

"I love you," he says with his lips.

"I love you too," I confess, my breath catching from the sincerity of the moment.

Out of the corner of my eye, I notice movement to the side. I divert my gaze from Alexander and see Stella waving her hands. She winks and gives two thumbs up. I want to laugh, but then I notice Christopher behind her, who can't take his attentive eyes off me. Catching my gaze, he smiles and raises his glass in a salute. I feel a weight lift off my shoulders. Christopher is a wise man, and I'm sure he'll understand everything.

Chapter 54

Alexander

Tonight, I hardly sleep at all. I haven't been this nervous since my university days. I don't know how I managed to resist staying at Sophie's home when she kissed me so tenderly in the car and urged me to come up. But I held back. Because I want to talk to her first, and then we'll see how she reacts to my words.

Buoyed by the success of last night, I rush to Sophie's house at full speed. I arrive ten minutes early, but she's already standing by the entrance, engrossed in her phone, shivering from the cold. I honk the horn. Sophie immediately looks up and meets my gaze. She smiles. I'm ready to do anything to see that happy smile as often as possible.

"Why are you standing in the cold?" I turn on the seat warmers and crank up the heater to full blast to warm her up quickly.

"I was waiting for you," she smiles.

I never thought I could feel such all-encompassing tenderness. They say, "You don't know what you've got until it's gone." It is fucking truth.

I lean into Sophie and steal a kiss from her lips. She responds eagerly.

I was so afraid she wouldn't want to see me. I was trembling before entering the banquet hall yesterday. I've never been this nervous even during exams. And how calm I felt when she agreed to talk to me. I keep silent about what I felt during our dance and public kiss. It seems that's when I became billions of times richer, simply because she's by my side.

No money on Earth can compare to the amount of love Sophie shares. It's hard to grasp that her feelings are directed solely at me, that she truly loves me.

We drive to the café with our favorite tracks playing. Once, we listened to them while cruising the city streets at night, and now we calmly drive in broad daylight, not hiding our feelings and humming familiar refrains.

In this simplicity of the moment lie the happiest minutes of life with a loved one, which you don't remember in the mundane routine but etch into your memory and recall in moments of solitude.

I give us time to enjoy hot, aromatic coffee and bagels before broaching serious topics.

"So why didn't you reply to my message right away?" Sophie sets her spoon aside and looks at me with a mischievous smile. There's not a hint of judgment or anger in her gaze. That's reassuring.

I wipe my mouth with a napkin and decide to speak honestly. There's no point in hiding anything. We've already learned that it leads to nothing good.

"I saw you with your boss and drove away, turning off my phone to avoid causing trouble."

Sophie leans back in her chair, surprised.

"So, it was not a figment of my imagination... I mean... I saw your car that evening."

"I hoped to go unnoticed," I chuckle, taking a sip of coffee from my mug.

She's silent for a few seconds, then blurts out:

"Christopher and I... There's nothing between us."

"Sophie," I reach across the table and cover her hand with mine, "I know."

"Then why did you hesitate to respond?" She looks at me intently.

"I wanted to tell you in person."

"You knew I'd be at the party?" She squints. Her pretended indignation makes me smile.

"Of course, my channel covered this party. I had a guest list," I shrug, popping another piece of bagel into my mouth.

"You sly fox," Sophie tosses a crumpled napkin at me and laughs, then adopts a serious look. "Tell me what happened that day."

The time for the most important conversation has come. I don't need to prepare for it; I've been ready to bare my soul to Sophie for a long time now. If she accepts all my flaws, then I'll be the happiest person in the world. And if not... well, so be it. I'll accept whatever decision she makes.

"Christine and Laura set me up. They concocted a story that Laura wasn't feeling well, to lure me to her place. But they forgot to play their roles until the end: I caught them laughing in the kitchen, as if nothing had happened. Laura was crying, begging me to stay. She got too carried away with this game, which I'm thoroughly tired of. I told her she couldn't contact me anymore and I stopped paying alimony."

Sophie frowns, processing the information she's received. Her hands nervously fidget with the edge of the tablecloth, and her eyes scrutinize my face.

"And Christine?"

"What about Christine?" I'm surprised. "She's a grown young lady. It's time for her to learn from her mistakes and live her own life. I'll support her financially, of course, but nothing more. Let her learn from her failures, pick herself up, and move on."

"Are you sure you shouldn't keep an eye on her? She might get into trouble," I hear concern for Christine? After what she did to Sophie?

Once again, I admire Sophie's wisdom and strength of character.

"She needs to grow up. She won't be able to do that under my constant supervision. She'll become a copy of her mother, and I wish her a decent future, not to become an alcoholic at twenty and end up with liver cirrhosis."

Sophie nods.

"Then why did you... break up with me?" She bites her lip. I want to hug her right away and never let go. To envelop her with care and warmth, so I never see that sad look again.

"I was scared of my past," these words are difficult for me, but I continue. "I saw the wrecked apartment, you drunk, hysterical, and I was afraid you'd leave me, like Laura wanted to do back then. Find someone better than me and replace me with them. But I forgot that you're completely different. I scared myself and ran away from my own problems like a fucking coward. Not from you."

Sophie squints, then opens her moist eyes and looks straight into my soul. Please don't cry, I beg. My heart can't take it. Unsettling thoughts start to flicker in my mind.

"When did you decide to come back?"

"On Saturday, when I came to you," I smirk, recalling that evening. "Pierce and John opened my eyes to what a jerk I've been."

"You're not a jerk," she shakes her head and stands up from the table. I'm ready to jump up to follow her, but Sophie surprises me —

she sits right on my lap and hugs me around the neck. "You just got tangled up. It happens. Thank you for sharing with me," she whispers in my ear and kisses my cheek.

Everything inside me explodes, as if a rock guitarist in a creative burst of euphoria breaks the strings of his instrument.

"I've told you before, you're the wisest one I know," I pull her body closer to mine.

"At least a hundred times," Sophie laughs, burying her nose into my neck.

"I love you," I brush my cheek against her forehead.

"I love you too," she kisses my collarbone.

"Christmas is coming soon," I remind her of the approaching holidays.

"Yeah, time flies so fast," Sophie sighs, her warm breath brushing against me.

"I plan to spend it with family: mine and my bride's parents."

A few seconds of silence. Sophie straightens up abruptly and looks me straight in the eyes.

"Whose parents?"

"My bride's," I smile and reach into my jacket pocket for the red box that's been waiting since Sunday. "Sophie, will you marry me?"

I open the lid with its golden ornament and reveal the platinum ring with an oval emerald surrounded by tiny diamonds. I watch Sophie's astonished face as she shifts her gaze between my eyes and the ring.

"Are you serious?" she whispers.

"As serious as can be," a nervous chuckle escapes me involuntarily.

Sophie breathes heavily, then with a joyful cry, she throws her arms around my neck and squeezes me tight.

"I do, I do, I do," she whispers in my ear, covering my face with kisses.

I slide the ring onto her slender ring finger and admire the sight. Once, I would have been horrified at the thought of proposing to someone, but with Sophie, everything is different. She has radically changed my life for the better, and I want to do the same for her.

"Now we need to break the news to my parents," she fidgets nervously on my knees. "They'll be shocked..."

"They won't. I've already talked to them."

"What?!" Sophie exclaims, looking shocked at me again.

I burst out laughing. It seems like everyone in the café is now watching us like we're crazy.

"I asked your father for his blessing," I shake my head, remembering how sternly her father looked at me when I showed up at Sophie's parental home.

"Wait, when did you manage to do that?" she claps her eyes, trying to mentally count something.

"On Monday."

"Does Mom know about this?" Sophie squints.

"Of course, I went through a long interview with her too," I chuckle.

Sophie's mom should work as HR at a large company. She practically asked me to fill out a whole questionnaire before hugging me like family and praising the choice of the beautiful ring. *"It will complement her eyes perfectly,"* she sniffed when she saw the green emerald.

"Holy moly, Mom's like a secret agent!" Sophie blurts out unexpectedly and giggles. "I was wondering why she insisted so much on talking to you."

"You talked to her?" I'm surprised because I asked her parents not to mention the surprise beforehand.

"Yeah," Sophie looks embarrassed, averting her gaze, "I told her a little about our story and Laura... Sorry."

"It's okay," I encourage her with a kiss on the nose. "She knows. I talked to her about it."

I recall the serious conversation in the kitchen, alone with Sophie's mom. She listened to me calmly and didn't once look at me with judgment. Of course, she said I was a fool to miss out on such a gem as her daughter, but she didn't criticize and just advised on how best to approach. Nothing new; I was ready for an honest conversation myself.

"What about your parents, and Christine?" Sophie asks with a panicked horror, covering her mouth with her hand. The ring sparkles in the morning sunlight. It's still hard to believe she said yes.

"Trust me, they'll be happy to see such a charming girl like you as my life partner. And Christine already knows, I talked to her. It'll take her some time, but I bet she'll handle it," I nod confidently and cover Sophie's lips with a kiss.

Enough thinking about others; it's time to enjoy moments for just the two of us.

Epilogue

The night city sprawls at my feet. It twinkles with a million golden lights, as if a generous handful of sparkles were scattered onto a black textured canvas. The sky is clear, and the bright moon illuminates the warm summer night.

I hear Alexander even before he opens the hotel room door and takes a step across the threshold. In the reflection of the panoramic windows, I see him entering the room, holding a bottle of champagne and two glasses. He's whistling a familiar tune to himself.

Today marks exactly one year since I met the man of my dreams. It was in this same place and this very room where we spent our first night together. Today, we'll celebrate our first wedding night.

"What a beautiful night, isn't it?" he smiles, placing the bottle on the coffee table.

I turn towards Alexander and watch as he pours the drink into the glasses. The black tuxedo sits perfectly on him, and the wedding ring, shining with silver, adds a touch of masculinity. I suggested he forego such symbols, but he looked at me as if I were crazy and said he wants a constant reminder of happiness in his life.

Alexander takes the filled glasses and moves towards me but freezes a meter away, surveying me from head to toe. I twirl around, showcasing my wedding dress once again. I chose a simple white silk gown with thin straps, an open back, and a boat neckline. Simple and elegant, without unnecessary details.

"You look stunning, Mrs. Bailey," Alexander admires.

"To match my husband," I overcome the distance between us, taking my glass and kissing his lips.

Finally, we're alone on our special day. The entire day was spent with parents and friends, first at the registry office and then at a restaurant. We opted for an intimate wedding, inviting only close ones. Alexander's parents showered me with kisses on both cheeks at every convenient moment, giving compliments and praising their son for an excellent choice, making me blush.

My parents, in turn, welcomed Alexander into the family with open arms. Mom liked him right away. She was thrilled with the charismatic and caring man. Especially when he helps with chores when we visit for holidays or just barbecue. Dad took a bit longer to warm up to him. But that's just how dads are.

Once, after a couple of glasses of whiskey, dad admitted that he can't believe his little daughter grew up so quickly and will soon start her own family. We all ended up crying then. Well, my dad ruined this magical moment when he asked us to hurry up with grandchildren. I told him not to count on them anytime soon. I still plan to finish my education and climb the career ladder. We'll see where it goes from there.

Christopher, by the way, personally gave me a bouquet of flowers when he heard that I was getting married. It was hard not to know about it because Stella announced it to the entire office. She and I seem to be good friends now, though she doesn't know how to keep a secret. Also, I got a permanent job after the second successful project. I dread how I'll juggle work and my master's degree starting this fall.

My former best friend couldn't come to the wedding. Christine got herself into trouble again. Liam pulled her into a bad crowd, and she started using drugs without any boundaries. Alexander's patience soon ran out, and he couldn't bear to see his daughter ruining her life anymore.

There was a big scandal. Liam hid somewhere from Bailey's anger. The decision to send Christine to a rehabilitation center and then to study at a university in England, Alexander made independently. Although, of course, Christine blamed me for everything. Saying that I want to get rid of her because I'm not ready to share Alexander with her.

Complete nonsense.

On the contrary, I wanted them to reconcile and actively encouraged Alexander to make amends with his daughter. But he's not ready for that yet. When he is, I'll support him.

No one has heard from Laura in a long time, not even her own daughter. It seems she found herself a new sponsor. I hope everything worked out for her in life, and she got her act together.

Pierce and John came to the wedding with their girlfriends and were just as happy as we were. They wished us all the best and never to put each other through this crap again because they don't want to clean up this mess one more time. We laughed together at this joke.

In retaliation, I chuckled slyly when Pierce's girlfriend caught the bride's bouquet, and he stood there with his eyes wide. I aimed on purpose.

"If you only knew how much I love you, my wife," Alexander hugs me with one arm with a satisfied smile.

"I love you more, my husband," I nibble on his chin.

"Oh, no, you don't," Alexander shakes his head and takes my glass, placing it on the table.

He lifts me off the floor and carries me to the bed. The hot scenes that happened here a year ago flash vividly and clearly in my memory.

"I don't want to take your dress off; stay in it a little longer," Alexander's voice is hoarse as he covers my neck with wet kisses.

I squirm on the sheets, unable to contain my desires any longer. I've been dreaming about this all day, looking at my magnificent husband. I wrap my legs, still in sandals, around his torso and hug him by the shoulders.

"What an impatient wife I have," Alexander smirks, feeling the straps of lingerie under the dress.

I completely dissolve in him as he plunges into me fully and makes me scream with uncontrollable sensations. Sex with Alexander is always intense and feels more like a union of two souls than a dirty affair.

I hope we won't lose this fire but carry it throughout our lives.

Half a year later

The glass cologne bottle with a clang falls onto the marble floor of the bathroom. It seems like I owe Alexander two of those already. But I'm not thinking about that right now. I stare in shock at the plastic stick lying on the edge of the sink and take two steps back, not realizing I'm stepping on glass shards piercing into my bare heels.

I slowly sink onto the closed toilet lid and touch my burning cheeks with icy palms. God, what should I do?

"Are you alright? I heard a noise," Alexander opens the door and scans the room until his concerned gaze falls upon me frozen in place.

"What happened?" He rushes to me and grabs my leg, which is bleeding. "I'll get the first aid kit now."

He steps around the puddle of cologne and opens the lower drawer, pulling out a white container with a green cross on top. He places it on the countertop, opens it, and accidentally knocks pregnancy test, which falls straight into the sink. I see in the mirror reflection how Alexander frowns and then retrieves a plastic stick.

"What's this?" He turns to me with the stick in his hand, twirling it between his fingers until he finds the result.

I stay silent. My thoughts are too far away. I dread what's coming next.

"Sophie, are you pregnant?" He asks with a sigh.

I nod and swallow convulsively, not fully realizing that it's true.

Alexander closes the distance between us and envelops me in his arms, lifting me off the ground. I feel like I'm about to be sick from excitement. Or is it sudden morning sickness? I don't even know anything about how pregnancy works!

"Put me down!" I pound Alexander's chest with my fists.

He puts me back in place and sits next to me on his knees.

"Dear, what's wrong?" He asks, gently tucking a strand of my disheveled hair behind my ear.

"I'm not ready," I shake my head. "What am I going to do? What kind of mother will I be? I haven't even finished my master's degree yet. What will I tell at work? How will I give birth? What will I do with the baby afterward?"

Alexander chuckles, embracing my face with his palms.

"Sweetheart, come on," he kisses the tip of my nose. "I'm here, and I always will be. We'll handle this together. We'll attend young parent courses, learn how to swaddle plastic babies. And besides, we have mothers who've been through this. They'll help. We'll figure out your work. I'm sure they'll give you maternity leave, and then you'll easily return to your job. You're an irreplaceable employee. We'll sort out your studies too. I'll talk to the dean, we'll settle this."

Tears stream from my eyes like wild rivers. Why did I get such a caring husband? After Alexander's words, I feel a little calmer. I'm not alone. Now I have the best husband in the world by my side.

"Baby," Alexander affectionately says and wipes tears from my cheeks, smiling gently, "you'll be a wonderful mother, you'll see. Our baby is so lucky to be under your heart."

I sob and pick up the test from the floor.

"Look," I point to the result.

"Hmm?" he looks puzzled, examining the letters.

"4 weeks," I wipe my wet nose with my sleeve. "We were in our favorite place back then."

I remember two weeks of paradise in Barbados, where we returned exactly a year later after that fateful trip. Hmm, every time we return from there with surprises.

"A truly magical place," Alexander snorts and hugs me tightly, kissing every inch of my skin.

In the circle of his arms, I feel like I'm in the safest place on Earth. Our baby is incredibly lucky. Alexander will be an amazing and loving father. I know that for sure.

Acknowledgments

Thanks to everyone who read the story of Alexander and Sophie! I know the emotional rollercoaster may have left you breathless at times, but now you can exhale and be happy for our love birds.

Thanks to my online readers whose unwavering support and genuine feedback have been invaluable to me as an author.

I would like to thank my family for standing by me throughout the writing process. To my mom, who watched me cuddle with my laptop even by the pool while on vacation in Rhodes in September 2022 (when the Forbidden Secret was taking shape). Thank you for reading my book and not believing that I could write such an ending. You know me too well :)

To my dad, who has guided me in my professional journey and steadfastly awaits the audio version of the book as a matter of principle (fingers crossed it arrives soon!)

To my grandmom, who is shocked by the morals of young adults. Thank you for reading the book in one day and calling me right away. Your opinion is always important to me.

To my designer, thanks to whom we can enjoy the beautiful design of this book. Thank you enduring my countless edits :)

And last but certainly not least, to my "A", who unexpectedly entered my life when I was writing the ending of this book. Thank you for your support and faith in me. And for blowing my mind every time you act like Alexander.

PS: You can find the first chapter of Forbidden Freedom on the next page ;)

XO Elisabeth

Turn the page to dive into Christine and Ethan's story in the second book of *Forbidden series*...

Chapter 1

Nowadays, England

"Christine, have you heard the news?" Selina asks in a hushed voice, trying not to disturb the silence of the library.

We sit at a long table between towering oak shelves filled to the brim with books. It's the epitome of British libraries in ancient universities. When I first arrived here, it felt like I had stepped into a Harry Potter movie.

Selina's long chestnut hairbrushes against my hands, tickling my skin. With this external attribute, she reminds me of my best friend. Or rather, my former best friend...

I shake my head, pushing away thoughts of the past. Enough, Christine, stop it. You promised yourself!

"What gossip have you heard this time?" I anticipate the topic of conversation, seeing her eyes gleaming with excitement.

Selina Howard - daughter of one of the Earls of England. Along with the title, she inherited a splendid estate more reminiscent of a castle; a subscription to gossips about the Royal Family firsthand; several brothers and sisters ready to tear each other apart for inheritance; a love for wagging tongues and afternoon tea with milk.

In short, the quintessential British dream.

"Why do you think it's gossip?" She rolls her eyes and leans back in her chair, swaying her long hair. I recoil from those that stick to the gloss on my lips. "Maybe it's urgent news related to our studies and doesn't require postponement?"

The local bookworm sitting across from us shoots a disapproving glance and points a finger in a "quiet" sign on the bulletin board. Then she briskly adjusts her old-fashioned metal-framed glasses and buries herself in a biology book.

Selina mimics her and makes faces. I smile at her antics. Here's a representative of a noble family, bound by blood ties to the British monarchy.

"Then spit it out," I soften the tone of my voice slightly and smile at Selina, pretending to be engrossed in a book on 20th-century architecture, which I need to present a report on next week.

Selina straightens up and leans closer to me again.

"Remember Mr. Fincher fell ill with a heart attack last week, and everyone was guessing who would teach art history today?" The fire in her eyes ignites with each word.

"Well, what about him?" I impatiently urge her on. I don't like it when she beats around the bush.

Her pupils dilate with anticipation of dropping a news bomb on me.

"A young, sexy professor will take his place!" Selina squeals, earning another disapproving glance from the bookworm.

In our university, there are indeed few young professors, but they never caused such a stir among Selina like news of a new teacher did.

"And what?" I inquire, fluttering my eyelashes in puzzlement.

Selina looks at me as if I'm daft.

"You don't understand," she shakes her head, waving her hands. "He's only a couple of years older than us. He's just twenty-six, and he's already a professor! It's a record for our university. They say he's unbelievably smart. Smart and handsome," Selina sighs dreamily and closes her eyes.

Hmm. When I enrolled in one of England's oldest universities and met the daughter of the Earl, I never thought I'd be involved in such a conversation. I thought that the rigorously bred representatives of high titles didn't engage in gossip. But it turned out to be quite the opposite.

Give them an inch, and they'll stick their curious noses into any hole without soap.

Although, it's more entertaining than cackling in the nuthouse where my father and stepmother threw me.

Nails dig into my skin, leaving red crescents. I close my eyes, banishing visions of the past in white coats with syringes in hand.

Twenty minutes and five rebukes from the bookworm, Selina and I land in the auditorium where the art history lecture will take place.

Selina bounces on the spot with impatience, gripping my wrist with strong fingers every time the door opens. (Her polo training from childhood clearly didn't go to waste. Her grip is such that a wet fish won't wriggle out). Each time, she sighs disappointedly when it's not the new sexy professor, but our classmate.

Soon, the door stops opening, all students settle into their seats and chatter amongst themselves. Five minutes have passed since the lecture started, and the professor is still missing.

Selina is already lying on the table, resting her head on her hands, keeping her gaze fixed on the door handle, which refuses to turn.

I distract myself with the book I brought from the library and make pencil marks in the notebook, necessary for the study report. I can't afford to mess up, or I'll be kicked out of university like a champagne cork. Straight to my father and...

"It's him! It's him!" Selina jerks me by the forearm with all her might, her eyes never leaving the figure of a man appearing in the doorway.

I lift my head to look at the new professor and lock eyes with an icy iris that pierces me with sharp spikes. A lump forms in my throat, and I can't swallow it. Because with a familiar gesture of his hand, the man adjusts his black locks of hair and walks to his desk. He sets down a leather briefcase and turns to face the audience.

My body starts trembling with a violent shiver. Even without his stretched-out Duran Duran T-shirt and worn-out sweatpants, I recognize him from a mile away.

Ethan fucking Blake. How did you end up here? Why now, after two years? Why in my university?

I take a deep breath, trying to withstand his heavy gaze.

I've built a good life for myself, and I won't let anyone, or anything ruin it! Not even you, a ghost from the past.

Printed in Great Britain
by Amazon